MANIA

AN ALEXANDER GREGORY THRILLER

LJ ROSS

ISBN: 978-1-912310-54-8

First published in March 2022 by Dark Skies Publishing

Author photo by Gareth Iwan Jones

Cover design by Stuart Bache

Cover design copyright © LJ Ross

Typeset by Riverside Publishing Solutions Limited

Printed and bound by CPI Goup (UK) Limited

MANIA

AN ALEXANDER GREGORY THRILLER

OTHER BOOKS BY LJ ROSS

THE ALEXANDER GREGORY THRILLERS IN ORDER:

1. *Impostor*
2. *Hysteria*
3. *Bedlam*

THE DCI RYAN MYSTERIES IN ORDER:

1. *Holy Island*
2. *Sycamore Gap*
3. *Heavenfield*
4. *Angel*
5. *High Force*
6. *Cragside*
7. *Dark Skies*
8. *Seven Bridges*
9. *The Hermitage*
10. *Longstone*
11. *The Infirmary (prequel)*
12. *The Moor*
13. *Penshaw*
14. *Borderlands*
15. *Ryan's Christmas*
16. *The Shrine*
17. *Cuthbert's Way*
18. *The Rock*

"Oh, I have lost my reputation! I have lost the immortal part of myself, and what remains is bestial."

—Cassio, in Shakespeare's *Othello*

THE OLD PALACE THEATRE

St Martin's Lane

Saturday, 8th January, at 7.30 p.m. prompt

Matinées Wednesdays and Saturdays at 2.30 p.m.

JASPER PUGH & SIR NIGEL VILLIERS

Present

KING LEAR

by
WILLIAM SHAKESPEARE

THE PLAYERS:

King Lear	Sir Nigel Villiers
Goneril, his daughter	Jasmine Kohli
Regan, his daughter	Olivia Routledge-Brown
Cordelia, his daughter	Frances Urwin
Albany, Goneril's Husband	James Slater
Cornwall, Regan's Husband	Kit Lawson
Kent	Samuel Elba
Gloucester	Will Cheyne
Edgar, his son	Dominic Reeve
Edmund, his son	Robin Ballantyne
Oswald, Goneril's Man	Christopher McCormack
Fool	Peter Gray

PRODUCTION BY JASPER PUGH & SIR NIGEL VILLIERS

DIRECTED BY MARGOT WINTERS

CHAPTER 1

The Old Palace Theatre, London

Opening Night

The storm raged all around him, echoing the turmoil that raged within.

Hard rain pattered down upon the ground in time with the drumming beat of his heart, while the wind howled shrill and fierce, forcing the hair back from his face to reveal a noble brow, lined and careworn by age and hard living. Through it all, thick smoke billowed like fog across a heath, clinging to his throat and clouding his vision.

Here, I stand...

Your slave.

He dragged in a laborious breath, wishing he could expel the foul-smelling air from his lungs, diaphragm heaving with the effort of restraint.

He lifted his arms upward, beseeching the elements, and tried to remember who he was.

A poor, weak, infirm, despised old man.

Thunder rumbled, a deafening sound that sliced through the darkness, and he was disoriented for a moment.

A despised old man.

Yes…yes, that was it.

He turned this way and that, while shards of white light broke through the murky fog to capture his face, upturned and confused, marred by madness. His feet began to stumble, as if dragging themselves across uneven grass, while his hands clutched the sides of his head.

And yet, I call you servile ministers…

"Bloody marvellous, isn't he?"

Doctor Alexander Gregory looked briefly at his friend, Professor Bill Douglas, who had whispered the words from his position in the neighbouring stalls seat.

"Very convincing," he agreed, softly.

He turned back to continue watching one of the world's leading actors perform his rendition of *King Lear* and was forced to admit that the delivery had been masterly, so far. The man's depiction of escalating mania, mirrored by the wild storm into which he'd been cast—created by an array of clever sound and lighting effects—was almost *too* realistic. In his line of work, Gregory was rarely fazed by the sight of a human being in crisis; in fact, it generally gave him a sense of purpose to be in the position to help them, if he could. Years spent working at Southmoor Hospital, which was one of a handful of 'special' hospitals in the UK dedicated to caring for the most dangerous kinds of patients had desensitised him to the usual behavioural tics one might associate with 'madness'—if one were to simplify a whole field of scholarly enquiry into a single, catch-all phrase.

And yet, as he sat in the shadows of the theatre, immersed in The Bard after an enjoyable evening with his friend, Gregory found himself unnerved by the role play. He couldn't say why, exactly; perhaps the mannerisms of a soul in torment were a little *too* accurate, or the rasp to his voice just a shade *too* convincing.

But then, he supposed that was the mark of a fine actor.

He tried to relax in the stiff, velvet-upholstered seat and ordered himself to lighten up. They were watching a work of great fiction, and he ought to enjoy the opportunity to switch off, for once, not seek out problems where there were none to be found.

There came another crackle of thunder and, somewhere in the rafters, a lighting technician flashed the powerful beam of a spotlight on the stage and then, briefly, around the room. Gregory blinked, and, as his eyes refocused on the solitary figure weaving drunkenly through the mists of white smoke, he noticed that the actor was not only stumbling but seemed to be on the verge of falling.

That was taking it too far, he thought. *Perhaps even the finest actors were not immune to a spot of self-indulgence, when it came to their interpretation of Shakespeare…*

No sooner had the uncharitable thought entered his head than it was replaced by a far more compassionate one. Perhaps the man was drunk, or under the influence of some other narcotic? Sir Nigel Villiers would hardly be the first person of means and opportunity to develop a toxic habit that might, from time to time, interfere with his work.

Gregory leaned forward again, studying the man's deportment for clues.

Sweating heavily, he noticed, but that could easily be a result of the hot stage lighting trained upon him. *Wide, unfocused eyes…unsteady on his feet…* but that could be affected for the sake of his art. Villiers was playing Lear, after all.

Sensing his discord, Douglas put a hand on his friend's back, urging him to relax. "Leave it back at the office," he murmured.

Gregory's lips twisted into a smile. There was very little he could conceal from his old friend and mentor, and even less he would ever wish to.

"Sorry," he muttered. "Occupational habit."

"*Ssh!*" A woman seated nearby threw what could only be described as a filthy look in their direction, and Gregory held up his hand in apology, settling back into his seat once more.

By now, Villiers faced the crowd, swaying on his feet in time to the thrumming of invisible rain. He could not see their faces, and could barely see the edge of the stage. His throat felt tight, his chest even tighter.

I will be the pattern of all patience…

I will say nothing.

From the wings, the eponymous 'Fool' in the story—an actor by the name of Peter Gray—prepared to make his stage entrance, taking a step forward, only to falter again in surprise.

A poor, weak, infirm, despised old man…

Beside him, the director looked up sharply.

"He's repeating his lines," Gray hissed. "What do I do?"

Margot Winters was an experienced hand, but she could have done without the old coot messing up one of the seminal scenes on opening night, with a packed audience there to see it. She could already see the critics' snide response in tomorrow's papers.

"Let him play it out," she muttered. "It's all you can do."

On stage, Villiers was oblivious to his error. He was no longer an actor, no longer repeating lines he'd rehearsed and knew like the back of his own hand. He *was* Lear; cold, alone, abandoned to the heath, and the vagaries of his own mind. He sucked in short, gasping breaths as he tried to get the words out once more, uncaring of the twitters in the audience or the irritation of his colleagues behind the scenes.

And...yet...

He began to cough, wheezing violently as his knees buckled.

And yet...

He raised one arm towards the audience, reaching out, fingers grasping at empty air before his body collapsed to the floor.

"That's not in the script," Douglas said, as a couple of taut seconds passed by.

Gregory was only half listening, his bright green eyes trained through the semi-darkness on the figure lying motionless on the stage.

Definitely not in the script.

A moment later, 'The Fool' hurried on and began to improvise a few bastardised lines from his own short monologue.

"Where are you?" he said, in a voice that was not quite so confident as it had been in the dress rehearsal.

He made his way through the mist and came to kneel beside Villiers' body.

"Fie, my Lord," he said, tremulously, and gave his shoulder a none-too-gentle shove. "Er…what malady has forsaken thee?"

It wasn't Shakespeare, but it was the best he could do.

When a couple more seconds passed and Villiers appeared not to have heard him, nor even flinched, Gray began to feel concerned.

He looked back over his shoulder, to where his director stood.

She made a shooing motion, and he tried again.

"M—my Lord?"

He gave Villiers another shove and, in doing so, realised the man was unconscious, his face fixed in the same mad grimace he'd worn as Lear.

Oh, shit.

"Sir Nigel isn't well!" he shouted out, shedding his character in a burst of panic. "I—is there a doctor in the house?"

Gregory was already up and out of his chair before the sentence was complete, clambering over legs and bags to make his way to the aisle from the centre stalls.

"Here!"

He held up his hand, and some unseen force raised the lights so that he could see the narrow stairs leading from the aisle to the stage, past the orchestra pit. One or two other voices called out to offer their services, but he was faster, long legs covering the ground, dodging the ushers and members of the audience who had risen from their seats and spilled into the gangway to get a better view. Gregory took the steps two at a time and hurried across the stage to where Peter Gray remained kneeling beside Villiers' body, with three other people at his shoulder.

"Give him some space," Gregory said, in clipped tones. "Call an ambulance."

He knelt beside the man's body and checked his airways for any sign of a blockage, then for any sign that the man was still breathing while he put two firm fingers to Villiers' carotid artery.

No pulse.

Thinking fast, Gregory calculated that it couldn't have been more than two minutes since Villiers fell, which meant there was still time to save him, if he tried.

With quick, assured movements, he flipped Villiers onto his back, tipped his chin up slightly, and went to work.

Somewhere behind him, he heard a woman's voice calling to her husband, and the vibrating hum of the audience speaking in low, urgent tones while they watched this new drama unfold. As the seconds ticked by and his arms continued to pump the man's chest while he blew long breaths into his lungs, the chatter died down and the theatre grew silent, the storm having been extinguished so there was no longer an artificial wind to relieve the brutal, exhausting sound of Gregory's laboured breathing as he battled to save a man's life.

Until, after much ado, the curtain fell.

CHAPTER 2

One week later

Shad Thames, London

Gregory awakened to a persistent banging.

His first thought was that it was another migraine, which was becoming a more frequent occurrence alongside his old friend, Chronic Sleep Deprivation. His second thought was that it could be a ruthless hangover, considering he'd put away the best part of a bottle of red wine the night before. With a groan, he rubbed a hand against his brow and swung his legs off the bed, realising that the banging was now accompanied by an intermittent ringing of his doorbell.

"All right—I'm coming!"

What time was it, anyway?

He checked his watch, which he'd forgotten to remove before collapsing into bed.

Nine-thirty.

It was a novelty to be able to sleep so late on a weekday, but he shouldn't allow it to become a habit. Indeed, it was probably Bill who was banging at the door, having decided to come and dish out a few home truths about his shoddy timekeeping and slovenly attitude.

You're on sabbatical, Alex, but that doesn't give you carte blanche to become a slob, he'd say. *Come on, boy, pick yourself up and get back to work.*

Bowing to the inevitable, Gregory padded the short distance from his bedroom to the front door and, not bothering to check the peep hole, swung it open.

It was not Bill Douglas waiting for him on the threshold.

It was a man and woman he'd never seen before. Both were somewhere in their early thirties, dressed in what he'd have described as 'smart casual' city gear, consisting of jeans, worn-in leather boots, jumpers and jackets, in deference to the wintry weather. The man was tall, around the same height as himself, while the woman was of average height—though that was the only thing he could say was in the least bit average about her, from first impressions alone. He was, after all, a red-blooded man, and knew a good-looking woman when he saw one.

He also knew a police officer when he saw one, and, by his count, here were two of them.

In the seconds it had taken him to conduct a brief assessment, the woman's eyes trailed over his dishevelled state and made a thorough assessment of her own.

"Doctor Alexander Gregory?" she asked, with an air of disbelief.

He smiled. It was true that, at that precise moment, he bore no resemblance to his usual self; certainly, not anybody's stereotypical notion of a starchy clinician.

"The very same," he murmured. "You must be here to discuss Nigel Villiers."

She reached inside the pocket of her jacket to produce a warrant card, and her partner followed suit.

"I'm DCI Ava Hope and this is DS Ben Carter," she said, and Gregory flicked a glance at the little plastic-coated wallets to verify. "We're from the Met's Homicide and Major Crime Command."

Gregory nodded. "You'd better come in," he said. "Please, take a seat, and I'll just run and put a shirt on."

It was one thing to answer the door bare-chested to his old friend; it was quite another to remain so during police questioning.

He returned a couple of minutes later to find Carter seated comfortably on his leather sofa, one burly leg slung over the other, while Hope stood by the window looking out at the panoramic view of the River Thames.

"Quite a place you've got here," she said, sticking her hands in the back pockets of her jeans.

Gregory took her compliment at face value, although it carried a question. How did a healthcare professional like himself, even a successful one, manage to bag himself a place overlooking the river?

That was a long story.

"Thanks," he said. "Can I offer either of you a drink—coffee, tea..?"

"Ye—" Carter began.

"No, thank you." Hope cut across him with another of her blandly eloquent stares, which seemed to have the desired effect, since her sergeant's lips promptly clamped shut.

"I hope you don't mind if I make one for myself," Gregory said, heading to the galley kitchen which was open plan to the living room. "I haven't had my morning shot of caffeine, yet. Please, feel free to start."

Watching his deft movements from her position by the window, it struck DCI Hope that the good doctor had the capacity to be quite a chameleon. Not five minutes ago, he'd appeared unguarded and—frankly—hungover, with his dark curls framing a pale, albeit handsome, face with bold green eyes that, despite their arresting colour, were tired and bloodshot. He might have been a man ten years younger than she knew him to be, just another twenty-something suffering the effects of a heavy night on the town.

Now, he'd assumed another persona entirely. She saw what she'd expected to see from the start: an urbane man in his mid-thirties whose hair was now tamed and who—crucially, for her peace of mind—was now wearing a thin jumper over a pair of smart jeans. Although he was still pale and tired, his eyes were alert, as though a light had been switched on so that they blazed a vibrant, emerald green. She suspected those eyes had the capacity to see far more than most people would like, which probably made him so good at his job. It also made him dangerous.

She shelved the observation and came to the point. "As you say, we're here to discuss the death of Sir Nigel Villiers," she began.

"Surely you mean his murder?" Gregory put in. He turned briefly from spooning ground coffee into a silver cafetière. "The matter wouldn't be in the hands of your department if it was a simple heart attack," he added.

Hope and Carter exchanged a glance.

"We have reason to believe the death of Sir Nigel was suspicious, and we are investigating on that basis," she said, carefully. "It's too early to say whether his death was murder."

Which meant they hadn't ruled out suicide, Gregory thought, as he came back to the living area with three mugs, a steaming pot of coffee and a small jug of milk.

"In case you change your mind," he said, setting them down on the coffee table before taking a seat opposite Carter. "So, if Villiers didn't die of a heart attack, what was the cause of death? There were no obvious wounds or signs of aggression that I could see."

Hope took a seat beside her partner and leaned forward, studying Gregory's reaction closely. He seemed perfectly at ease in their company, which was to be expected, but she had certain boxes she needed to tick before she could trust this man.

"Sir Nigel's death bore all the hallmarks of a cardiac arrest," she said. "But, as a matter of routine post-mortem examination, his bloodwork was referred for toxicology analysis. The report came back yesterday, and the matter was escalated to our team. There was found to be toxic levels of conium maculatum in his blood—a substance more commonly known as hemlock."

Gregory frowned. "*Hemlock?*" he repeated. "As in—the poisonous plant?"

She nodded.

"That's very interesting," he murmured.

"How so, Doctor Gregory?"

He took a sip of coffee, thinking of all the things he could say about somebody having chosen such an old-fashioned weapon as their *modus operandi*.

Perhaps, once the preliminaries were out of the way.

"It's consistent with Villiers' behaviour prior to his collapse," was all he said. "He was visibly struggling to catch his breath."

Hope nodded, while Carter made a note.

"I understand you gave Sir Nigel mouth-to-mouth during the course of trying to resuscitate him," she said. "Can I ask whether you've experienced any ill effects, yourself?"

Gregory considered the question, then shook his head. Tempting though it might have been, he couldn't blame any of his neuroses on having accidentally ingested a dose of hemlock.

"I'm glad to hear it," she said, though her eyes remained watchful. "When Sir Nigel collapsed and it became apparent to his co-star, Peter Gray, that something was wrong, you were the first to volunteer your services as a doctor. Can I ask how you happened to react so quickly? You are—forgive me—a psychiatric doctor, rather than a practising medical clinician."

Gregory admired her style. Subtle, but with an edge of steel.

"To become a psychiatrist, one first trains in general medicine," he explained. "But, aside from that, I have up-to-date advanced first aid training, which is"—*was,* he added silently—"mandatory for my role at Southmoor Hospital, where I'm often called upon to manage and deal with serious medical interventions. I also hold a postgraduate degree in clinical psychology, which is now my main field of interest. I can assure you, Chief Inspector, I have the necessary qualifications."

"I don't doubt it," Hope averred. "However, that still doesn't explain how you, above all others, reacted so quickly to the emergency."

"Instinct and experience," he said, succinctly. "I'd been watching Villiers' behaviour on stage from my position in the stalls and I felt a certain discomfort, which I know now came from having observed the prelude to his collapse. His movements were disoriented, his eyes unfocused, he was sweating and panting profusely. I felt it was more than merely a case of overacting the part of Lear."

Carter let out a short laugh, which was quelled by another mild look from his chief inspector.

"Nonetheless, that's quite a perceptive talent you have there, Doctor," Hope remarked.

He drained his coffee cup, eyeing her over the rim. "Unfortunately, it didn't help, on this occasion."

She couldn't argue with that. "Did you know Sir Nigel personally?"

Gregory shook his head. "Not at all," he said. "However, my friend and colleague, Professor Bill

Douglas, was an old friend of his from university. I believe they kept in touch, every now and then. That's how we came to have tickets for opening night—they were gifted."

Carter made a note, although they were already aware of that small nugget, having learned the same from an earlier conversation with Professor Douglas.

"Would you mind telling us your movements that evening?"

It was all routine, he knew, but DCI Hope had an uncanny knack for disarming a person, which was another skill he could only admire.

"Let's see," he said, thinking back to the previous Saturday. "I'd spent Friday night in Cambridge with Bill. He lives there and teaches at the university."

He didn't bother to add that they were in the process of re-opening their profiling unit because, if his so-called 'perceptive talents' were on the money, he'd say DCI Hope was already well aware of the fact.

"How would you describe your relationship with Professor Douglas?" she threw in, and caught him off guard.

His relationship?

Gregory thought of his old friend and mentor and wondered how to distil all the important facets into words. He was more than a colleague, more than a friend…he supposed Bill had been a father to him.

However, that wasn't what she really wanted to know.

DCI Hope wanted to know whether there was any romantic feeling that might induce either one of them to lie for the other.

"The relationship is purely platonic," he said, though it irked him to have to explain. "Bill is a professional colleague, a friend and mentor. We've worked together for years—but, if you think that might lead him to give a false alibi to the police, you're very much mistaken."

Hope nodded her understanding. "Very well. You were telling us you'd spent Friday night in Cambridge?"

"Yes. We had breakfast, talked over a few past cases, then, at around three o'clock on Saturday, we took the train together into London and came back here. I changed clothes and, since the weather was good, we walked along the river towards the centre of town. We had a drink at a little bar—"

"The name of the bar, please?" Carter interrupted.

"*Brasserie Max,*" Gregory replied. "It's attached to the Covent Garden Hotel. We arrived around five-thirty, decided to stay for a quick bite to eat in the restaurant, and left at around six-forty-five. We walked around the corner to The Old Palace Theatre on St Martin's Lane in time for seven o'clock, or thereabouts. We picked up a couple of glasses of dubious red wine at the theatre bar and took our seats in the stalls in time for curtain up, at seven-thirty."

He paused, sending them both a placid look.

"Does that satisfy you both as to my alibi for last Saturday—and Professor Douglas's, for that matter?"

"For now," Hope replied, with the ghost of a smile, and then reached for the coffee. "D' you mind?"

"Please, help yourself."

Upon which note, Gregory realised, the preliminaries were complete.

"So," he said. "Would you like to tell me how I can help you? It's obvious you've already spoken with Bill, who must have told you the same story I have."

Hope took a swig of coffee, savoured the taste, and added 'Coffee Connoisseur' to his list of attributes.

"The fact you have a good alibi for your movements during the period Sir Nigel Villiers is likely to have been poisoned, not to mention a lack of any apparent motive to do him harm, is convenient for us," she admitted. "I won't beat around the bush any longer, Doctor Gregory. We're aware of your background in criminal profiling, and our superintendent has specifically requested that we engage your services to try to tie this up quickly and discreetly."

"Why?"

She blinked. "Why—discreetly?"

"No." He shook his head. "Why has your superintendent requested me? What's the connection?"

"Oh. He knew the victim—the deceased—personally. In light of their friendship and the fact Sir Nigel was such a well-known personality, he—we—all feel he deserves a timely investigation."

Gregory thought of all the unnamed sex workers, homeless and disaffected individuals who lost their lives each year. Did they have anybody in the corridors of power to ensure they received a timely investigation? He doubted it, but that was a conversation for another day. For now, there was the hemlock, and the curious case of a dead stage star to attend to.

But, he didn't accept immediately. He'd been burned by the lure of an interesting case before, and it had taught him to be cautious. Four years earlier, when he'd worked alongside his friend to provide scientific profiles of violent criminals to police forces around the country and beyond, they'd enjoyed one success after another. That is, until the Andersson case. Their profiles were only ever intended to be used as a tool for the investigating team, never as gospel. So, when they'd been asked to profile the killer of male sex workers in the Soho district of London, they'd used their collective knowledge of many similar cases and personality types to create a generic profile which was intended to help the police to narrow down their enormous pool of suspects. Unfortunately for them, the mounting pressure and public outcry about their lack of progress having more to do with institutional police homophobia than having no useful leads, led the investigative team to make reactive decisions that were not fully considered, and the investigation became an exercise in saving face rather than seeking justice. Before they knew it, he and Douglas had been dismissed while the police set up an elaborate 'honey trap' for a man they were convinced fit the bill—and perhaps he did, on the face of it. That man, Carl Deere, was prosecuted with the full force of the law. His name had been smeared in every newspaper and across every television channel, and he was sentenced to a full term of life imprisonment.

There was only one problem: it turned out he *wasn't* their killer, after all.

When the murders continued despite Deere being safely behind bars, the police soon realised they'd locked up the wrong man and the papers had a field day with accusations of incompetence. Gregory didn't know who had been responsible for what happened next, but he remembered waking up one dreadful morning to find his name plastered across the front pages of *The Times*, alongside a lengthy article detailing the ways in which he and Douglas, and not the police, were really to blame for the incarceration of an innocent man. They'd been hounded for weeks by paparazzi and reporters, while their so-called 'friends' in the Met had remained silent throughout.

He could have defended himself, he supposed. Could have told them the true purpose of a profile or pointed out the many other times their work had helped bring violent offenders to justice, but the horse had long since bolted the stable and anything that came afterwards lacked credibility.

All these thoughts and more passed through Gregory's mind and, if he'd been that starchy psychiatrist DCI Hope had expected to find, Gregory might have declined her offer. But, for all his natural caution when it came to further joint ventures with the police, his desire to seek out the truth was a more powerful motivator, matched only by his desire to help find the person who'd been driven to kill.

"I'll read the file," he said. "When do you want to start?"

DCI Hope looked down at a newspaper lying discarded on the coffee table. The headline read, 'SIR NIGEL DIES ON STAGE DESPITE HEROIC EFFORTS OF NOTORIOUS CRIMINAL PROFILER'.

She lifted her eyes again, and there was a challenge in them.

"What other plans do you have for the day, aside from reading the newspapers?"

Touché, he thought.

"I'll get my coat."

CHAPTER 3

New Scotland Yard was located on Victoria Embankment, in the district of Westminster. The headquarters of the Metropolitan Police Service occupied a building with a long pedigree of law enforcement, having previously been home to Whitehall Police Station, and was neighboured by several other giants in the world of domestic law enforcement and security, including the Ministry of Defence. As with so many great cities immortalised on screen and in novels, the streets in that part of town called to mind pictures of men and women in dingy, camel-coloured anoraks reporting into unmarked offices, and of spies keeping tabs on one politician or another through long-lensed cameras from grimy, third-floor windows. Consequently, as DCI Hope's car made its steady way along the Embankment towards The Yard, Gregory half-expected to spot a young Michael Caine walking along the riverbank with the *Ipcress File* tucked under his arm, and not the colourful stream of tourists who followed guides with large yellow umbrellas as they traipsed their way along its famous pavements.

It was not the first time he'd visited the Met's stronghold and yet, each time, Gregory was struck by its austerity; the building itself had been constructed sometime in the 1930s, but its classical minimalism did not inspire so much as intimidate, which was a convenient by-product given its purpose. However, some effort had been made to modernise its frontage, with the addition of an oval-shaped glass entrance pavilion, presumably to reflect the Met's desire to manifest a transparent face to the wider community that it served.

Whether it had succeeded in that desire was debateable but, as Gregory picked up his visitor badge and followed DCI Hope and DS Carter through the security turnstiles and into the wide lobby area, he could not deny the place was a hive of industry. Staff of all ranks and roles bustled about their business, moving up and down the towering glass lifts which stood in the centre of the room. The three newcomers followed suit, and soon Gregory found himself rising upward to the office levels where, after a cheerful *ping*, the doors swished open, and he was led further into the heart of the beast.

"I've arranged a briefing with the team," Hope said, as they scanned through another set of turnstiles. "It's the fastest way to bring you up to speed with what we know, so far."

"Which isn't a lot," Carter warned him, before excusing himself to retrieve some files while they made their way to one of the meeting rooms.

Gregory felt like a prize cow with all eyes upon him as they walked along the main gangway between rows of identical-looking desks until they reached a door marked 'CONFERENCE ROOM B', whose walls were made of reinforced opaque glass.

"Look," she said, once the door clicked shut behind them. "While we're waiting for the others to arrive, I might as well tell you that there are a few amongst them who don't think much of offender profiling—"

"In other words, they think I'm a quack," Gregory said.

She couldn't help but laugh.

"Well, you said it."

"It's all right, Chief Inspector," he said, and leaned back against one of the desks while she set the coffee machine to brew. "It comes with the territory."

She cleared her throat.

"There—ah—there were a couple of objections, after what happened in the Andersson case," she said, and he found himself grateful that she was clearly not the type to beat around the bush. Here was a woman who spoke her mind freely and openly, even when social propriety might have made it awkward for her to do so.

"Of course," he said, smoothly. "I'm notorious—remember?"

She turned to look back over her shoulder, caught his smile, and then turned back again, feeling flustered.

"I wouldn't joke about it, if I were you," she said. "There are people here who worked the case and still feel angry about what happened."

Gregory's eyes turned cool.

They felt angry?

Were any of their names dragged through the mud? Was their reputation hung out to dry?

"It's an incredible thing—perception," he said, after he'd taken a moment to compose himself. "How differently one person can view the same set of facts versus another. Have you ever heard of *abnegation*, Chief Inspector?"

She set a mug of coffee on the long conference table beside him.

"Can't say that I have."

"It's a fancy term for 'denial'," he explained. "Freud first coined it to explain the psychological phenomenon whereby people who are faced with a truth that is too painful or uncomfortable for them to bear, simply reject it and insist the opposite is true, despite overwhelming evidence to the contrary. It often happens in cases where an individual has acted poorly and is ashamed of the fact."

Hope was a quick study. "I understand what you're saying," she said. "Look, I wasn't a part of the Andersson case, but I know as well as anyone that it ruffled a lot of feathers. Tensions were running high and pressure to close the case was coming from every conceivable direction. When that happens, it takes a strong backbone to keep a clear head. Sometimes, mistakes are made. I won't speak against any of my colleagues, Doctor, but what I will say is that I'm sorry that you were caught in the cross-fire."

It was the closest thing Gregory had ever had to an apology from any serving member of the Metropolitan Police, and it took him by surprise.

"Thank you for that," he said quietly, and opened his mouth to say something else, but the words were lost on the air as the door opened again and Carter entered with several other staff members in tow.

"Show time," she said.

"Quack, quack," Gregory replied, and made her laugh again.

Murder Investigation Team 8, or simply, 'MIT 8', was one of eighteen teams within the Metropolitan

Police's Homicide and Major Crime Command. Aside from Hope and Carter, it consisted of twenty other detectives, plus three permanent administrative staff members—not all of whom were in attendance. In fact, seated around the beech wood conference table were only five others, each of 'detective sergeant' or 'inspector' rank, all of whom were men in their mid-forties answerable to the young woman at the head of the table.

Gregory thought of his own limited dealings with Scotland Yard and knew that, despite any number of mandatory 'Equality and Diversity in the Workplace' training sessions, ingrained attitudes between the sexes weren't easily shifted within institutional hierarchies. Analysing the body language of those in the room, which varied from casual, splayed-leg macho to cross-armed and tight-lipped, he made a conservative estimate that at least three of the five who'd yet to introduce themselves were of the 'Old School' and didn't take too kindly to being given orders by a woman they'd rather be chatting up down at the local boozer.

She looked at each of them in turn.

"As you know, we're here to discuss progress on the Villiers case. Before we do, I'd like to introduce you to our visitor—this is Doctor Alexander Gregory, an experienced clinician and offender profiler. He's here at the request of the Super' and should be afforded every courtesy."

There was a warning in her tone that was unmistakable.

"It's only been a few days," one of them said. "Bit premature to start calling in the head doctors, don't you think?"

She looked him squarely in the eye. "In any case, but *particularly* in a high-profile case such as this, we should be thankful for all the help we can get. Now," she said. "Let's recap what we know. Can you run us through it, Ben?"

DS Carter stood up and moved to the whiteboard at the front of the room, where he drew a long black line to signify the timeline he was about to discuss. There were advanced software programs to construct timelines, connections, flow-charts and any number of document management services to assist with the running of a police investigation, but there was something comforting and simple about seeing the words set out in front of them in plain black and white.

"Working backwards, we know that Nigel Villiers was pronounced dead at St Thomas' Hospital at nine-twenty-seven p.m. on Saturday 8th January. He collapsed approximately one hour before then, at around eight-thirty, whereupon resuscitation attempts began within two or three minutes—by Doctor Gregory, as it happens."

The eyes in the room turned upon him again, this time with a degree of suspicion.

"Doctor Gregory is fully alibied and his movements for the relevant period accounted for," Hope added, for good measure.

Reluctantly, the eyes turned back to the board.

"Curtain went up at exactly seven-thirty," Carter continued. "Immediately prior to this, Sir Nigel was in his dressing room, alone, for fifteen minutes before curtain call—from around seven-fifteen."

"According to several of his co-stars and his wife, Lady Rebecca Villiers—who was also in attendance at the theatre that night—it was a longstanding habit of his to be left alone for a quarter of an hour before any performance," Hope told them. "He liked to take some time to clear his head and prepare himself before facing the audience."

"Everyone arrived at the theatre earlier than usual, given that it was opening night," Carter continued. "The theatre manager, Jasper Pugh, gave a speech to the full cast and crew at six o'clock on the stage, followed by the director, Margot Winters. After then, at around half past, everybody dispersed to get ready for the performance. Hair and make-up artists were in Sir Nigel's room for roughly twenty minutes, from half past six until six-fifty or thereabouts, following which he was joined by his wife, who wished him well, and several of his other co-stars popped in to do the same and share a glass of Dutch courage."

Carter paused, twiddling the pen between his fingers.

"According to the tox report, the hemlock found in Sir Nigel's bloodstream was of sufficient quantity to kill and would likely have been administered orally—through food or drink—no more than two hours before his collapse. That gives us a window of six-thirty onwards, give or take. As far as we can tell, Sir Nigel ingested a glass of champagne as part of a toast during the speeches, although that was a little earlier than our estimated window, at six o'clock. Following that, we know he kept a jug of water in his dressing room—it would have been there all evening and was prepared by his assistant, a bloke by the name of Marcus Hale, who confirms that he filled the jug with bottled Evian as usual while Sir Nigel was listening to the speeches on stage."

"He could easily have dropped something in his water," one of the other detectives said.

"Possibly, except hemlock isn't transparent," Hope replied. "It would have been obvious that the water was contaminated—unless somebody made a concentrated solution first. Added to which, the team went over the jug and glasses and found no trace of hemlock on any of them."

"The frustrating thing is that we haven't found the source," Carter said. "We know there was the champagne, the water jug, and a buffet of sandwiches and other nibbles available on a tray in Villiers' room. All of that has been tested and found to be clear of hemlock. Likewise, the dram of whiskey he had with his co-stars, shortly after seven o'clock."

"The fact is, there was a lot of movement, backstage," Hope said. "Lots of coming and going, knocks on the door, people passing in and out…"

"Except when Villiers was alone for fifteen minutes," Gregory said softly.

"Yes, apart from then," Hope agreed. "Everyone we've taken preliminary statements from agrees that he was a vibrant man of sixty-one, in the prime of his life. He was always punctual and well-rehearsed, the consummate professional. He'd enjoyed a distinguished stage and screen career for more than forty years and showed no signs of stopping or slowing up—"

"Yeah, well. Hemlock didn't just find its way into his bloodstream by accident, did it?" a detective by the name of Wilson interrupted her.

There were smirks amongst the men, but Hope merely smiled.

"I'm glad you thoroughly understand the parameters of your job, Roger. We're all here to discover whether Sir Nigel ingested hemlock against his will or if it was a planned suicide. That's why they call it an investigation."

The smirks now dealt with, she nodded to Carter, who picked up the thread of his summary.

"The fact is, almost anyone could have gained access to Villiers' glass, his water, champagne or the selection of food and drink that was delivered to his room and available from around five-thirty, that evening," he said. "The food was delivered by an off-site catering team, who provided similar trays of sandwiches and fruit to other members of the cast. The company has been a longstanding partner of the theatre for over ten years."

"Who placed the order?" Hope asked.

"The theatre manager, Jasper Pugh, or his assistant, Jacky Martin," Carter replied, having looked into it. "I have the name of the person who took the order and the delivery courier. The food has been tested and came back clear."

Hope nodded. "Post-mortem analyses of the contents of Villiers' stomach haven't come back yet," she said. "But, depending on when he last ate, there's every chance his stomach acids would have degraded any meaningful samples, so I'm not going to hold my breath."

While she was speaking, Gregory flipped through the photocopied pages of the file in front of him, paying particular attention to an inventory of items found on Villiers' person and in his dressing room, and on the images taken of the room.

His eyes traced over the small space, with its classic, bulb-lined mirror and rack of costumery;

the side table upon which the water and tray of food had rested; the glass of drained whiskey sitting on his dressing table beside a framed picture of his wife and what appeared to be children or grandchildren...and then, Gregory's eye fell upon something else sitting innocuously on the dressing table, half-concealed by the glass.

Multi-vitamin tablets.

He wasn't any kind of expert on pharmacology, or indeed on poison hemlock, but he did know that a noxious substance could more readily be absorbed into the bloodstream in powdered or capsule form. If someone had a mind to, they could have ground down the hemlock flower and substituted a harmless vitamin capsule for something deadly.

"Excuse me," he said. "Have you tested the bottle of multi-vitamins?"

Hope nodded. "They're a standard mix of vitamins and iron," she said. "According to his wife, he took them religiously."

In his line of work, Gregory mapped patterns of behaviour in order to better understand underlying disorders or differences in personality type. When it came to violent offenders, he also mapped patterns of offending—symbolism, execution, choice of weaponry or geography, for starters. In one of Fate's great ironies he'd often found that, while he was mapping them, offenders were also mapping the behaviour of their victims, taking meticulous notes of their daily habits or preferences for use against them at some later date. That being the case, who was to say that someone close to Villiers hadn't known of his daily habit and, with a little planning, substituted the pills, only to switch them back again before the arrival of the police?

It was certainly possible.

As for suicide…

"Do we have any reason to believe Villiers would have taken his own life?" he asked.

Hope shook her head.

"Absolutely none," she told him. "The problem is, we don't have any reason to believe someone would have wanted to kill him, either."

Gregory disagreed.

"He was well known," he said, and thought of all the people who developed unhealthy obsessions with their idols. Most of the time, it came to nothing, but there were always outliers. "Did he have any super fans? Anyone who'd been bothering him, lately?"

"We've asked his assistant, Hale, to put together a list of any fans who regularly got in touch," Carter told him. "Sir Nigel had a big following but, from what he could see, there wasn't anybody to be especially worried about. Given his demographic, Villiers' fan base generally consisted of young ingenues looking to catch a break, or older female fans who'd been following him since Day One and liked to send him things like knitted tea caddies and pictures of their cats."

Hope thought of the cat she had at home and wondered if, one day, she'd find herself knitting tea caddies...

It was a slippery slope.

"We've taken Villiers' laptop, which was at the theatre, as well as his home electronics—the Digital Forensics team are going over them now, in case there's anything interesting," she said, shoving all thoughts of cats and knitting to one side. "Likewise, his financial records, although that may take some time."

Gregory nodded. "I understand that suicide can't be ruled out, at this point, but, if we assume a degree of foul play, then my question is this: aside from his co-stars, all of whom we have to assume had *opportunity*, if not necessarily motive, who else had access to the theatre or was on the premises to be able to administer the hemlock?"

"The scenarios are endless," Hope said. "Either we have an opportunist who was unknown to Villiers and managed to gain access to his food or drink in order to contaminate it, or we have somebody who was well known to Villiers and would have been able to gain access at any time."

She ran an agitated hand through her hair and let it fall away again.

"The theatre had a capacity of seven hundred," she said. "Add in the cast and crew, and you're looking at more like seven-fifty. We've been contacting each of them for statements, and then it's a process of cross-checking and interviewing...we can hopefully eliminate many of them, but, since we don't know precisely how the poison was administered, we can't rule out a chance meeting between Villiers and some unknown person."

In most cases, Gregory thought, a killer was known to their victim. However, when that victim was a famous actor, ordinary rules didn't always apply. This was precisely when an offender profile could be an enormous help to an investigation, because it would allow the police to focus their resources on possibilities that were most likely to bring them a swift return, rather than shooting in the dark.

In that moment, he made up his mind to help, and began running through the facts in his mind, pairing them with what he knew of historic cases.

"We've got a lot of ground to cover, a wide pool of suspects and no time," Hope said. "The papers aren't letting up, and neither are the brass—"

At that very moment, the 'brass' entered the room, and Gregory watched all seven detectives unconsciously square their shoulders in deference to the new arrival.

Detective Chief Superintendent Simon Campbell was a slight, balding man of around sixty, whose Glaswegian accent had long since been shaved and buffed so that it would be barely recognisable to any of his old school friends back in Dalmarnock—not that it mattered, since he hadn't chosen to keep in touch with any of them.

"Sorry to interrupt you all," he said, with a genial smile. "I thought I'd stop in to see how things are progressing. Ah! I see you managed to persuade Doctor Gregory to lend his talents to our investigation."

"Yes, sir," Hope replied, and turned as if to make the introductions. "Doctor, this is Detective Chief Superintendent—"

But Gregory had already risen from his seat, briefcase held loosely in hand.

"DCS Campbell and I are already well acquainted," he said, eyeing the man who'd led the Andersson case and been responsible, in Gregory's view, for much of what had gone wrong with it. He strongly suspected it had been Campbell's notion to feed him and Douglas to the press, to save his own miserable hide so, if this was the man who'd asked for him, specifically, there could only be one reason for it: the superintendent wanted to put in place somebody he could blame if Villiers' killer was not caught.

Well, he would not be the fall-guy a second time.

He turned to DCI Hope.

"Thank you for allowing me to be present at your briefing, and to have sight of the file," he said, pushing it back across the table. "Unfortunately, I won't be able to help you, on this occasion. I wish you every success with your investigation."

He nodded to the others and, a moment later, he was gone.

Gregory barely made it to the end of the street before he heard swift footsteps approaching from behind.

"Alex! Wait, just a minute!"

To his surprise, the superintendent himself had deigned to follow him.

"Simon," he said. "I don't think we have anything further to discuss."

The air around them was cold as it rolled in from the river, but his voice was colder.

"I understand how you must feel—"

"I doubt that very much."

Campbell sighed. In the ordinary course of things, he'd have been able to rely on the natural gravitas of his position to command respect, but he could see a different approach was needed here, and he didn't delude himself that Gregory felt any kind of respect for him, or his position, given their shared history.

"I understand your anger, and I'm sorry for it. I handled myself badly, four years ago."

"Thank you. Now, if you'll excuse me—"

Campbell put a hand on Gregory's arm.

"Let me buy you a quick pint at the Red Lion," he said. "We can talk it over."

"You've had four years to say anything worth saying," Gregory told him. "You knew where to find us."

Campbell tried to look contrite.

"I know. Look, whatever you may think of me doesn't matter, because this case isn't about either of us. It's about a much-loved man who died before his time. He deserves the best we can give him, as do his family."

"You have a good team in there investigating already."

Campbell nodded quickly, reminding Gregory of one of those little toys which sat on the back seat of a car with its head bobbing up and down.

"Yes, but you can see the extent of the challenge they're facing. They've got a line of suspects a mile long and no leads. If they knew the *kind* of person they were looking for—"

"They might be looking for nobody."

Campbell looked out towards the water and expelled a long breath, which fogged on the air.

"I can't believe it of Nigel," he said, eventually. "He's the last person to have taken his own life."

Gregory thought of the patients who had walked through his consulting room door at Southmoor full of smiles, well-dressed and confident. They were the same ones who would talk about everything and nothing—anything to fill the silence—and had often been able to hold down high-powered jobs or a busy family life. They were also the ones he'd found with a handmade noose around their necks, or an empty pill bottle beside their beds.

"Appearances can be deceptive," he said.

Campbell spread his hands in mute appeal.

"That's why we need two profiles, Alex. An offender profile, discussing the type of person who could have killed in that way, and a victim profile, all about Nigel."

It would be an interesting task, there was no denying that, but the past could not be forgotten, and Gregory rarely made the same mistake twice. He opened his mouth to issue a final rejection but, sensing it was forthcoming, Campbell interjected with one final, devastating argument.

"Bill Douglas was Nigel's friend, too," he said, softly. "Have you spoken with him, to ask whether he'd like to be a part of the investigation? It might be important to him, if not to you."

Cunning bastard, Gregory thought.

For, of course, he was perfectly right. Despite everything that had gone before, Bill would want to help bring his friend's killer to book, or at least find out the answer to how he died. He was not in any position to reject the opportunity to work with the police without discussing it with him first.

His eyes passed over Campbell's face with ill-concealed resentment.

"I'll talk to Bill," he said, and left it at that.

CHAPTER 4

The man was seated in the corner of a café, head bowed over the news app he'd loaded onto his phone, one long forefinger scrolling through the headlines of the day. Every now and then, he let out a vocal sound of irritation, loud enough to bother those seated at neighbouring tables and have them glance over with expressions of mild concern.

'*Heroic efforts of criminal profiler…*' he read, while gnawing at the edge of his nail. '*Police praise doctor's lifesaving attempt…*'

"Would you like to order anything else?"

He jumped a little in his chair, not having heard the waitress approach.

"No," he snapped.

She felt a flush run up her neck and a film of sweat cake her skin. She didn't like this man and never had, but he kept coming back and, invariably, she was the one who drew the short straw and was forced to wait on him.

The pity of it was, when he'd first come into the café, he'd caught her eye. Some men had that effect, and he was one of them: strikingly handsome and, in the beginning, well dressed.

But now?

Now, he was unkempt and rude, without a kind word to say, let alone any kind of tip for her trouble.

"Well, I'm afraid this is one of our busiest times of day, so I'm going to have to ask you to vacate the table if you're no longer eating or drinking," she said. "I hope you unders—"

She trailed off when he looked up at her, pinning her with eyes that seemed so full of darkness and… and something like *hate*.

The force of the emotion was strong enough to bring tears to her eyes.

"I'm not moving," he muttered. "So, get me a coffee, if you must."

No 'please' or 'thank you', she noted, and she'd been hoping he'd just leave without ordering anything. She'd seen the other customers looking over at him, as if he were some sort of oddball, which he was. The man brought a sense of acute discomfort wherever he went.

"What kind of coffee—?"

"Jesus," he muttered. "Does it matter? Black. Black coffee."

She flipped her notepad shut and stalked back to the counter to make it up for him.

"Mr Sunshine back in today, then?"

Jill, one of the other waitresses, kept her voice beneath the level of the coffee machine.

"Oh, yeah. He's on fine form, today," Anika replied. "He could freeze a person's tits at fifty yards."

Jill sniggered. "Wonder what his story is," she mused. "He has one of those faces…as if I've seen him before, you know?"

"He has that look about him," Anika said. "But it's funny how a person can become less attractive the more you get to know them, isn't it?"

"True," her friend said. "When he first came in, I thought Christmas had come early. Now, I can't see him in the same way."

"He gets uglier by the day," Anika agreed, glancing over the counter to where he had resumed his hunched position at one of the little wooden tables.

"I wonder what's upset him so much?" Jill said, leaning against the counter beside her.

"God knows," Anika murmured. "Whatever it is, I wouldn't want to be on the receiving end. There's something about him that frightens me."

Jill chuckled and gave her friend a bolstering pat on the back.

"He's harmless," she said, breezily. "Probably just one of those political fanatics, all riled up about the latest cutback."

Anika smiled, but her eyes strayed back to the man at the table, remembering how he'd looked at her.

Gregory spent the remainder of the day wandering the streets of London, soaking up its atmosphere while he thought about whether to become embroiled in the Villiers case any further than he was already. Setting aside his reservations about DCS Campbell and any ulterior motives the man may have for wanting to bring he and Bill on board, he knew it may turn out that Nigel Villiers had simply had enough of life and decided to choose a particularly dramatic moment to end it all, live on stage in front of hundreds of people.

Why, then, didn't that possibility ring true?

The hemlock.

Poison of the herbal variety was no ordinary choice for a person wishing to end it all, but it was in keeping with Villiers' theatrical bent. After all, hadn't Socrates chosen hemlock tea as his means of execution, having been found guilty of corrupting the Athenian youth? For a man who'd lived and breathed many of the great works of classical fiction, perhaps Villiers thought to take a leaf out of Socrates' book and go out in style.

On the other hand, if the hemlock had been administered by some unseen, malevolent hand, that would put an entirely different complexion on matters. For one thing, the choice of poison was symbolic, and one could infer that somebody believed Villiers deserved to die painfully and publicly.

But, why?

It all came down to perception, again. Over a sixty-year lifespan, it was possible Villiers had committed any number of major and minor infractions; the question of degree was in the mind and eye of the beholder. Gregory already knew Villiers had no criminal record, aside from a couple of pops for cannabis when he was a young man, which was hardly something to kill over. To the outside world, he was an award-winning actor who had saved The Old Palace Theatre from ruin, over a decade ago, partnering with its then manager, Jasper Pugh, to revive the old, beloved place and use some of his considerable industry clout to convince his actor friends to come along and do a rendition of *The Cherry Orchard,* or *Waiting for Godot.* Big names sold big tickets, and The Old Palace had indeed been saved, its walls preserved for another generation to enjoy. He'd been the toast of London's Theatreland, his face projected onto the side of famous skyscrapers in moody black and white to advertise *King Lear,* and every prediction had been for another roaring success.

Had someone begrudged him that success?

In cases such as these, it might have been traditional to look to the understudy—who, of course, would be a pinched-looking, grasping, Uriah Heap of a man, ready to jump into Villiers' still-warm shoes—but there was no such person. Quite simply, there had been no understudy for Nigel Villiers, because he was a unique commodity.

His personal life, perhaps?

From what Gregory had seen, there were no grubby tales of affairs or scandal to mar Villiers' reputation; he was a married man of over thirty years, not having chosen to trade in the wife who'd helped him build his career and borne his children, for a younger model. Theirs was a fairy tale love story, so the papers always said, about two young stage stars who'd met on the set of *Romeo & Juliet* at Wyndham's, and married scarcely three months later. Rebecca Villiers was a name in her own right, an active philanthropist and regular talk show guest—the kind of person the *Daily Mail* might have described, somewhat nauseatingly, as a 'National Treasure'. The couple had three children, two of whom were also actors making their way in America, and a third who was rebelling against his parents' fame while trying to make his own way as a musician.

Gregory could hardly blame him. He knew, only too well, how a parent's influence could cast a long shadow.

He shivered, and picked up his pace along the south bank of the river, moving between the crowds queuing to pick up their lunch from one of the many street vendors and pop-up cafés that lined the boulevard, his mind far, far away.

"Alex?"

He didn't hear his name, at first.

"*Alex*!"

He paused, turning to see an attractive woman of around thirty jogging towards him from the opposite direction.

"I thought that was you!"

He stared, trying desperately to remember her name. It was obvious that he *should* remember, judging by her open, smiling demeanour. Was she a patient?

"Hi," he said, blandly.

Some of the light dimmed in her eyes. "You don't remember me, do you?"

He could have lied, but he was beyond that, now. "No, I'm sorry."

She let out a harsh little laugh. "Well, that does wonders for my ego," she said, and lifted her chin. "We spent the night together after a conference, a couple of years ago."

Suddenly, it came back to him.

A country hotel. Two days of interminable lectures. Too much wine, afterwards.

"Sarah," he realised. "Or, I should say, Doctor Sarah Jepson."

Intelligent. Funny. Looking for more than he wanted to give, at the time.

"Ten points," she said. "I was going to ask how you've been, but you look like shit."

He grinned. "Flatterer."

A small smile tugged at the corner of her mouth, which she quickly dispersed. He wasn't forgiven, yet.

"What have you been doing with yourself?"

"Same old," he said, not wanting to get into it. "Er…how've you been?"

"Busy…busy."

There was an awkward silence.

"Well—" he began.

"Do you—" she said.

They laughed.

"I was just heading back to my flat," he said. "But I haven't had any lunch yet. Have you eaten?"

She hated herself for being tempted. Very tempted. It had been disappointing not to have heard from him, the last time, and she was forever telling her patients to exercise good judgment.

If only she listened to her own advice.

"I've got forty-five minutes before I need to get back to the office," she said, and her private practice was less than a ten-minute walk away. "I could manage a bite."

Gregory spread a hand towards the various street vendors.

"What do you fancy?"

There was a question, she thought.

CHAPTER 5

"You look exhausted."

Professor Bill Douglas made his observation from the doorway of Gregory's flat later that evening.

"Too kind," he said, ushering him inside.

"You aren't getting enough sleep," Bill continued, divesting himself of several layers of winter clothing.

Gregory made a non-committal sound. "How was your day?"

"Long," Douglas admitted, collapsing onto the sofa, which let out a protesting wheeze beneath his weight. "The Ministry of Justice asked me to put together my recommendations for how to reduce rates of recidivism amongst certain types of offender…you might as well ask, 'How long is a piece of string?', but I did it, anyhow. Talked to them about recovery programmes, investment in people, early interventions…but they don't want to hear about restorative justice. It's not popular, you see."

Gregory recognised his friend's frustration. As an eminent academic, Bill was often called upon to produce research papers to inform new governmental policies, which took considerable time and effort, only to find them thrown on the slush pile or wilfully ignored in favour of more populist decision-making by whichever political party happened to be in power at the time. The average voter didn't want to feel sorry for an offender; they wanted them locked behind bars, with more 'bobbies on the beat'—even though there was no reliable evidence to say that an increased police presence on the streets made any palpable difference to crime rates.

Douglas sighed, and rubbed a hand over his chin, which sported a well-trimmed beard he'd recently grown and was beginning to enjoy.

"Heard from the police, yesterday," he added, with a yawn. "Standard questions, really. They wanted to know my movements, how I knew Nigel…that sort of thing. Have you heard from them, yet?"

Gregory uncorked a bottle of Bill's favourite wine and set it on the side to air, before turning to face him.

"As a matter of fact, they came to see me today."

"Oh? I'm surprised they made a house call."

"They wanted something," Gregory said. "Once I'd confirmed my whereabouts, which must have corroborated your account of our movements last Saturday, they asked me if I—or, rather, *we*—would come on board and assist them with their enquiry."

Douglas' eyebrows flew into his hairline.

"I understood that Nigel had died of a heart attack," he said. "That isn't the case?"

Gregory gave a quick shake of his head, and folded his arms across his chest.

"Technically speaking, yes, but it's not the full story. They found a fatal level of poison—hemlock—in his bloodstream," he said. "It would have brought on asphyxiation and eventual cardiac arrest."

"Poor Nigel," Douglas said. "I can't imagine…well, we must help—"

"We were requested specifically by their superintendent," Gregory interjected. "A man by the name of Simon Campbell."

"Ah," Douglas said, slowly. "I see."

"I went along to The Yard today to hear the facts and take a look at the file, before I knew who was behind it," Gregory continued. "It's unclear whether Nigel took his own life or had his life taken from him, but they want us to produce two profiles covering either eventuality."

"You're reluctant?"

Gregory reached for the bottle of wine, pouring a healthy splash into two glasses.

"I remember the last time," he said.

"Hard to forget," Douglas agreed, and took one of the offered glasses. "I wouldn't blame you, for not wanting to be a part of it. It's a high-profile case, and we couldn't trust Simon not to throw us to the wolves again."

Gregory sipped his wine thoughtfully. "But—?"

"But," Douglas agreed, toasting his glass. "Nigel was my friend. So is his wife—and I know his family. I can't stand by and not use my knowledge to help, even in some small way."

Gregory had known what the answer would be, and was prepared for it, but he couldn't prevent the sinking feeling in his stomach.

"You're under no obligation to join me," Douglas said, quietly. "You've had enough to think about, these past few weeks, and more to come, with the professional conduct hearing coming up."

Gregory took another gulp of wine, and thought of the letter sitting on his desk inviting him to come and defend himself in front of a panel of his peers. He'd breached several codes of conduct by accepting his own mother as a patient at Southmoor; the mother who, suffering from Munchausen syndrome by proxy, had murdered his two siblings in their infancy and almost killed him, too. She'd been detained under the Mental Health Act since the eighties and, consequently, hadn't recognised her own son as a grown man, especially since he'd changed his name years before. To her, he'd been her psychiatrist, nothing more. He was the man who tried each week to help her recover, who listened to her ravings with a placid, professional face. All the while, he'd craved understanding and, if he was brutally honest, just one scrap of remorse, so he could try to forgive her and move on with his own life.

But, of course, there had been no apology, and then she'd killed herself, removing any possibility of there ever being one forthcoming.

Did any of it amount to an adequate defence against a charge of professional misconduct? Would they understand the small, sad hope of the boy he'd once been? The hope that, one day, his mother might recognise him and express how sorry she was, how she'd loved him, all along, and that it was merely her illness that had prevented her from being the mother she'd always longed to be—and that he'd always longed for?

He doubted it.

"I can handle it," was all he said.

Douglas wasn't fooled. "How are you holding up?"

Gregory thought of the sleepless nights and of the nightmares whenever he did manage to drift off; he thought of the hallucinations he thought he'd left behind and the bursts of energy compared with long periods of malaise.

"I'm too much in my own thoughts," he said, and came to a decision. "I'll help with the Villiers case—it'll be a good distraction."

"If it gets to be too much, you'll tell me?"

Gregory turned to his friend and thought, not for the first time, what a wonderful father he might have made.

"You'll be the first to know."

A few minutes passed in companionable silence, before Douglas spoke again.

"You know, in days gone by, hemlock was used to treat mania," he said. "In mild doses, it acts as a sedative."

Gregory smiled.

"I'll keep it in mind."

CHAPTER 6

The following morning, Gregory awoke before the dawn and threw open a window to let the cold breeze wash over his body. He welcomed the shock, and breathed deeply of the crisp, frosty air until shards of sunlight began to break through the layers of steel-grey cloud, burnishing the River Thames a glittering, molten silver. He watched its slow, inexorable progress towards the sea for long minutes, thinking of how the river hardly changed and how much it must have seen in the millennia since human beings had decided to settle on its banks. Battles, fires, parades worthy of kings and queens, executions, industry... and, more recently, tourist boats chugging back and forth, some of them in the shape of giant ducks.

It took all sorts.

Turning his mind to more pressing matters than boats resembling waterfowl, Gregory spent a couple of hours at his desk researching the late Nigel Villiers, scribbling down notes and printing articles of particular interest, building his own dossier from which he would begin to construct a profile. Following a lengthy discussion with Bill the previous evening, he had a good idea of the kind of man his friend perceived Villiers to have been, which broadly matched how the rest of the world had seen him. Apparently, Nigel Villiers had been a character at university, forty years earlier; part of the Cambridge Stagelights, he'd acted with contemporaries who had gone on to make successful careers of their own. Whilst he'd read Modern Languages at Magdalen College, Villiers hadn't excelled himself academically, having been far too interested in his newfound vocation and in the endless opportunities for *fun*. There were shades of Sebastien Flyte in him, Gregory thought, remembering Evelyn Waugh's character in *Brideshead Revisited*. A privileged man from a privileged background, who could afford to be unconcerned about having left university scraping a third-class degree because a glittering career awaited him just around the corner. Bill recalled how talent scouts and theatre producers had ear-marked Villiers for prestigious parts in the West End, even before he'd graduated, and life had been mapped out for young Nigel.

How, then, had the two men struck up such an unlikely friendship?

Bill admitted that, back in those days, he'd been drawn to the glamorous world Villiers inhabited; to the parties, the people and punting on the River Cam, all of which were a contrast to his own upbringing and expectations, which were of hard work and gratitude for the enormous opportunity he'd been given. Douglas had earned his place at Cambridge, you see—not because of any longstanding family connection, but because he'd been the brightest student in his school. He'd been a scholarship boy with limited means, which he'd conserved as much as possible. Villiers had taken a shine to him after a chance meeting on the college rowing team, finding Bill's particular brand of intelligence and wit a valuable boon to his eclectic circle of friends, and the lure of champagne and tuxedos had been too great to refuse.

But what of the man himself? Gregory had wondered. *What of Nigel's character?*

For all his wealth and entitlement, Bill remembered him fondly as a vibrant personality and, if he'd ever upset anyone, it was never maliciously done. Feckless or thoughtless, perhaps, but never intentional.

Which, of course, didn't remove the possibility that sometime, somehow, Nigel Villiers had caused very grave upset, and had paid for it with his life.

Shortly after noon, Gregory dipped beneath the colourful Art Deco canopy of The Old Palace Theatre, where he found DCI Hope waiting for him. She was dressed simply again—no frills, no make-up—and her hair was damp from a brief rain shower earlier.

The lack of artifice suited her.

"I didn't think I'd be seeing you again," she said, in her usual forthright manner.

"I didn't think you would either," he said. "No DS Carter, today?"

"There's plenty for him to do back at the office. The team are working flat out to try to tie this thing up. No Professor Douglas?" she countered.

Gregory shook his head.

"He has commitments back at the university," he said. "But we're working on the profiles together—I'll copy any relevant information to him."

"Fine by me," she said, with a shrug. "Shall we?"

With that, she led the way inside the foyer, where they were met by one of the ushers.

"Are you looking to buy tickets for the matinée today?" he asked. "I'm sorry to tell you, we're completely sold out."

Hope took out her warrant card and made the introductions.

"We're here to see Jasper Pugh," she said. "Where's the theatre manager's office, please?"

The usher stammered out some directions and scuttled off, presumably to warn his friends that the fuzz was in the building.

"I thought there was no understudy for Nigel Villiers," Gregory muttered. "It's barely been a week, and the show is back up and running. Isn't that a bit quick?"

"You know what they say—'the show must go on,'" Hope replied. "They've recruited some bloke called Alan Midsomer, who's not quite in the same league as Villiers but he's a decent pick at short notice. No previous connection with the deceased, by the way."

Gregory smiled, thinking that she always seemed to be one step ahead of him.

"What's the story with Pugh?" he asked, keeping his voice low as they made their way along a carpeted corridor towards the manager's office.

"Longstanding friend and colleague of Villiers," she said, equally softly. "They've known each other for years and co-own this theatre—that is, until Villiers died. His share passes to his wife, now."

Gregory nodded.

"Pugh is currently in a relationship with one of the actors in the production—a young woman by the name of Jasmine Kohli."

"Was there any nepotism involved in her casting?"

"I wondered that," Hope said, throwing a smile back over her shoulder. "It seems you're as cynical as I am. But, no, by all accounts they only met after Kohli joined the production, not before."

Presently, they arrived outside a smart, white-painted door with a small brass plaque that read, 'MANAGER'. Hope knocked and, a moment later, they heard a disembodied voice inviting them to 'come'.

Did people still say that? Gregory wondered.

Apparently so.

CHAPTER 7

Jasper Pugh's office was large, which was by no means obvious given the fact it was stuffed to brimming with antiques and collectibles from the theatrical world. It was a trove of memorabilia, with countless framed photographs and preserved copies of show programmes from the 1920s and 30s, their edges yellowed with age. In the corner of the room, there was a cardboard cut-out of a famous actress who'd recently finished her run at the theatre, while in the centre of it all was an enormous captain's desk in polished mahogany, behind which a tall, slender man was seated. He was dressed impeccably and with absolute conformity to stereotype: the shirt he wore being pin-striped and open-collared, allowing room for the red silk cravat knotted around his neck. His hair—a shade of brown that defied conventional ageing—was brushed back from a tanned forehead, and, when he smiled, his teeth were a blinding shade of white.

"DCI Hope? Good to see you again," he said, rising to shake her hand before turning to Gregory. "I seem to recognise you?"

"This is Doctor Alexander Gregory," Hope told him. "He performed CPR on Sir Nigel, last Saturday, and will be assisting us with our enquiries as a police consultant."

"Oh, yes…yes, of course, I remember now," Pugh said, sadly. "I didn't get a chance to thank you for your efforts, Doctor."

He held out a hand to him, which Gregory took.

"You have my condolences," he said.

"Thank you," Pugh replied. "It's been very hard for all of us. To be honest, I don't know that it's really sunk in yet."

He let go of Gregory's hand and indicated a couple of leather armchairs arranged in front of his desk.

"Please, make yourselves comfortable. Can I offer you a drink?"

"No, thank you," Hope said, and Gregory was intrigued to observe her in action, noting the subtle softening to her voice. He imagined a lot of people were persuaded to talk more freely, because of it.

"So, how can I help you?" Pugh asked, settling back into his chair. "I gave my statement to one of your colleagues last week—DS Carter, I think it was."

"You did," Hope said. "We're grateful for that. However, certain evidence has come to light which has thrown up further lines of enquiry, and we need to go over everybody's movements on the night Sir Nigel died once more."

"Evidence?" Pugh frowned. "I thought Nigel had a heart attack?"

"He did, sir."

Hope did not elaborate, and continued to look at him with an open, friendly expression.

"Well, whatever it might be, I'm sure there's a simple explanation," Pugh said, in the kind of falsely optimistic tone a parent might use to congratulate a child who'd placed last in every race. "I'll help you however I can."

"We were hoping to take a walk through the theatre, to get a lay of the land," Hope said. "Do you have any objections?"

"None at all," he said. "We have a matinée performance at two-thirty today and, naturally, I'd rather there wasn't an obvious police presence when our audience begins to arrive. They're like vultures when it comes to gossip, and I feel it's my duty to the theatre and to Nigel to protect its reputation as far as possible."

"We'll be done before then," she assured him.

"Very well, then."

"Before we look around, I'd be grateful if you could recap your movements for us, on the night Sir Nigel died?"

Pugh looked between the pair of them, and the penny dropped. "Certainly, but...look, is this now a *murder* enquiry?"

"We are treating Sir Nigel's death as suspicious," Hope replied.

Pugh was shocked. "But..." he blustered. "That can't be the case. Nobody would want to harm Nigel, *nobody*—"

"It's important not to jump to conclusions," Hope said. "We're exploring all possibilities."

He nodded, looking pale and suddenly older than he had, only minutes before. "Poor Nigel," he said, rubbing a tired hand over his eyes. "He was one of my closest friends, you know. He was, to coin that detestable phrase, one in a million."

Hope and Gregory adopted joint expressions of compassion.

"You wanted to know my movements?" he said, distractedly. "Of course. Let's see...it was opening night, which is always more nerve-racking than one imagines, even after you've been in the business for as long as I have."

"How long is that?" Gregory asked.

"Thirty-two years," Pugh said, and nodded towards one of the pictures on the wall, which was of himself as a much younger man. "I grew up in Hastings and wanted the bright lights of the city. When I first came to London, I thought I'd tread the boards myself—I was a dancer, really, not an actor. That one's of me as part of the ensemble in *The Nutcracker* at Sadler's Wells, taken in December of '81."

Dutifully, they turned to look at it, and made noises of appreciation.

"I was never going to make it big," he admitted. "I just didn't have the same passion as the others, and I preferred to live life, not hide myself away for hours on end rehearsing. I suppose that's how Nigel and I became friends: we both shared a certain...*joie de vivre.*"

"How did you meet?"

"Through his wife, Rebecca," Pugh said. "She and I were in a production of *Pygmalion* together— it must have been around '83 or '84—and we got along famously. Becca was playing Eliza, of course, and I'd managed to land Freddie—Lord knows how. Anyway, she and Nigel often held parties, and I was invited along to one of them. We became firm friends, and Nigel helped me to move into the production side of things, introduced me to the right people...that sort of thing. Around ten years ago, we decided to join forces and step in to revitalise this old place."

He gestured widely, to encompass the theatre building.

"He sounds like a very useful person to have known," Gregory remarked.

"I admit, he was," Pugh said. "I won't deny that our friendship had its benefits, but what many people don't understand is that Nigel was a very discerning man. He met a lot of people who wanted to know him because of what he could do for them, but that's a privilege he afforded only to those he deemed worthy of his effort. He had no time for those who didn't make their own luck, or whom he didn't find interesting, in some way or another."

"Interesting?" Gregory queried.

"You know," Pugh said, waving a hand in the air. "Funny—or intelligent. He admired those who could hold their own, and detested hangers-on."

And preferred to remain the patriarch, Gregory surmised.

"You were telling us about opening night," Hope said, steering the conversation back.

"Yes. I spent most of the day here at the theatre dealing with last minute disasters, fighting fires…all the usual detritus you'd imagine before a big event."

"I'm afraid neither of us are familiar with the theatrical world," Hope said, with another of her smiles. "Perhaps you could give us an idea of the kind of fires you're talking about."

Pugh let out a gusty sigh. "Last minute changes to stage direction from Margot, which meant tweaking the props. A malfunction in the curtain which needed to be fixed…two of the ushers not turning up for work. Dealing with the histrionics of those cast members who'd decided, sometime between the dress rehearsal and opening night, that they were suddenly no good, unworthy and unwilling to show their faces on stage. Impostor Syndrome is rife in our world, so I'm usually called upon to administer a pep talk and remind them of how marvellous they are, et cetera, et cetera."

"Who needed a pep talk, on that evening?"

"Well, believe it or not...*Nigel*," Pugh said, and pulled a face. "Look—I don't like speaking ill of the dead."

"No ill has been spoken—yet," Gregory murmured.

"Well, it was very unusual for Nigel to be temperamental," Pugh continued, wanting to make that very clear. "He had a reputation—rightfully so— for being consistent and calm before a performance. He didn't tend to get stage fright because it was his vocation, you see. He was born to do it."

"But last Saturday was different?" Hope said.

"He didn't seem himself," Pugh admitted. "He was edgy, nervous...a bit irritable, if you know what I mean. I remember wondering if something else was on his mind. Stage psychology is a bit like sports psychology, in that regard. Outside distractions can affect an actor's performance. They need to be in the right head space."

"Did Nigel mention anything that was upsetting him?" Hope asked. "*Anyone*?"

Pugh thought about it, then shook his head.

"No, I'm sorry, he didn't. After the speeches at around six o'clock, he went back to his room and I left him to it, so that hair and make-up could do their work. I popped my head around the door at seven and found most of the others gathered in his room for a pre-curtain drink, and he seemed more like his usual self, so I joined them for a minute or two and then left."

He paused, swallowing a sudden constriction in his throat, and was embarrassed to find tears clouding his eyes.

"That—that was the last time we spoke, before he died. I think I said something terribly trivial, like, 'break a leg'. How I wish I'd known…there was so much more I'd have liked to say to him."

Pugh's voice faltered on the last sentence, and he rose from his chair to look out of one of the narrow, upper windows overlooking St Martin's Lane, too proud to break down in front of strangers.

When he turned back, his voice was recovered.

"If anything has been amiss, I'll do all I can to help you, Chief Inspector. If someone has hurt Nigel, I want you to find them, lock 'em up and throw away the key."

There was that retributive spirit Bill had spoken of, Gregory thought, but he understood the impulse for revenge. When it came to loved ones, it was a rare soul who could forgive those who harmed them, and, for many victims of crime and their families, it was often a bridge too far.

Had he truly forgiven his mother, for instance?

The jury was still out.

CHAPTER 8

"Quite a character, isn't he?"

DCI Hope ventured the opinion once they were safely out of earshot, getting lost in the corridors of The Old Palace Theatre as they made their way in the vague direction of the dressing rooms.

"Pugh? Yes, he's exactly what I'd have imagined a theatre manager and producer to look like— although, of course, as part-owner, he probably has much more say in the running of the theatre than might be the case for the ordinary manager."

"He doesn't appear to be overbearing," Hope said, fairly. "In fact, he seemed devastated by the loss of his friend."

"He's a former actor," Gregory pointed out.

Hope grinned. "And I thought I was the cynical one."

"Who's next on the list?" Gregory asked. "I assume you chose this time of day knowing that most of the cast would be here, preparing for the matinee performance."

"You don't miss a trick, do you?" she said. "Of course, you're right. I was hoping to catch each of them for five minutes, to give you an opportunity to meet them and for me to rattle them a bit."

"I don't remember seeing that in the official guide to police interview techniques."

"It's in the footnotes," she said, flashing him a quick smile.

Presently, they reached the end of a corridor and emerged onto a half landing, from which three narrow staircases spouted off in different directions.

"It's like an Escher painting," Gregory remarked.

Ava darted a quick glance in his direction, thinking of the Escher prints she had on her bedroom wall at home. She'd never met anyone else who appreciated his work, but some sense of self-preservation held her back from saying as much.

"Yes, it is," she said. "I think Pugh said to bear left from here."

They took the left staircase which led them downstairs, past the stage door.

"To get here for half past five, Villiers left his flat in Mayfair at five o'clock, taking a pre-booked taxi his wife ordered for them both. They arrived together and then separated, so that she could meet friends for a pre-theatre drink across the road at The Ivy restaurant, while he entered the theatre through this door, just like all the other cast members," Hope said, pausing briefly to push open the door and glance down the alleyway outside.

"Any CCTV?"

"Nothing indoors, as you can see," Hope replied. "There's an ancient camera above the door here but, when I requested the tape, I was told it had been decommissioned years ago and was mostly there as a deterrent. There's a camera up there beside the streetlamp, so we've contacted the local council to see if we can get the footage. It'll only be partial, judging by the angle, but it might help with the process of elimination."

Gregory nodded, considering the light and the local vicinity. For an alleyway, it was well-lit and not long enough to be classified as dangerous; they could see pedestrians walking at either end. Set against that, owing to the season, darkness would already have fallen by the time Villiers arrived at the theatre and that could hide a multitude of sins. However, the stage door required an access code, without which it was not possible to enter.

"If there was an unknown perpetrator, this wouldn't have been an ideal point of entry," Hope said, reading his mind again. "They'd have to know the security code, which was changed only recently to coincide with the new production."

Unless somebody told them the code, Gregory thought.

"Are there any other access points?"

"A couple of fire doors—again, inaccessible from outside—and the main entrance."

Gregory knew that the main doors were kept open from around ten o'clock in the morning, to allow people to come in and buy tickets from the box office, in the foyer of the theatre. It would be easy enough for someone to come in, ostensibly to buy a ticket, ask to use the facilities and find a nice hidey-hole while they waited for Villiers to arrive backstage. The foyer was not 'policed', and it was possible for people to slip through the net.

While he turned over the possibilities in his mind, they followed the staircase down and then up again, through a swing door marked, 'PRIVATE', until they reached a long corridor with a row of doors, each with a different name taped on the front.

"Villiers' former dressing room is the largest, at the other end of the corridor nearest the stage," Hope told him. "Shall we start at this end and work our way along?"

Gregory followed her lead, and approached the first door marked, 'PETER GRAY'.

"Ah, The Fool," he said, and raised a knuckle to the wood.

Seconds later, it was opened by the man himself, who was dressed in costume but not yet made up.

He looked at the pair of them, but his eyes lingered on Gregory.

"DCI Hope," she said, showing him her warrant card. "This is Doctor Gregory. May we come in for a quick chat? It's about Sir Nigel."

Gray looked as if he might have refused, but then relented.

"You'd better come in."

As it happened, Peter Gray was very far from being the fool he portrayed on stage.

Having done three years' medical training before deciding his talents lay in another direction, Gray had been a jobbing actor for the past fifteen years, accepting a steady stream of stage and television roles which might have led the average viewer to remark that, 'they recognised his face' without necessarily being able to put a name to it. Despite being in possession of an enthusiastic agent, Gray was yet to receive a leading role that might have elevated him into the kind of sphere to which he aspired because, whilst enthusiastic, his agent had neglected to tell him that talent alone was not sufficient to have production companies beating a pathway to his door. Age and time were against him and, unfortunately for Gray, his looks, although pleasant, were not enough to build marketing campaigns around or invite offers to play moody romantic heroes, more was the pity.

Gray was unaware that he wore the weight of this disappointment on his sleeve, but then, he was not in the habit of meeting behavioural specialists on any regular basis.

"Thank you for your time, Mr Gray," Hope said, once they'd packed themselves into his cubby-hole. "We know you have a performance to prepare for this afternoon, so we won't keep you for very long."

He nodded and sat down on the chair at his dressing table, which was more of a plank of wood fitted against one wall of the room, atop of which an IKEA mirror had been fitted to give it some pazazz.

"I suppose you want to tie up all the loose ends, after Nigel's death," he said, but his eyes strayed to Gregory again.

"We do have some questions," Hope said, and flipped open her notebook. "I understand you were the one to raise the alarm upon finding Sir Nigel in distress on stage. Is that correct?"

He nodded, and went back over his movements up until he realised Villiers was unresponsive.

"That's when I called out to see if there was a doctor in the house, and—"

He stopped and looked at Gregory afresh.

"I'm sorry—I've just remembered who you are," he said. "You were the doctor who tried to help Nigel."

Gregory nodded.

"Well, thanks for all you did," Gray said, and reached for the glass of water sitting at his elbow. "I'm sorry, I'd offer you both something, but as you can see, things are a bit limited in here…"

He gestured around the room, which was smaller than a prison cell.

"Please, don't trouble yourself," Hope smiled. "We just have a few standard questions to ask. Firstly, I wonder if you could take us back over your movements on the day in question—what time did you arrive at the theatre, for example?"

Gray choked slightly on his water, and coughed a bit, thumping his chest with one balled fist.

"My—movements? What do you need to know that for? I thought Nige' had a heart attack?"

"It's a question of being thorough, Mr Gray."

"Do I need a solicitor?"

Hope raised an eyebrow. "I don't know, Mr Gray. Do you feel you need a solicitor to answer these questions?"

Gregory held back a smile.

"No, I s'pose not," he said, and let out a nervous laugh. "Um, well, I got here at about five-thirty. That's when most of us piled in, because we know Jasper and Margot had a few words to say at six."

"What did you do, once you got here?"

Gray took another long gulp of water, his throat feeling suddenly dry.

"Um, I don't know. I came in here, I lounged around a bit, went over my lines…that sort of thing."

"Did you see anyone else during that time?"

His eyes skittered between the pair of them, and then fell away.

"No—nobody. I stayed in here until six, or a couple of minutes before, and then made my way to the stage to hear the speeches and clap along."

"Did you speak to Sir Nigel during that time, or see anyone who did?"

Gray frowned, then shook his head.

"I'm sorry, I can't remember," he said. "I might have said 'hello', but everyone was milling around, and my attention was on Jasper and then Margot, not on Nigel."

"He didn't want to give a speech?" Gregory queried.

For the first time, Gray became animated.

"Actually, I did find that unusual," he said, leaning forward. "Nigel was part-owner of the theatre, and he's never been shy of public speaking. I'd have thought he would have said a few words but…he mustn't have felt like it, or maybe he was already feeling unwell."

"Did you happen to notice whether Sir Nigel was upset or out of sorts?" Hope prodded.

"No, I'm sorry. I've been over this in my mind for the past week, wondering if I should have noticed him looking pale or something like that, but..." He shrugged. "I'm sorry. Aside from being a little quieter than usual, he looked just like himself."

They asked a few more questions before excusing themselves, shutting the door carefully behind them.

"I don't think you need me to tell you the most obvious take-away from that encounter, do you?" Gregory said.

Hope shook her head. "Even I can tell when somebody's lying through their teeth," she said. "The question is—why?"

Gregory nodded. "Shall we see who's behind Door Number Two?"

CHAPTER 9

They found all three of King Lear's daughters gathered in the dressing room of the eldest sibling, Goneril, a character played by a striking-looking woman by the name of Jasmine Kohli. She answered the door on their second knock, still laughing at something one of the others had said, but her face fell immediately upon catching sight of Hope and Gregory.

"This is the backstage area," she said, brusquely. "If you're looking for the box office, you need to head back to the main entrance."

"Ms Kohli? You might not remember me—" Hope began.

"I'm sorry, I don't remember every person I meet. Now, I'm going to have to ask you to leave. This area is clearly marked, 'Private', and you shouldn't be here. If you don't leave, I'll have to call someone to have you shown out."

Hope and Gregory both happened to know security was very limited at The Old Palace Theatre, but they weren't about to split hairs.

"DCI Hope, from the Metropolitan Police," she said, with admirable restraint. "This is Doctor Gregory, our consultant. We were hoping to have a word—"

"Who is it, Jas?"

An actor they knew to be Olivia Routledge-Brown appeared in the doorway and her attention was immediately caught by the tall, dark-haired man.

"Oh, my God! You're the doctor who helped Nigel, aren't you?"

Her big, blue eyes widened expressively.

"We all wished we could have thanked you, on the night," Olivia gushed, reaching for both of his hands and holding them in what DCI Hope considered to be an over-the-top manner. "Why don't you come in?"

Gregory found himself being tugged inside, while Hope followed with decidedly less enthusiasm.

"Fran, this is Doctor Gregory," Olivia was saying to the third woman in the room. "You remember, he's the guy who performed CPR on Nigel, last Saturday?"

"Oh, my goodness!" Frances Unwin, another up-and-coming star of the London stage, rose to her feet and enveloped Gregory in a hug. From her position by the door, DCI Hope might have been irritated, were it not for his comical expression of surprise, which was priceless.

"Sorry to break it up, but I wonder if I might ask the three of you some questions?"

All three pairs of eyes turned to her.

"This is DCI Hope, from the Metropolitan Police," Jasmine explained.

"Is anything wrong?" Frances asked, relinquishing her hold of Gregory to clasp her hands to her chest. "I mean, of course, it's awful that Nigel had a heart attack, but he *was* of a certain age, and he *did* like the best of everything…"

"Yes, we were only saying the other day, it's a lesson for us all to watch the cholesterol," Olivia put in, and the others made sounds of agreement. "My grandad had a heart attack around the same age, and you know, he loved his fry-ups—"

"Unfortunately, our enquiry as to the precise cause of Sir Nigel's death is ongoing." Hope cut short any further discussion of starchy fat, since they didn't have all day and, as it happened, she'd enjoyed a bacon bap that very morning and didn't need the guilt trip.

"Are you saying there was something suspicious about how he died?" Jasmine asked.

Hope turned to her.

"That's what we're hoping to find out, Ms Kohli. Perhaps you'd like to take a seat?"

The three women settled themselves on a battered old chesterfield which took up the entire length of one wall of the dressing room.

"The first thing I'd like to ask each of you is what time you arrived at the theatre, last Saturday?"

As their natural leader, Jasmine spoke first.

"We're sharing a flat beside Notting Hill tube station," she explained. "We left at the same time and shared a taxi across town."

She rattled off the address.

"We got here about five or ten past five," Jasmine continued.

The others nodded.

"All right," Hope murmured. "What did you do, once you got here?"

"We each went to our dressing rooms," Jasmine replied. "I wanted to go over my lines, and I think Olivia wanted a word with Margot—is that right?"

Olivia nodded again.

"I wanted to ask if I could play a scene slightly differently," she said, and launched into a lengthy explanation of the reading of her character and associated stage direction. "I couldn't find Margot, so I went to my dressing room and started to get changed."

"Around what time was this?" Hope murmured.

"It must have been quarter-past-five," Olivia said.

"Does the Director have her own office?" Gregory asked.

"Yes, it's not much, but she has the room next to Nigel's, at the end of the corridor—oh, I should probably say, 'next to Alan's'. It's so hard for him, having to step in after what happened."

DCI Hope had met the man, briefly, and thought that, on the contrary, Alan Midsomer seemed inordinately pleased with his lot, even with the spectre of Nigel Villiers hanging over him.

"Did you go along to the speeches at six?" she asked.

Three heads nodded.

"I was a couple of minutes late, because I had a wardrobe malfunction," Jasmine explained. "My zip got caught at the back, and I had to go and hunt for somebody to help. In the end, I gave up, because everyone was down on the stage, anyway."

Hope made a note.

"How would you describe the mood at that time?" she asked them.

They looked amongst themselves.

"Sort of...as you'd expect," Frances said, with a nervous little laugh. "People were a bit on edge because it was opening night and that's just normal. There was also a bit of excitement, for the same reason."

"How would you describe Sir Nigel's mood at that time?" Gregory asked them.

"Well, now you mention it, I suppose he was a bit less cheerful than usual," Olivia said, and looked to the others for confirmation. "Wouldn't you say?"

"I thought he seemed tired," Jasmine said, with a shrug. "Thought he must be getting a bit too old to be burning the candle at both ends. I'm sorry to say it, but, when he started repeating his lines on stage, my first thought was, 'That'll be because he was out too late the night before'. I feel sorry that I thought it, now."

The other two put comforting arms around her, and were at pains to tell her she couldn't possibly have known.

"I wondered if he'd been hitting the booze," Frances admitted. "Nigel liked a drink—always the best of whatever tipple was going—and, honestly, I don't know how it didn't affect him more than it did. He was always so sharp and switched on, you know? But, that night, when we were listening to the speeches, I thought he looked like he wasn't really listening, or he was a bit out of focus."

"What made you think that?" Gregory asked.

"I don't know, really," she said, feeling a bit awkward now that she'd said it. "I was just strange for him to be so quiet. He didn't seem engaged with what Jasper or Margot were saying and then, later, when we popped into his room for a pre-curtain drink, he was smiling and saying all the right things, but it seemed his mind was somewhere else entirely."

"Did he mention anything to you that was unusual, or say he'd been concerned about anything?" Gregory prodded.

The three shook their heads.

"Nigel wasn't really the kind of person to confide like that—or, at least, not to us," Olivia said. "We worked very well professionally, he was warm and welcoming, but he wouldn't talk to any of us about personal matters."

Frances agreed, but Jasmine looked away.

"He wasn't the sort of person who *needed* to confide," she said, and there was a hard edge to her voice. "He was untouchable."

Gregory shook his head.

"Death comes to us all, in the end."

Hope and Gregory continued to make their way down the corridor, speaking to the people who had, for a time at least, become Nigel Villiers' adoptive family.

"It really *is* like one big, extended family," Margot Winters confirmed, once they reached the little room that passed for her office at the far end of the hall. "Relationships are compressed in the theatre. You interact with people intensely during a relatively short space of time, so you end up making fast friendships."

"Or the opposite?" Gregory asked.

She gave an awkward shrug. "Yes, I suppose that's equally true."

"Tell us about the dynamics in this production, Ms Winters," DCI Hope said. "There must have been some of the cast who got along better than others, for instance."

Winters leaned back against her desk and folded her arms, in a gesture that was classically defensive.

"What does this have to do with Nigel's death?" she prevaricated. "I can't see how backstage gossip can help him, now."

"You'd be surprised," Gregory said, with a guileless smile.

"It's important for us to have as full a picture as possible," Hope put in, swiftly. "It may seem like gossip to you, but it's valuable for us to understand where tensions may have lain."

Winters heaved a big sigh, and then let it wheeze out again.

"Look, you don't understand," she said, with just a touch of condescension. "At some time or another, they've all been at one another's throats, or mine, for that matter. *Especially* mine," she tagged on, with a self-deprecating laugh.

She reached for a fat wad of papers on the desk behind her and held it in front of them. A quick glance told them it was a script of *King Lear*, heavily annotated.

"You see all the notes?" she said, letting it drop back down onto the desk. "That's just the tip of the iceberg. Numerous things have changed since the actors met for their first read-through. Just when we think we have a scene just right, one of them will pipe up and tell me they don't like this or that, while another one positively loves it. Honestly, it's like herding cats, sometimes."

"My sympathies," Hope murmured, and Gregory hid a smile. When your world was one of discovering and investigating some of the worst damage one human being could inflict upon another, he supposed it was hard to get too worked up about mundane matters of people management.

"Anyway, this naturally creates a certain amount of tension between those involved, but it's short-lived and seldom leads to anything more—certainly not anything of the kind of gravity you might imagine."

"All the same, is there anybody who was consistently difficult—particularly with Sir Nigel?"

Margot chewed on her lip for a couple of seconds, obviously torn between feeling like she was telling tales and helping a police effort.

Civic duty won out.

"Well, I suppose I should say that Jasmine and Sir Nigel didn't really see eye to eye," she admitted. "They were different in so many ways: he was a privileged white, middle-class man whereas Jas has had to survive in an industry that often overlooks women of colour...hell, women in general—and *I* would know."

She thought briefly of all the times she'd been passed over for a male counterpart, all the times she'd had to fight to keep a job, even after she'd won it. Then, because she could be honest with herself, wondered how many of those times were because somebody else was better suited, and how many of those times were because of some sort of gender bias.

It was hard to tell the difference, especially in her own mind.

"Nigel...well, his humour could be a bit tone deaf," she continued. "I tried to mention it to him, but he was set in his ways and had no desire to change them."

"I suppose there was no great incentive," Hope remarked. "Would anybody have challenged him, in his position?"

There was a meaningful silence, which was all the answer they needed.

"I suppose the only person who might have challenged him was Jasper," Margot did say. "They'd known each other long enough, for one thing. But it complicated matters that—"

She broke off, obviously wondering if she was saying too much.

"That Jasper had struck up a relationship with Jasmine Kohli?" Hope finished for her, and watched relief pass over the other woman's face.

"*Yes*," she said. "I'm afraid Nigel didn't really approve of their…ah, friendship, and told Jasper as much. It might have affected the extent to which he'd have listened to any well-meaning advice, if he'd lost respect for the person trying to give it, if you catch my drift."

Gregory nodded.

"How do you know this?" he asked, and the woman bristled.

"Well, I wasn't listening at key holes, if that's what you think!" she said. "Half of the company heard them going at it, a couple of weeks ago."

"Do you remember anything else of what was said between them?" Hope asked.

"Not really," Margot replied, more calmly. "As I told you, there are often outbursts in the weeks leading up to a new run, and it wasn't out of the ordinary for Jasper and Nigel to have an argument one day and be the best of friends the next. I only remember Nigel saying something about not mixing work with pleasure, and Jasper saying something in return about that being rich, coming from him."

"What do you think he meant by that?" Hope asked, once again beating Gregory to it.

Margot shrugged.

"Nigel met Rebecca while they were in the same production," she said. "I assumed he was referring to that."

Hope smiled, and made a note.

"Ah—moving on to what happened that evening," she said. "Could you tell us where you were, from around five o'clock?"

Margot ran both hands through her short mop of curls and then hugged herself again.

"Well, I got here early, at around two o'clock. I needed to check on the sets, speak to the crew... all that jazz. It always takes longer than you think to go over all the fine details, and I like to be on top of things."

"I understand most of the actors arrived at around five o'clock?" Gregory said, after she'd run through her movements before then. "Where were you from then until...say, half past?"

She began rubbing her arms, as if cold.

"I was in here," she said.

"The whole time?" Hope asked, not looking up from her notepad.

"The whole time," Winters confirmed, in a tone that brooked no argument. "Now, if there's nothing else—?"

"Of course," Gregory said. "Thank you for your time."

CHAPTER 10

Lance Beckett had been born Winston Sugden on 1st January 1960, heralding not only a decade defined by swinging, flower power and the continued might of The Beatles, but a sickly, sallow-faced boy who would go on to lead a life of grand expectations that were seldom met.

Winston's mother, Vera Sugden, had been enamoured of one of the young, up-and-coming actors of her generation, and had spent every Friday and Saturday night shivering outside the Stage Door of whichever theatre he happened to be playing, her hair done in the latest style and wearing her best dress and shoes. Her diligence had finally paid off one rainy Saturday night, when the young Arthur Kane had found himself the worse for wear after a bad night on stage and one too many Campari and sodas to make up for it. Unable to drive himself home, and having insulted or alienated most of his colleagues in the theatre, he decided to accept Vera's kind offer to find him a taxi.

She had a homely, unthreatening look about her, after all.

Whether or not he realised that the price of procuring the taxi ride would be having to endure her company on the journey home is unclear, but one thing is for certain: Arthur *did* choose to accept her generous offer of a warm body to lose himself in, though he had barely any recollection of it the following morning, upon wakening to find her shiny, eager face lying beside him.

Vera had it all planned out, you see.

They'd be married, of course. Nothing too fancy, because that was *du trop*. It was fashionable to want something low key and beautiful…a little artsy, just like her beloved Arthur, who would be handsome in a blue suit and tie, with his blond hair brushed back from his perfectly symmetrical face. She'd wear a lacy white number with flowers in her hair, and she'd get her cousin Eileen to curl it for her. Things might be hard in the beginning—he was still just starting out on his long journey to stardom— but that would soon change, she just knew it. Vera would be the glamorous partner of London's brightest star; she'd have her hair coiffed regularly at Vidal Sassoon and wear the latest fashions, whether they suited her, or not.

It was everything she'd ever dreamed of.

Arthur saw all of this shining from her myopic blue eyes that dreary Sunday morning, and some animal sense of self-preservation prompted him to leap from the covers to put some distance between himself and the woman who was, to all intents, a stranger to him.

Don't do anything stupid, his mother had warned him, when he'd left for London. *There'll be lots of girls chasing you, after that film you did. Just you mind yourself, my lad.*

Swallowing bile, Arthur tried to remember if he'd used protection, and his eyes scanned the bedside table and the floor with rising panic.

But there was no comforting little plastic packet to console him.

As it happened, the question of what Arthur might have done upon finding that he'd fathered a child during the long hours of a night he couldn't remember was lost in the sands of time, because, mere days after his interlude with Vera, he was killed in a car accident whilst driving along Edgware Road, and that was that.

At first, Arthur's comfortably middle-class family refused to acknowledge young Winston; grief combined with disappointment upon meeting the boy's mother combined in a perfect storm of rejection. However, with a certain amount of focused harassment, alongside one or two well-placed threats to smear their son's name, Vera was able to secure some of the finer things for her little boy, onto whom she transferred her former idolisation of his father.

Winston would *have* the best of everything and would *be* the best at everything.

She'd see to it.

Sixty-one years later, Lance Beckett thought of his childhood and wondered what life might have been like if he'd simply remained 'Winston Sugden'. If he hadn't inherited his father's looks and his mother's calculating brain, both of which allowed him to succeed in life—but, only to a degree, beyond which he'd never been able to rise.

There was nothing so painful as mediocrity.

His grandparents had paid for a private education, and he'd made the best of it; enough to allow his grandfather to have a word with an old chum in Cambridge, who owed him a favour. That favour was repaid with a crisp white acceptance letter, and Winston had soon left the stifling confines of his mother's home for a new life, with even greater prospects than before.

You're a genius, Win, his mother would say. *You can do anything you want. You could be famous, like your father...*

Conversations of that kind would usually descend into flights of fancy, wherein Vera concocted new, entirely fictitious anecdotes about his late father's elaborate romantic gestures, and of how they'd planned to marry...oh, what a cruel world to have snatched him so soon, like Jimmy Dean, and so on, and so forth.

So, it was with some relief that he arrived in the Junior Common Room on the first day of a new term, and perhaps curiosity about his own lineage had drawn him to an advert pinned on the notice board:

CAMBRIDGE STAGELIGHTS
Open auditions this Thursday
Contact Nigel
Magdalen, 3rd Floor

At first, things had gone so well. Winston was young, good-looking and well-spoken—elocution lessons having been a stipulation of his grandparents' agreement to continue paying for his education—and passably smart, if you overlooked an abundance of polyester. He'd met Nigel Villiers and a group of other bright, young things, and felt an instant sense of homecoming.

"You should think about changing your name," Nigel had blurted out, one day. "Honestly, if you're going to be trying for all the romantic parts, you need something a bit more inspiring than

Winston bloody Sugden. It screams Elephant and Castle, when you want the girls to be screaming other things."

He did have a point.

They'd been reading *King Arthur* at the time, and there was a Beckett play lying discarded on a table nearby, which was how 'Lance Beckett' was born.

He remembered they'd held a makeshift christening, with champagne in lieu of holy water. He remembered the first time he'd told a girl his new name and seen her blush. When his first offer had come through, to play Lysander in *A Midsummer Night's Dream* on the London stage, he'd jumped at the chance, thinking it was his Big Break. There'd been a couple of television movies after that, an episode of *The Avengers* and some bit parts in *Murder, She Wrote* and *Columbo,* as time had worn on. He'd put it about that the producers of the Bond franchise had seriously considered him for the role Timothy Dalton ended up taking, but of course, that had been pie in the sky.

Lance Beckett was a name nobody would remember; not even his own mother, who was in the final stages of dementia and would continue to call him 'Arthur' until she drew her last breath.

He often found himself wondering whether it would have been best never to have known about Arthur Kane. Never to have had the fancy education his grandparents bought him, nor the expectations that education instilled. Maybe it would have been better to have been plain, old Winston Sugden, and to have lived a peaceful, satisfied life of obscurity, never to have tasted even a morsel of that thing called 'fame'.

For, now he'd tasted it, he craved it, and the craving was never satisfied.

CHAPTER 11

A widespread belief that the late Nigel Villiers had died of a heart attack meant that his dressing room was not immediately designated as a crime scene. It had been left open to all and sundry, so that, by the time the case was referred to DCI Hope, there was very little chance of there being any useful trace evidence to be found by even the most hawk-eyed forensic officer. The room was covered in fingerprints, old and new, and although Villiers' personal effects had been confiscated for inspection eventually, it was possible that anything of interest could have been tampered with, removed or otherwise disposed of long before Hope and her team ever set foot inside The Old Palace Theatre.

Nonetheless, she and Gregory decided to pay a visit to Villiers' old dressing room, if only to complete a visual picture of the terrain. They were admitted by his successor, Alan Midsomer, who was the only person inside the theatre walls who seemed entirely unaffected by the recent tragedy.

"Hello there," he said, cheerfully. "You're that *lovely* police officer I spoke to the other day."

It was a statement, not a question, and had been delivered in a manner Gregory found distinctly over-the-top.

"DCI Ava Hope," she reminded him. "This is Doctor Gregory, who's consulting with us on the death of Sir Nigel. I wonder if we might come in for a moment?"

Midsomer held open the door and indicated they should enter.

"How can I help you?" he asked, flopping down onto a red velvet sofa.

The room was noticeably plusher than some of the others they'd seen, as befitted the star of the show. Roses had been arranged in vases of varying size and there was a small seating area, which allowed several people to crowd around a tiny coffee table and discuss Shakespeare or, in this case, suspicious deaths.

"Actually, we were hoping to have a quick look around the room—we won't be long, Mr Midsomer, but—"

"Ah! I see," he said, and jumped up again. "Say no more, say no more…"

He bustled about, scooping up a mug of half-drunk tea which held a suspiciously amber hue, slung a long scarf around his neck and stuffed a packet of Superkings into his back pocket.

"I'll nip outside for a quick smoke," he said. "Ten minutes be enough, d'you reckon?"

He didn't wait for a response, but swept from the room in a cloud of heavy aftershave.

"You didn't want to ask him anything?" Gregory asked.

Hope shook her head. "He's been thoroughly vetted, already," she explained. "He was in Edinburgh at the time Villiers died, and had no personal connections that we can see. His story checks out."

Gregory nodded, and put the man from his mind—for now.

"So, you believe this is where Villiers was most likely to have been poisoned?" he said, casting his sharp eye around the space.

"Yes," Hope replied. "The champagne that was offered onstage was a 'help yourself' scenario, so there was no way of ensuring Villiers would be certain to pick up a contaminated glass."

Gregory had known cases where the objective was not one specific victim, but anyone who happened upon a contaminated batch of food or drink. Worse still, he'd known men who'd contaminated baby food with shards of metal in order to blackmail supermarket chains for large sums of money, playing Russian Roulette with the health and safety of tiny infants.

"Without knowing the source of the hemlock, it's impossible to say for certain whether Nigel was a victim, let alone an *intended* victim," he said. "But, in the absence of any indication of blackmail or threatening behaviour, we have to assume the toxin met its intended recipient."

She nodded. "No CCTV in here, as you can see," she said, gesturing to the bare corners. "Not that I'd expect there to be. People don't like to feel watched while they're getting changed, after all."

"It all depends on who's doing the watching," Gregory murmured, catching her off-guard again. "However, I take your point. It would have been handy to have had some nice, clear footage of an intruder creeping in here to sprinkle hemlock in Villiers' tea."

"Where would be the fun in that?" she said.

Gregory grinned.

"At one point in the evening, Villiers had a roomful of people in here," he said. "Some sitting on that sofa, perhaps, while others stood around or perched on the chair over there."

His eyes traced the space, and then he closed them briefly, remembering the photographs taken of the room as it had been.

"The food tray was on the sideboard," he said, raising a finger to point to a mid-century cabinet sitting against one wall. "But, from what we've heard,

Villiers wasn't seated anywhere near it. He kept to his chair right there, beside the dressing table."

He opened his eyes and nodded towards the mahogany captain's chair with an upholstered leather seat.

"There were a couple of drinks beside him, including the water jug, but it would have taken a fair amount of luck and good timing for someone to slip something into his drink while he wasn't looking," Gregory said. "It would have been an obvious manoeuvre, and very risky. However, if we assume Villiers didn't self-administer, I'd say we're looking for someone with a taste for drama in all forms, and perhaps quite a high appetite for risk."

"What makes you say that?"

"The choice of poison, for one thing," Gregory replied. "It's traceable, and it's unusual. That tells me it was chosen deliberately, possibly for its symbolism or previous association with the death of Socrates. The kind of person who does that wants to be perceived as clever, which is how they perceive themselves. They likely have grandiose ideas about their capabilities, in general, and that isn't the kind of personality who would shrink from the task of dropping a bit of powdered poison into a glass, while nobody's looking. Not forgetting, they may be adept at sleight of hand or misdirection, especially if they have any theatrical training."

While Hope listened, she found she could imagine the kind of personality as clearly as if they were standing in the room beside her. Unfortunately, the vision was nameless and faceless, but that would change.

"Of course," Gregory continued, from all we know of Villiers, the person I've just described could easily have been the man himself. It's a hell of a way to go out, and a way of being remembered for a long time to come."

"But why would he choose hemlock?"

Gregory stuck his hands in his pockets and thought before answering.

"At Socrates' trial, in 399 BC, he was found guilty of two charges. The first was for impiety against the pantheon by failing to acknowledge the same gods the city acknowledged, and the second was for corrupting the youth of Athens by asking them philosophical questions—"

"The nerve," she said, deadpan.

"Quite," he said, with a smile. "Socrates was sentenced to death by hemlock poisoning and, rather than fleeing the city as he could have done, opted to stay and drink his punishment because it was in line with his previous teachings around civic obedience to the law."

"So you're saying he martyred himself?"

"You could say that," Gregory agreed. "He was widely considered to be a man of integrity, and his execution has been interpreted as a poor statement on the democracy at the time. If Villiers took the hemlock knowingly, it's possible he could have been trying to make a statement about himself being a wronged yet honourable man."

Hope folded her arms and stared around the room, at nothing in particular.

"It would make sense, if his character had been maligned in any way, but he was widely revered. He has a clean record, as you know."

Gregory caught his own reflection in the dressing table mirror and looked away swiftly.

"Not everything is recorded," he said quietly.

CHAPTER 12

Lance Beckett took the Tube from his small, rented studio in King's Cross—an area not known for being the finest in London, but it was on the up nowadays, which meant he could pass it off as a deliberate move on his part to be living somewhere fashionable.

It's important to keep up with fashion, Winston, his mother used to say.

Even now, she enjoyed having her hair done by the mobile hairdresser who visited the nursing home once a week and always asked about the latest trends. The hairdresser, a lady called Roisin, would *uhm* and *ahh* over her demands for blonde highlights, whilst curling rollers into his mother's sparse tendrils and spraying the usual amount of Elnett to hold it in place.

He patted his own hair, which had been thinning over the years, a fact he'd been able to disguise by the addition of an artist's cap worn jauntily to one side. He'd grown a bit of facial fuzz, since he'd seen a lot of younger men sporting well-trimmed beards, and he was pleased to note it carried the added benefit of covering the jowls that seemed to have developed along his jawline, which had once been razor sharp. He'd taken some time with his appearance, given the important appointments he had scheduled for that day, and hoped the money he'd splashed in Harvey Nic's was worth it.

Looking around the crowded train carriage, he caught a woman's eye, and gave her one of his trademark smiles—the kind that had once earned him the role as Lysander, but never Romeo.

She looked away quickly and immersed herself in her Kindle.

Probably reading some smut, he thought, unkindly, while trying to swallow the acid flavour of rejection.

Presently, the train pulled into Oxford Circus, and he followed the wave of shoppers filing along the platform towards the exit to street level. He hated being lost amongst the crowd, unnoticed and unrecognised, and a memory flashed into his mind of a time when Nigel had once complained to him about the ignominy of being accosted by strangers.

I wouldn't mind, old boy, but sometimes all one wants is to have a quiet dinner. Is it too much to ask?

Nigel had said, one night when he'd treated them both to dinner at Nobu restaurant, a known celebrity eatery.

It becomes terribly dull not to be able to walk down the street without some dreadful paparazzo or another snapping away, he'd said, another night, when he'd taken Lance to Annabel's for an aperitif before supper.

He'd made all the right noises, sympathised, and said how bloody awful it must be, whilst taking care to wax lyrical about how he, Lance, had all the anonymity he could ever wish for and could pursue his art in a true and authentic way.

Which was, of course, utter rubbish.

He'd sell his soul for another taste of the limelight. He'd make a Faustian pact...whatever it took just to have that woman on the Tube look at him and smile back.

Lance walked along Oxford Street, cursing the new shoes he'd bought, then cut south through the streets of Mayfair towards Berkeley Square. This was another part of London entirely; the province of Claridge's and designer clothing, of supercars and fine dining, where old and new money combined to create a few square miles of cushioned wealth. As he passed the glittering windows of Old Bond Street and paused to look at some of their wares, he found himself comparing the new leather shoes he wore with a more expensive pair on display. Inevitably, he found them wanting.

How proud he'd been of them, only that morning.

Now, they seemed cheap and tacky, and he imagined all eyes were upon him, watching the 'poor' man, the impostor, walking amongst them. Dismayed, he hurried on, turning up the collar of his jacket against the chill, wishing he'd been able to afford a new overcoat. He couldn't have worn the old one hanging in his closet; it wasn't smart enough for Mayfair.

That would all change, soon enough, he thought. *The first thing he'd do with the money is buy himself a whole new wardrobe.*

Maybe a hair transplant…

With these pleasant thoughts circling, Lance made directly for a tall, elegant building flanked by Doric columns on one side of the square, taking care to puff out his chest a bit as he approached the liveried doorman. He had a persona to maintain, and it hadn't let him down, yet.

"Good to see you again, Mr Beckett," the man said, with a certain obsequiousness Lance found entirely appropriate.

"Javier," he said, with a nod. "I'm here to see Lady Villiers—"

"Is she expecting you, sir?"

"Naturally," he lied.

Javier, who had taken the measure of Lance Beckett almost from their first meeting, knew that Mrs Villiers had given express instructions to decline all visitors who weren't already authorised for entry on the list he kept inside his breast pocket.

However, exceptions could always be made, for the right price.

He made a show of retrieving the list, and ran a white gloved finger down the printed names.

"I'm sorry, sir," he said, in a serious tone. "I'm afraid I don't have you on the list for today."

Lance eyed the man with distaste, but decided to play along.

"There must be some mistake," he said. "Check again."

"I could ring Lady Villiers—"

"No need for that," Lance said, knowingly. "I'm one of her late husband's oldest friends, and I'm sure she wouldn't like to think of you having kept me waiting out here for so long. No sense in you coming in for any trouble, is there?"

He made a show of his own, reaching for his wallet.

"That's very considerate, sir," Javier said, and watched him count out a crisp twenty. "Unfortunately—"

He paused, allowing Lance to count out two more twenties before speaking again.

"Now that I think about it, I'm sure Lady Villiers must have made a mistake with the list. Allow me—"

He held open the door, and the money was exchanged in the blink of an eye.

"Have a nice day, sir," Javier said, pocketing the cash.

"Greedy bugger," Lance muttered, and made his way into the marble foyer.

Sir Nigel and Lady Villiers' Berkeley Square apartment spanned the third and fourth floors of one of the oldest buildings in that part of town. Having once been home to a peer of the realm, it had fallen into disrepair sometime during the 1960s and had since been purchased and refurbished by a Russian oligarch who'd been looking for a convenient way to invest some of his abundant, off-balance-sheet cash in London real estate, since none of the football clubs happened to be for sale at the time. Accordingly, the building had been refurbished and individual units sold for eye-wateringly-high prices at the turn of the new millennium, which happened to coincide with a particularly lucrative movie franchise Sir Nigel had been a part of and in which he'd had a financial share.

'Apartment 3' was an eclectic mix of modern art and plush fabrics, decorated in a minimalist style intended to give free rein to the enormous selection of framed stills of Nigel and Rebecca Villiers that were arranged artfully on its expansive white walls. The visual homage might have been off-putting, but Marcus Hale had long since learned to ignore the eyes watching him from black frames, especially when he was supposed to be concentrating on the lady who was naked and willing on the long white sofa beneath him.

It wasn't love, unless you counted a love for *money*, but he certainly liked her enough to give it his best shot.

Thinking of England, and all that…

Finally, she cried out, and he sent up a silent prayer of thanks before joining her, and then collapsed onto the cushions at her side.

"I'm a terrible person," Rebecca Villiers said, as she always did, during the first five minutes post-coitus. "Nigel is barely cold in his grave…"

He's not even in a grave yet, Marcus thought, but held his tongue.

"Of course you're not a terrible person, darling," he said, obligingly, and wondered whether it was time for lunch.

"We have to stop this, Marcus," she said. "We really must."

He sighed, and realised that she was going to need more convincing before lunch. Really, he deserved a medal...or an Oscar.

He turned to her, his eyes adoring and his words imploring.

"You'd break my heart," he said. "Rebecca, I can't live without having you—"

He administered a thorough kiss, and began to think of something to stir his interest, when the apartment buzzer sounded.

A reprieve, he thought.

"Oh, God," she whispered. "Who the hell is that?"

Rebecca rolled off the sofa and began pulling on her clothes, scooping them from the floor where he'd taken care to discard them in a convincing display of passion. He watched her for a moment and thought that, for a woman in her mid-fifties, she really wasn't half bad. Nothing like the women in their early twenties whom he preferred, given the choice...but, whatever she lacked in age and suppleness of skin, Rebecca more than made up for in financial generosity, useful contacts and, he had to admit, *eagerness*.

A positive mental attitude went a long way, he'd always found.

"Get dressed!" she hissed, as the buzzer sounded again.

Marcus heaved himself from the sofa, yawned, then collected his clothes before sauntering towards the downstairs cloakroom.

Rebecca Villiers watched his retreating body for a lustful moment and then, smoothing her hair into place, checked herself in the hallway mirror before opening the door.

CHAPTER 13

"Rebecca!"

Lance Beckett stood in the open doorway, his arms spread wide.

"Lance?" she burst out. "What are you doing here?"

"Well, after what happened to Nigel, I wanted to come and offer my condolences," he said, sombrely. "You must be *devastated*."

She realised he was waiting for a response, so she made a sound of agreement and tried to remember the appropriate response of a grieving widow.

"I—yes, I can hardly believe it," she mumbled.

"You don't look entirely yourself," he said, taking in her heightened colour and uncombed hair. "I can only imagine…"

She realised he was waiting to be invited inside, and cursed the doorman.

"It's very good of you to call round, Lance, but really, this isn't a good time—"

His eyes strayed somewhere over her shoulder, and she realised he'd spotted Marcus—clothed, she hoped.

"I see I've interrupted you," he said, in a tone that made her squirm.

"Yes, um, Marcus is—was—Nigel's assistant, as you know," she said, and wished she didn't sound so damn *guilty*. "He came over to—ah—tie up a few loose ends and talk about the future, you know, that sort of thing."

"Of course, of course," Lance said, but still, he made no move to leave.

"Um, well, perhaps you'd like to come in for a coffee?" she felt obliged to ask.

"That would be lovely," he replied, ignoring every social cue telling him that his presence was unwelcome. "Just one coffee, then I'll leave you to... tie up those loose ends."

Rebecca had never liked Lance Beckett but, at that moment, she positively *hated* him. Why Nigel had ever remained friends with him for so long was a mystery but, hopefully, this would be one of the final times she'd be forced to make small talk with the man.

"Marcus, you remember Lance Beckett?" she said, leading him into the living area where Marcus was now immaculately dressed and seated beside a glass coffee table, looking every inch the professional.

He rose to his feet. "I haven't had the pleasure, Mr Beckett, but, of course, I know you by name and from the big screen," he said.

Listening to him, Rebecca marvelled at Marcus' ability to administer flattery at the drop of a hat. Not many men of twenty-eight would remember a man like Lance Beckett, but he prided himself in always being prepared, and that included knowing all of Nigel's close acquaintances and friends, of which there were many.

Only belatedly did she wonder whether the words of love he'd whispered to her less than ten minutes' earlier fell into the same category of 'flattery on tap'.

She'd worry about that later.

"Coffee? Tea?" she asked.

"I'll have a brandy, if there's one going," Lance said, and his eyes strayed to the well-stocked bar on the other side of the room. "Let's raise a toast to an old friend—it's what Nigel would have wanted."

Rebecca clenched her jaw while she prepared his drink.

"Thanks, you're a darling," he said, raising the glass. "To Nigel, our old friend, gone but never forgotten…"

He knocked back three fingers.

"To Nigel," Rebecca murmured, taking a sip of soda water while her eyes strayed across the room to where Marcus watched them both with a hint of…was that contempt? She supposed she couldn't blame him.

"So," Lance said, and began to prowl around the room admiring the *objets d'art*, as he always did. "How are you holding up? Need a hand going through anything?"

"We have everything in hand," Marcus said, smoothly.

Lance had to admire his style. "I'm sure you do," he drawled. "Incidentally, when's the funeral?"

Rebecca flushed again. "I'm not sure," she said. "The police haven't released Nigel's body, yet."

Police?

"But…surely that's for the hospital to determine?" Lance said, looking between them. "Nigel had a heart attack, didn't he? What do the police have to do with it?"

Rebecca looked surprised. "I'm sorry, I thought they would have contacted you, by now," she said. "They need to do some further enquiries, and another autopsy. They found something poisonous in Nigel's blood, you see, and they don't know how it got there."

Lance looked down into his glass, swirled the remaining liquid, then knocked it back like medicine. "Do they—ah—do they suspect foul play?" he asked.

"They're being a bit cagey about it," Rebecca admitted. "They told me they're now treating his death as suspicious, which sounds a lot like they think…they think it was…"

"Murder?" Lance finished for her.

He set his glass on the nearest table, while his mind went into overdrive.

Things had just become very interesting.

"Well, I'll leave you to your grief," he said suddenly, all charm once more. "I'm sure the police investigation is just a lot of box-ticking, darling, and everything will blow over soon enough. Incidentally, why haven't I seen it in the papers, yet?"

"There's a press embargo," she told him quietly. "Which reminds me, Lance, *please* don't repeat what I've told you. The police are keen to try and keep their investigation under wraps for as long as possible without the bloodhounds coming for us. It was bad enough, having all the journalists sniffing around last week."

"Of course, my sweet, I'm the soul of discretion."

He cast a final glance in Marcus' direction, and smiled.

After departing The Old Palace Theatre, Gregory excused himself and made directly for a little café just around the corner, where he had spent many a pleasant afternoon with his own thoughts and where he knew he could mull over the facts, hearsay, circumstantial evidence and impressions that were swirling around his mind.

'*What*' plus '*why*' equals '*who*'.

It was the winning formula put forward by the late Robert K. Ressler, a former FBI agent and author, who played a key role in profiling violent offenders during the 1970s and was credited with first coining the term 'serial killer'. Despite there being no suggestion of serial murder, in this case, he agreed with the basic logic. He took out a small notebook and a fountain pen, and began to make notes on the first of two profiles he had been tasked to produce:

PSYCHOLOGICAL PROFILE
Subject: Sir Nigel Anthony Villiers ('NV')
Victim(s): None known, query suicide.

Police Liaison(s): Detective Chief Inspector Ava Hope (Head, MIT-8, Metropolitan Police); Detective Sergeant Benjamin Carter (MIT-8, Metropolitan Police).

In compiling this profile, I have considered all information made available to me from the scene (including location, time of day and year) and have analysed any forensic data drawn from the physical evidence, which has been limited. I have read and considered all available witness statements, secondary statements and in-person interviews conducted in the presence of DCI Hope, as well as the autopsy and toxicology reports prepared by the pathologist, though I understand a second autopsy is scheduled. In addition, I have considered the type and manner of death, logistical means and the personality traits of the victim that may determine the likelihood of self-harm. If further evidence comes to light following the submission of this profile, it will be updated accordingly...

"What can I get you?"

Gregory looked up sharply.

"I'll have a black coffee and one of those ham and cheese paninis," he said. "Thanks."

The waitress looked at him for a long moment, then at the scribbles on his pad. "Coming up," she said eventually.

Did it show? he wondered. *Did people see the shadow of murder reflected in his eyes and feel frightened?*

Constructing a profile was not a cheerful task. It involved thinking of past offences and offenders, drawing upon his years of experience dealing with individuals who, even on the most charitable analysis, were seriously disturbed. It required him to assess the likely personality type of the profile subject, considering childhood indicators and crimes leading up to the main offence, factoring in geographic location and means, and, of course, potential motive. The process of peeling away the layers of projection and falsity a perpetrator might throw up, to reveal the festering mass beneath, was not a task for the faint-hearted. It took a certain kind of courage to face the darkest corners of the human mind without fear; but then, Gregory had faced his own mind—the hardest of all—and emerged unscathed, so he knew it could be done. All the same, he needed to remember that it was not everybody's idea of the dream job, and it wouldn't hurt him to crack a smile, once in a while.

Putting thought into action, Gregory made sure to thank the waitress with a friendly smile before resuming his notes:

This profile contains a list of personality and behavioural characteristics of the subject, as well as a suggested sequence of events leading to his death. This profile should be used by the Metropolitan Police to help them to determine the likelihood of suicide versus foul play, giving due weight to any further evidence that may come to light. Please note, it should not be used conclusively, but as a guide to assist in the process of their broader investigation.

Sequence of events:

NV collapsed on stage at The Old Palace Theatre, London, at approximately 8.30p.m. on Saturday 8th January. Despite twenty minutes of focused CPR effort, I was unable to resuscitate NV (please see addendum to this Profile, setting out the special circumstances, background and basis upon which this commission was accepted). First responding paramedics on scene at The Old Palace Theatre and members of the Accident and Emergency Department were unable to resuscitate, and NV was pronounced dead upon arrival at St. Thomas' Hospital, London, at 9.27p.m. Cause of death has been determined as acute respiratory failure following the ingestion of the neurotoxin conium maculatum, commonly known as 'poison hemlock'—toxic alkaloids having affected NV's nervous system, causing him to display symptoms including nausea, shortness of breath, confusion, muscle seizures, blue-tinted lips and eventual paralysis through a lack of intrapulmonary blood flow to the body, thereby starving it of oxygen. There was, and is, no cure. It is therefore accepted that, even if the emergency services had arrived at the scene sooner, or had a ventilator been applied immediately, neither may have been sufficient to prevent NV's death, following the ingestion of the toxin in sufficient quantity. True time of death is therefore determined to be soon after NV collapsed on stage, at approximately 8.30p.m. Please note, the presentation of NV's symptoms bore all the hallmarks of, and led those present to assume he had suffered from, a cardiac arrest. It was only during the course of their routine examination that the police were made aware of the presence of the toxin in NV's bloodstream, in sufficient quantity to prove fatal. Following this, an investigation into 'suspicious death' was launched.

The toxicology report provided to me by the police indicates a level of toxin sufficient to kill within a two-hour ante-mortem window, which indicates that NV ingested the toxin sometime between approximately 6.30p.m. and 8.30p.m. The running time of the play was approximately three hours commencing 7.30pm, including an interval of twenty minutes, which was due following the completion of Act 2, at 9p.m. or thereabouts. It is therefore possible to narrow the relevant window of opportunity during which the toxin might have been ingested. Whilst the source of the hemlock and time of ingestion is unclear, according to eyewitness accounts from backstage cast and crew, supported by audience accounts, NV ingested nothing other than water during his 'on-stage' time, which he sipped occasionally from a glass taken from a large bottle of Evian kept in the wings, which was shared by other members of the cast who displayed no symptoms of illness themselves. Common sense analysis would therefore rule out the possibility of NV having ingested hemlock during on-stage time, suggesting ingestion prior to curtain up, sometime roughly between 6.30 and 7.30p.m.

Information provided to the police by NV's wife, Rebecca Villiers, and his personal assistant, Marcus Hale, indicates that he left his home in Berkeley Square,

London, at precisely five o'clock on 8th January, taking a taxi with RV to The Old Palace Theatre. They arrived at 5.30p.m., whereupon RV left NV in an apparently well state to meet friends at The Ivy, whilst NV proceeded through the Stage Door using his access code. External CCTV footage has been requested to confirm this timescale, but no internal CCTV cameras are available in that part of the theatre. However, considering witness accounts from fellow cast and crew, it seems that NV went directly to his dressing room without calling on anyone or running into anyone along the way—a fact which seems unusual, given the flow of inward traffic between five and five-thirty, which is when most of the other actors arrived at the theatre.

The external catering team, 'A1 Eats', a longstanding partner of The Old Palace Theatre, delivered several food trays to the theatre between 5.15p.m. and 5.30p.m., arriving through the main entrance—which has been confirmed by front of house staff. In a statement from their courier, they state that a tray was taken to NV's dressing room shortly before 5.30p.m. The door was open, and they found the dressing room empty with the lights off, so they entered, left the covered tray on a side cabinet and moved onto the next delivery. It is to be noted that:

- It is unusual for the catering team courier not to have seen NV at that time, even passing one another in the corridor, although not impossible.

- *The courier confirms that, to the best of their memory, all other dressing rooms were occupied by 5.30p.m. or shortly thereafter.*

At six o'clock, all members of the cast and crew assembled on stage to hear opening night speeches from Jasper Pugh, NV's co-producer and co-owner of the Old Palace Theatre, as well as Margot Winters, the Director. Champagne was offered as a toast from a tray of pre-poured drinks and NV apparently drank a glass taken from this tray. It is not known who poured these glasses, but if the toxin was administered by an outside person with an intention to harm NV, it seems unlikely they would have chosen this method—there were no guarantees NV would have chosen the correct glass, unless handed to him, and eyewitness accounts state that he helped himself. Between 6.30 and 6.50p.m., NV was joined by hair and make-up artists, whose statements both corroborate those timings, and confirm that NV was joined briefly by his wife, RV, at 6.50p.m. At that time, she confirms that she wished her husband well but did not stay for a drink, nor consume any food, before taking up her seat in one of the boxes. Between approximately 6.50 and 7.15p.m., NV was joined by several of his cohort, who had a pre-performance drink in his dressing room. Witness accounts broadly tally, stating that he drank at least one glass of brandy from a seat beside his dressing table, but did not appear to have any food. At 7.15p.m.

NV was left alone to prepare for his performance and joined his fellow cast members on stage in time for curtain up at 7.30p.m.

There are two windows of time during which NV's movements are unaccounted for, between approximately 5.15 and 5.30p.m., and then between 6.00 and 6.30p.m. During the former, NV was not in his dressing room, while we can assume NV could have been alone in his dressing room during the latter. In either case, NV could have been in the company of another person who has not reported the same in their witness statement.

Gregory paused, considering the facts which represented a pattern for Nigel Villiers, as opposed to those that were subject to change and were therefore unpredictable to a third party or potential offender.

Although access to the backstage area of the theatre via the stage door is protected by a security code, and there were several ushers on site from around six o'clock in the main foyer and auditorium, there was little else in the way of security to prevent a third party from gaining access to the backstage area at any time during the day. Likewise, there are no internal CCTV cameras in the backstage area, although there are two in the main foyer which are being analysed by police personnel for any unusual activity. However, if a third party who was unknown to NV intended to contaminate his food, drink or any other substance suitable for ingestion (e.g. multivitamin tablets photographed at the scene), they would have needed advance knowledge of NV's movements in order to perpetrate the crime. The elements of NV's timeline that might have been predictable are:

- His arrival at the theatre, at 5.30p.m.

- His attendance at the speeches, at 6p.m.

- His fifteen-minute window to prepare, at 7.15p.m.

Other behavioural predictors might have been:

- A tendency towards alcoholic beverages, confirmed by many of his co-actors, as well as his wife and personal assistant. The pathology report also confirms a moderate alcohol level in NV's bloodstream.

- A tendency to take multi-vitamins.

- A tendency to drink Evian water.

No physical evidence has been recovered from NV's dressing room, nor the remains of any hemlock or packaging to suggest NV or a third party administered the toxin in his dressing room. There was no sign of forced entry, or any other aggression, and other forensic evidence may be unreliable owing to the poor or mixed sampling taken from a highly-contaminated scene. It is therefore surmised that the toxin was ingested knowingly by NV, or unknowingly at the instigation of a third party able to gain access to administer without NV's knowledge and remove any trace afterwards.

Personality and behavioural factors:

NV was, by all accounts, a gregarious man with a classic extrovert personality type. He held a position of power within his community, not merely because of his success in the realms of acting and production, but because of his amassed wealth and co-ownership of the theatre—which, in conjunction with Jasper Pugh, gave him heightened powers to hire or fire, and to supervise the direction of any given production. It seems NV often chose to help those he deemed 'worthy', which demonstrates a certain arrogance had developed over time that was not unexpected given the above factors, and seems in keeping with his character, taking into account anecdotal reports of his younger self—longstanding friends, including Professor William Douglas (co-author of this profile) have confirmed NV was always confident, assured and a 'natural leader' who had a tendency to garner many friends, but not necessarily able to provide a consistent or meaningful degree of friendship to all those he met. In other words, whilst a person held his interest, they became NV's focus but, after that time, they could feel left in the cold. Notwithstanding this, NV was able to sustain friendships and relationships throughout his lifetime, including his marriage—although, given the above factors, it is uncertain whether these relationships were mutually beneficial or one-sided, and furthermore, whether they were founded on a superficial basis.

Although generally well-liked and respected, it has been noted that NV could, from time to time, display an outmoded sense of humour and give casual offence. He has been described as 'invincible', 'indomitable' and 'untouchable', which could suggest he was aware of how his humour and actions might be perceived, but was unwilling to change because he knew that he was unlikely to suffer any negative consequences.

NV was considered by those who knew him to be an intelligent man who graduated from Cambridge University, but he possessed a poor academic record, which indicates a degree of complacency in respect of formal learning structures or the need for them, as well as a grandiose opinion of his own ability to succeed irrespective of academic outcomes.

On the night of his death, it was noted by some that he was more reserved than usual (choosing not to make a speech, for example) and that he appeared tired, but nobody reported him mentioning any specific cause.

The above observations would generally reduce NV's associated 'risk' as a suitable victim, since he would be more likely to fight or cause a commotion, should he have become aware of any contamination or attempt to contaminate. Therefore, if a third party was involved, they are likely to be a perpetrator whose confidence matched or exceeded NV's own, and were unconcerned by an elevated chance of discovery.

Suicide or murder?

NV has no medical history of depressive disorders or other mood affective disorders, and had not received any negative news pertaining to his health or otherwise. He was not taking any regular medication, aside from multivitamin tablets and the occasional headache tablet, though he did drink more than an average quantity of alcohol on a weekly basis. This did not appear to have a suppressive impact, considering he remained generally in high spirits, but the possibility of NV having used alcohol to self-medicate cannot be discounted. It is possible that, as an intelligent man, he was aware that many of his relationships were superficial in nature or one-sided, and this can create a sense of emotional isolation. To the best of our knowledge, he enjoyed a long and happy relationship with his wife, RV, but should that prove to be false, it could have provided another reason for NV to feel isolated. This, combined with his withdrawn or otherwise anxious 'out of character' behaviour reported by Jasper Pugh, Peter Gray, Jasmine Kohli, Olivia Routledge-Brown and Frances Unwin on the evening of 8th January, means we cannot discount the possibility that NV chose to self-administer the hemlock. Furthermore, the choice of hemlock is significant, because it demonstrates: a degree of planning and organisation as opposed to a 'spur of the moment' decision; a preference for a 'neat' death, or *alternatively, a dislike of bloody or 'messy' deaths; and, a preference for a symbolic or theatrical death. Whilst it would have been difficult to predict exactly when NV would collapse, the properties of hemlock poisoning are widely known or available, even to laypersons, therefore it would have been possible to predict with some degree of accuracy at what time NV would be likely to collapse following a certain dosage given in advance. The timing of NV's collapse happened during Act 2, Scene 4 of King Lear, which is a particularly dramatic moment, and was therefore likely to create maximum impact. The symbolism behind the choice of poison as well as the timing of NV's collapse could indicate a need to have his death remembered, possibly as a final act of egoism.*

Further information regarding NV's financial affairs, personal history and relationships is needed to determine whether he had any known reason to consider ending his own life—on balance, it would appear highly unlikely that NV would choose this course of action without an external catalyst...

Gregory set his pen down and reached for the cup of coffee which had, at some point during his furious scribbling, materialised on the table beside him. He ran through the possible catalysts for suicide in his mind, ranging from terminal cancer to infidelity, to financial ruin back to reputational scandal.

None of them was known to the police, but it was early days, yet…

No sooner had the thought entered his mind than his mobile phone began to buzz against the tabletop.

DCI Hope.

He answered the call and, after a brief discussion, set the small block of plastic back down on the table, already reaching for his pen to update the summary he'd just outlined.

The police had found a potential catalyst for suicide, after all.

———

Anika watched the man from behind the counter and thought that, if possible, he appeared even more disgruntled than on the previous day.

"Can't keep away, can he?" Jill said, coming to stand beside her.

"I wish he would," Anika replied.

"Maybe he has a crush on you," her friend joked, and gave her a playful nudge. "Maybe we've misjudged him all this time, and he just doesn't know how to talk to women."

"I don't think so," Anika murmured.

"Do you want me to go and take his order?"

"No, I'm just being silly. I'll do it."

But it was with a sense of trepidation that Anika made the short journey from the counter to the table where he'd stationed himself with an assortment of newspapers, notepad, pen and mobile phone.

"What can I get you?" she asked him, not bothering with any of the pleasantries she might have afforded other customers.

As usual, he seemed surprised by the question, and she wondered why he bothered to come out to a café if he had no intention of ordering any food or drink. While he processed the question, her eyes fell to the notepad on the table, widening slightly at the vicious circles drawn in black biro, the angry-looking spider diagrams and lists of names, times and dates.

He moved his hand to cover it, and her eyes snapped up again to find him watching her, this time with a thoughtful, intense expression.

He gave his order, and she hurried away, eager to be gone from the man whose eyes followed her and continued to follow her, all the way back to the counter.

CHAPTER 14

As the sun made its slow descent towards the horizon, Gregory meandered back through the higgledy-piggledy streets of London towards the Yard, to reconvene for a late meeting with DCI Hope and DS Carter. Though the festive season had been and gone, its echo lingered alongside the tattered remains of Christmas decorations yet to be swept away, and, for once, he was glad. For many years, he'd wished away the woollen jumpers and jingle bell rocks, their gawdy colours and saccharine melodies too much a reminder of all he'd never had.

Which, of course, wasn't quite true.

There *had* been well-meaning foster families who'd tried their best to wash away his nightmares with chocolate yule logs and games of Cluedo or Monopoly by the fireside. But, as was so often the case, good intentions seldom matched reality, especially in the case of a young boy whose stomach was so damaged by his mother's best efforts that it could not hold down the sickly-sweet confectionary. It had taken time and healing before he'd been able to enjoy ordinary foods without fear of illness. He'd learned to exercise caution where his mother's cooking was concerned, but he'd also learned what it was to be hungry—so hungry, it burned the lining of his stomach—and desperation drove him to eat the meals she prepared and drink the oddly-flavoured milk she poured, all the while knowing he would be writhing on his bed later that evening.

Thinking of it brought his mind back around to the late Nigel Villiers, and the question of whether he had knowingly ingested poison or been the unwitting victim of a similarly disordered mind. His mother's illness had driven her to poison her own children, and he wondered fleetingly whether someone of a similar bent had been driven to kill in order to elicit the same psychological response, deriving their satisfaction from the glory that came from knowing, even privately, that they had wielded such power over a man who had been so powerful in life.

It was the ultimate reversal.

His mother had slowly poisoned her children in a warped bid to reclaim her errant husband's attention, but had somebody poisoned Nigel Villiers because they craved a different kind of attention from the media? Did they like knowing the truth and watching the police flounder, all the while congratulating themselves on their superiority?

It wouldn't be the first time.

He thought of the serial killer David Berkowitz, better known as the 'Son of Sam', who was eventually caught in 1977 after a yearlong crime spree in New York, during which time he killed six people and wounded another seven. He'd left notes at the crime scenes, one of which had read, "I am a monster. I am the 'Son of Sam.'" He'd sent several more notes which allowed the police to piece together enough clues to catch him. As a psychiatrist, Gregory queried whether the man's flagrant interaction with the police and the press was a bragging exercise or, on a deeper level, an admission that he needed to be stopped and brought to justice. Either way, he'd enjoyed his five minutes of fame, that was for sure.

But perhaps the most famous of all killers who'd enjoyed taunting the police and the papers with their exploits was the self-styled 'Jack the Ripper', who might have walked the very pavement Gregory now walked, back in 1888. Had he enjoyed the fear that had rippled through London that summer, or the frisson of excitement that came from wondering whether he would be apprehended? Little could he have known that more than a hundred years would pass and, still, nobody had any conclusive notion as to his identity.

It had been too easy, for old Jack.

Presently, the iconic twirling sign of 'New Scotland Yard' came into view, and Gregory made his way once again through the foyer, where he was met by DS Carter. The Yard was quieter than it had been the previous day, and the impending darkness gave its glass frontage an eerie, empty feel that wouldn't have been out of place in a dystopian film.

"The boss tells me you've got a working profile, for us," Carter continued, casting a glance towards the quiet man at his side. "That's quick work."

"I know the first few days are crucial to a police investigation," Gregory said. "I won't be the one to hold you up."

Carter nodded, approvingly. "What made you want to do it—profiling, I mean?"

It was an idle question, asked as they made their way to another of the glass fronted meeting rooms on the office floor, and Carter couldn't have known that the answer went to the very heart of why Gregory had sought a career doctoring the mind.

"Prevention," he said, simply. "Although it's true that my patients are usually referred to me *after* the commission of an offence, and police forces approach me *after* a crime has already been committed, by playing some small part in helping to bring the offender to justice, or help them to heal themselves to whatever degree, I'm also intercepting them before they commit even more crimes. It's small comfort to the families of their victims, but it has the wider benefit of preventing harm to others."

Carter nodded. "It's the sword or the shield, in our world," he said, gesturing for Gregory to enter the meeting room. "Force or service, depending on your point of view. I won't pretend that I feel much in the way of compassion for the kind of animals we sometimes bring into lock-up, but I respect you for having the mettle to try to help them, when others would just put them down."

Gregory turned to him. "The fact is, Carter, a lot of them end up putting *themselves* down," he said quietly, and thought of Cathy Jones, who'd wrapped a long set of rosary beads tightly around her own neck. "I'm not naïve enough to think I can help all of them, but I can learn from their behaviour and apply that knowledge to the next case, and then the next."

"I guess nothing much surprises you," Carter said.

Gregory smiled, and shook his head. "There's still room for surprises, when you're dealing with the frontier of the human mind. Its scope is limitless."

"How d'you ever hope to understand it?" Carter asked him. "Seems to me, there's a syndrome for everything, these days, and more being invented all the time."

"That's just labelling," Gregory said. "The trick is never to lose sight of the individual. There might be twenty thousand people in a square mile of London who've been diagnosed with the same mood disorder, but every one of them is a person whose symptoms and behaviours might present entirely differently. It's the same with violent offenders: they've each killed people or hurt them in some other way, which has an agreed label, and their reasons for doing so might appear similar, at first glance—childhood trauma, revenge, love, jealousy, money, and so on. But their individual reasoning and methodology will always be unique. It's about finding the broad patterns to narrow down the pool and then taking it from there."

Carter asked the million-dollar question.

"You ever make a mistake, Doc? Ever think you had somebody pegged, only to find you were wrong?"

Gregory thought of Carl Deere, but, in that case, the profile he'd created hadn't been wrong. The content turned out to be a near-perfect match, once he'd been falsely apprehended—the only thing that hadn't matched were the facts in that case, and it represented the all-important difference between guilt and innocence. Theodor Andersson might have been the guilty party, however, as far as he was concerned, Deere had all the red-flag markers and personality-type indicators capable of violent offending...it just so happened that he hadn't.

That they knew of.

"It's like I said, people can always surprise you," Gregory replied, and hoped that would never prove one day to be true of Carl Deere, wherever he may be.

CHAPTER 15

"Digital Forensics have come through with two solid leads."

DCI Hope said the words every Senior Investigating Officer longed to say, and thanked whichever deity was responsible for cutting her a break.

"You said on the phone that they'd recovered threatening messages?" Gregory said, and took a swig of the instant sludge which passed for coffee in large, government-funded offices.

"Here, see for yourself," she said, handing him a printed sheet containing copies of the e-mails recovered from Villiers' account. "These were found in his 'Deleted' folder."

Gregory cast his eye over four e-mails, each sent a couple of days apart over the course of the week prior to Villiers' death:

From: socrates@untraceable.gr

To: SirNigel@outlook.com
Monday, 3rd January, 15:03p.m.
Dear Nigel,

I do hope you don't mind me calling you, 'Nigel'. I know you so well, after all. You've had a wonderful life, haven't you? The best of everything, every door opened for you, every light turned to 'green'. Everyone thinks you're marvellous, don't they? Too scared to say otherwise, at least to your face. But times have changed. You're over the hill. A relic from a bygone era where it was okay to call people 'coloured', use women like chattels and get away with it. But your time is up, Nigel. I know all about you and your cronies. I know what you did, and it's time the truth came out.

Do the right thing, Nigel. I'll be watching.
S.

The e-mail had been deleted on the same day, at 5.47p.m., but a second e-mail had been sent the very next morning:

From: socrates@untraceable.gr
To: SirNigel@outlook.com
Tuesday, 4th January, 09.15a.m.
Hello again, Nigel.

Did you receive my last e-mail? It was rude of you not to reply, if you did. Don't you understand that I'm giving you an opportunity to right past wrongs?

I don't want to have to force the issue. Get in touch, and I'll tell you what needs to happen, now.

I'll be watching.

S.

That e-mail had also been deleted, almost as soon as it was received, at 9.18a.m. Another arrived, this time two days later:

From: socrates@untraceable.gr
To: SirNigel@outlook.com
Thursday, 6th January, 13.09p.m.
Nigel,
Your lack of response is disappointing. I would have thought a man in your position would care more about his reputation, but perhaps you think I'm bluffing? Is that it, Nigel? In that case, I suggest you think back to the Summer of 1979 and reconsider, very carefully.
I'll be watching.
S.

The e-mail had been deleted later that day, at 4.05p.m., and a final one received the next day, a mere twenty-four hours before Villiers' death:

From: socrates@untraceable.gr
To: SirNigel@outlook.com
Friday, 7th January, 6.03p.m.

You know what you need to do, Nigel. Look to Socrates for inspiration. The time is ripe, and your legacy can remain intact, such as it is. Think of it as a reprieve, for a man is nothing without his reputation.

S.

The e-mail had been deleted at 6.27p.m., and no more received, after then. Gregory re-read the contents once more, for good measure, then sat back in one of the uncomfortable plastic chairs around the conference table to mull it over.

"What do you make of it?" Hope asked him, when the silence stretched on. "You were right about the connection with Socrates, for one thing."

"Have you been able to trace the sender?" Gregory asked, because gathering facts was paramount before he'd venture an opinion.

"The team are working on it," Carter told him. "But I wouldn't count any chickens. The sender's e-mail server is based overseas and seems to be routed across various encrypted networks, so our chances of tracing the sender are about as high as my chances of scoring a date with Rihanna."

Hope snorted.

"Yeah, you'd be lucky."

"Stranger things have happened," Carter said, a bit put out by her quick agreement. "A girl told me I looked a bit like Idris Elba, once."

"In dim lighting, maybe," Hope shot back.

Gregory heard their easy banter and understood it. He'd worked with many policing teams over the years and one thing that was common in all of them was a healthy sense of humour; it was critical, to do the job they did and remain sane.

"It looks a lot like the sender was pushing for Villiers to take his own life, doesn't it?" Hope prodded, gnawing on her lip as she tried to read his mind. "Why else refer Villiers to Socrates? He must have been talking about the way he died—with the hemlock—and suggesting he do the same, or risk being outed for some past misdemeanour."

"Nigel wouldn't be the first high profile personality to commit suicide rather than face the consequences of a shady past," Carter agreed, breaking open a packet of salt 'n' vinegar crisps to quieten his grumbling stomach. "It's weird nothing came up in our searches before now, though. I would have sworn Villiers was squeaky clean."

"Nobody's ever that," Hope said, and turned back to Gregory, who saw so much and said so little. "In the preliminary profile you sent me, you said you thought it was highly unlikely Villiers would have committed suicide without some sort of external catalyst. Wouldn't you say this is exactly the sort of catalyst that might have sent him over the edge? The sender's right about one thing, which is that reputation meant everything to a man like him."

Gregory nodded. "That's still true," he agreed. "And this certainly throws up an interesting line of thinking. But the fact that Villiers deleted the e-mails strikes me as even more interesting."

"Why?"

"In the first place, he was a technological dinosaur," Gregory said. "His wife, his assistant and several of the other members of the crew said in their statements that he could be a hard man to track down, because he didn't always bother to keep a mobile phone with him and didn't check e-mails on any regular basis."

Hope nodded. It was a fair point. "And, second?"

"Secondly, on a psychological level, deleting the e-mails could demonstrate a kind of dismissal of their content," Gregory said. "You said this was his personal e-mail account, rather than his work account, yes?"

Hope nodded.

"In that case, who would've had access to it? Who might have found these e-mails and read them?"

"Not Hale, for one thing," Carter said. "He managed Villiers' business e-mail accounts, his diary and so on, but not his personal correspondence."

"That we know of," Hope put in. "The fact is, you're right. Villiers wasn't tech savvy, at all. He probably hadn't updated his password in years, and we already know the laptop he kept at the theatre, supposedly for work use, was hardly used and not even password protected."

"Which means anybody could, in theory, have accessed his e-mails and read the threatening messages," Gregory surmised. "Which might explain why he chose to delete them."

And yet…

Something still didn't add up. He only wished he knew what it was.

"You said Digital Forensics turned up another lead?"

Hope nodded, and pulled out a slim folder, which she handed to him.

"We may not be able to trace the name of our mysterious sender, but perhaps we won't need to," she said, tapping the top page.

It was a printed sheet from Villiers' personal bank account, with a few individual payments highlighted in neon yellow. The amounts were not insubstantial by ordinary standards, but a brief glance at Villiers' broader spending habits told Gregory that it wouldn't have cost him any sleep.

"It's a series of irregular payments to the same account," Carter said. "There's no standing order or direct debit, just ad hoc payments, made roughly once a month or bi-monthly. The amounts vary, but they're usually a grand a piece, at least, and they've increased over time."

"You're thinking that the person who sent Villiers those threatening e-mails might also have been extorting money from him?"

"It's possible, isn't it?" Hope said, leaning forward. "Payments to that same account go all the way back, at least six months. I've asked to see records beyond that time, and I'm wrangling with the powers that be to provide me with the named account holder, so we can pay them a visit. I'm hoping they'll come through, tomorrow morning."

Gregory nodded, but still couldn't shake the feeling that something was missing from the picture.

"The kind of personality who styles themselves as Socrates, one of the world's greatest philosophers, and suggests that a renowned actor use hemlock poisoning as a penance for his past misdeeds is not usually the same kind of personality who can be bought with money," he said.

"You can be philosophical and greedy," Hope pointed out. "They're not mutually exclusive."

Gregory flashed an appreciative smile. "You're not wrong," he said. "But, in my experience, offenders who justify their actions by reference to higher causes tend to be obsessive. They prefer rituals, symbolism, rites, religious practices…or all the above. They are, at least in the beginning, highly organised and don't deviate from plans and processes they've set out for themselves. They live by a code and, above all else, they are fearless in their pursuit of what they consider to be 'right'. It would be more consistent for that kind of personality to find any money from Villiers tainted or unworthy of them."

He leaned forward and linked his fingers on the tabletop, so their hands were almost touching.

"In my working profile of the personality type to have killed Villiers, I've outlined somebody who is relatively unimportant in life; someone who feels side-lined or perpetually in the shadows. Ignored, overlooked, undermined or unappreciated, at least from their own perspective, but who maintains a feeling of superiority over those around them. They are intelligent, but not the *most* intelligent person in the room. They are good-looking, but not the *most* striking in the room. In certain circles, they might be the star, until a bolder, brighter star arrives and outshines them, with very little effort, at all. They're often forgettable, and, the problem is, they're smart enough to *know* that they're forgettable. It breeds resentment."

He paused, looking between them both.

"You know yourselves that those who kill aren't always Ted Bundy," he said. "They're not all articulate, reasonably-attractive people. More often, they're commonplace, and frustrated by their own mediocrity. They might be hyper-sensitive to their own perceived deficiencies or faults that could have been used to undermine them, routinely, from childhood. I could throw around words like 'projection' or 'transference', but their need to act out repressed aggression on a proxy, a symbol of all they hate or all they haven't achieved, might be their way of dealing with their overall grievances against life, or against other people *like* the proxy, whom they feel has wronged them, or people like them."

Hope let out a short, frustrated sigh.

"The problem is, what you're saying makes sense," she said. "I can imagine that kind of person killing in the name of their ideals, but I can't imagine them extorting money beforehand."

"There are always exceptions to every rule," Gregory cautioned. "Nobody said murdering idealists weren't also prone to impecuniosity."

When Hope smiled, it lit up her whole face, and Gregory found himself smiling too. From his position across the table, Carter watched them with a knowing eye.

"The fact remains, we have a series of suspicious payments that are unaccounted for, and a dead King Lear," she said. "Maybe there was more than one person who knows what happened in 1979."

"Villiers was at university in Cambridge, back in 1979," Gregory said. "If we're going to find out what happened, we need to go back to the source."

Hope nodded. "Any excuse for a day trip out of London."

CHAPTER 16

Lance Beckett approached *The Harlequin* pub with a spring in his step.

Only hours before, he could admit to having felt somewhat...*nervous* about this appointment, but not anymore.

Oh, no.

Everything had changed, and he was only sorry that he'd been too blind to see things as they truly were, long before then. He almost laughed aloud at the measly sum of money he'd been planning to demand in exchange for his silence on that other matter...

It seemed paltry, now, and demeaning.

Far too cheap.

Perhaps the knowledge in his possession should have given rise for concern, but he was too busy thinking of all the dinners he would eat at The Fat Duck. Too busy imagining the sensation of fine, hand-tailored fabrics against his skin. Catching sight of himself in the

157

window of the pub, he could already see the fresh crop of hair that would adorn his head, before long.

He'd be on top again, after all these years, and the offers would start rolling in.

I'm sure it's beneath you, Mr Beckett, but we wondered if you'd consider the latest Wes Anderson? He needs somebody with your kind of gravitas...

Netflix are doing a big-budget production of Romeo and Juliet, and you're their first choice...

No more Christmas pantos or school plays. No more 'guest appearances' at local supermarkets or panel appearances on talk shows nobody had ever heard of, on channels nobody ever watched. His eyes shone brightly, like a child's, and—just for a moment—he was happy.

Lance was still smiling when he arrived at the pub, which was one of the smallest and most secluded in London. Little more than one long galley, it was located directly behind the Sadler's Wells Theatre, in Islington, and only a short walk from his home in King's Cross. He knew the place well, and could remember a time, years ago, when he'd drunk there regularly with Nigel and some of the others...

Poor Nigel.

Still, he was dead and gone, while Lance still lived.

Look after Number One, his mother used to say.

He intended to do just that.

"You're late."

"Only by a few minutes," Lance said, and settled himself on the only other stool beside the little wooden table. It was an awkward perch, but the other occupant had already secured the comfortable bench seat, so there wasn't much he could do about it.

The pub was always dark, being old and panelled in oak throughout, with one long bar and very few windows. Small pendant lights shone dimly above it, to guide the hand of the lone barman, but the remainder of the room was lit only by flickering tea lights that had been placed on each round table, and a couple of vintage floor-standing lamps with embroidered shades. It was the kind of place that attracted well-off students who could afford to pay a little extra for their pint and enjoyed the artsy ambiance, as well as older professionals who were part of the production at the theatre or had come to watch it.

"Lucky you got a table," Lance said, in a vague attempt to make small talk. "It gets pretty bus, in here."

His companion said nothing, and merely sipped at their glass of white wine. Lance watched the action and licked dry lips.

"I could use a drop of that, myself," he said.

"Allow me," the other said, genially, and Lance relaxed a fraction. If that was going to be the tone of the evening, they'd get along well enough.

He thought about what the best opening gambit would be.

Should he just come out with his demands?

Should he wait a while, butter them up a bit?

A glass appeared in front of him, and he mumbled his thanks, drinking deeply.

"I was surprised to hear from you."

Lance cleared his throat. "Were you? Well, it's been a long time, hasn't it…" He trailed off, cursing himself for being all kinds of coward.

He should just say what he had to say, and leave.

"I—ah—well, the fact is, I wondered whether we couldn't come to some sort of arrangement," Lance said.

"I think you're mistaking me for Nigel," the other said, with a chuckle. "He was the kind of man to make arrangements."

Lance took another sip of wine, and tried again.

"I mean to say, we can *help* one another, in a mutually beneficial way."

"How so?"

Now it came to it, Lance was tongue-tied. "Well, let's just say that…certain information had come into my possession. Information that might"— *incriminate,* he'd been about to say—"look *unusual,* to outside parties investigating Nigel's death."

He paused, trying to gauge their reaction, but could see only the shadowed outline of their face and nothing at all behind their eyes.

He swallowed again.

"What information might that be?"

But Lance wasn't about to risk being overheard. Instead, he produced an envelope from his breast pocket in which he'd written down a summary of what he knew, took a discreet glance to either side, and slid it across the table.

"Certainly very interesting," the other replied, pocketing the envelope. "But you have no proof. Why would anybody believe the word of a washed-up actor with a gambling problem, over someone like me?"

They knew about his little habit.

Who else knew?

Lance ran a hand over his mouth, wiping away the sweat from his upper lip, and tried to remain focused. This was all part of the dance, the prelude to an agreement. They'd hurl a bit of muck at one another and end up shaking hands, in the end.

"The question is, do you want to risk it?" he said. He was proud of how bold he sounded, despite the trembling in his legs. "Mud sticks," he added. "Once the whispers start, people start thinking there's no smoke without fire…" he said, with an exaggerated sigh. "But if I've wasted my time bringing this to you, first—"

He paused, just long enough to allow them to come to a decision.

"Whilst I'm sure you understand that everything in this little envelope is mistaken, I do agree that reputational damage is always best avoided," the other replied, softly. "On that basis, I'm sure we can agree to help one another—depending upon what you have in mind, of course."

Lance smiled slowly.

That was more like it.

"How about we start with another glass of this lovely Sancerre, and take it from there?"

He waggled his empty glass and smiled like a cat.

CHAPTER 17

Anika gave a jaw-cracking yawn and hung her apron on its usual peg, before reaching for her jacket and handbag. It had been a long day, the new owners of the café having recently acquired a liquor license, so she was now required to work at least four late shifts per week rather than the regular eight till five she'd signed up for, originally. It wasn't that she was afraid of work—far from it—but it was hard enough missing out on all the school pick-ups; now, it would mean relying on the childminder to stay longer in the evenings and paying extra for the dubious privilege of not seeing her son.

Her chest began to palpitate as she thought of the spiralling costs of living in the city, and she rubbed an absent hand against it, to ease the pain.

How could she afford to continue working at the café, and pay for childcare?

How could she stand only seeing Ollie for snatches of time?

First thing in the morning, she'd try speaking to the owner again. Maybe she hadn't been clear enough in the explanation she'd given of her circumstances, and there were other staff members—like Jill—who didn't have dependants and wouldn't mind staying late in the evenings.

Surely, they'd be reasonable?

With these thoughts weighing on her mind, Anika made sure all the lights were turned off and the service area left clean and tidy for the next morning, then stepped out into the cold January night, making sure to lock the door behind her. Central London was like any other major city around the world: busy, frenetic and, at times, lonely, but it wasn't like New York. People did eventually sleep, and lights turned out, but not quite yet. People passed by, bundled up in winter coats and scarves, heads bent against the wind that whipped through the streets and stirred up the plastic bags overflowing the bin beside the bus stop.

Anika stooped to pick one up and stuffed it back inside, then made her way towards the tube station, feet aching and back stiff, but not as sore as her heart. She was one of thousands of people walking the streets of London that night, just another nameless face in her plain navy coat, jeans and trainers. She passed beneath the shining frontage of several theatres, each advertising their latest production in garish yellow lights which shone like beacons into the dark January night. She glanced at the names and faces plastered across the billboards, recognised some of them, and tried to remember the last time she'd been able to go to the theatre.

Cinderella, two Christmases ago, with Ollie.

She'd saved the money to take him to see a pantomime at a theatre in Finsbury, where she'd been forced to sit through ninety minutes of, 'Oh, no, you didn't!' and, 'Oh, yes, you did!' which had been worth it just to see the smile on her son's face.

There'd be no pantomimes this year.

To her annoyance, tears escaped her eyes, and she swiped them away with the back of her hand. Anika didn't often cry, these days, because it was wasted energy and, after all, what did crying achieve? Absolutely nothing. It didn't solve the problem of her partner, Damien, having left her for another woman two weeks before she gave birth to their son, seven years ago. It didn't change his having neglected to pay any child support, despite subjecting her to a humiliating and painful process of DNA checks to prove that the child they'd conceived in love—or so she'd thought—was his.

All to avoid paying a measly few quid every week, to keep clothes on a little boy's back and food in his belly.

How she wished she could throw the money back in his face…

But she couldn't.

She picked up her pace, tired of London and its grey pavements, weary of the drudgery of working in hospitality but unable to see a way out. She was an immigrant with limited qualifications, a single mother without A-levels or even GCSE's. If she had the time, she'd have studied for them at night school, but exhaustion and lack of funds prevented her. There was no family to help, no kindly neighbour who would sit and read with her. She'd taught herself to speak English and to speak it well, and she worked as hard as she could, but that was as far as she could go.

And so, she went back to the café every day and cleaned the dishes, served food with a smile, washed out the toilets. She answered the perennial question of, 'Where are you really from?' and parried some of the comments that followed from those who felt she didn't belong. She batted away the wandering hands of men and tried not to detest the rich, jobless women who gathered on Monday mornings to cluck, and look at her slim body and blonde hair with eyes full of malice.

They weren't as bad as some.

Anika thought of the man who'd come into the café again, that day, and of the angry scribbles on his notepad. There was something about him that made her skin crawl…

It was his eyes, she realised.

When they fixed on her, she felt pinned, like a butterfly. They never seemed to blink, and, worst of all, she could read nothing from their expression other than a general sense of loathing or a simmering anger that was liable to erupt at any moment.

He frightened her.

As the comforting lights of the tube station beckoned, Anika thrust him from her mind and hurried to catch the next train, her footsteps clattering down the metal escalator into the bowels of the Underground. She didn't stop to look behind and, even if she had, she wouldn't have noticed the man who followed several metres behind her, with eyes that were hard and unblinking.

———

Lance Beckett was on top of the world.

He couldn't remember how many glasses of wine he'd polished off before they'd decided to go back to his place to celebrate their new partnership; all he knew was they'd stumbled through the back streets of Islington laughing like a couple of old friends.

They'd talked of many things, but especially of Nigel.

Ah, Nigel.

What a self-serving, supercilious bastard he'd been, when he really thought about it. Lording it over all of them like the bloody Messiah, dishing out advice about how to act and how to manage his finances, as if he were a damn schoolboy and not a grown man.

"Always was a conde—a conde—condescending so-and-so," he slurred. "Right from the v-very beginning."

Lance stumbled, but a strong arm held him upright.

Not far to go, now.

"The—the trouble with ol' Nige' was that…that everything was handed to him on a plate," he rolled on. "Never had to fight for anything. Not Nigel…"

"Got a key?"

Lance blinked, and then nodded, leaning one hand against the brick wall of the building where he lived.

"Mmm hmm. Somewhere in here," he mumbled, and began searching the pockets of his blazer. "Wonder if he knew his wifey was bangin' the secretary?"

Probably.

He found the key, held it up proudly, then dropped it with a clatter of metal.

"Oops," he chuckled, and swiped it up again with clumsy fingers.

It took several attempts to get the key into the lock, but finally, it turned.

"Et voila!" Lance exclaimed. "Come in, come in."

And, just like that, he invited the spider in.

CHAPTER 18

It was late, by the time Gregory returned home.

He found it dark, since he'd left no welcoming light burning in the hallway, and it was cold, since he'd forgotten to turn the thermostat up. As a man who'd lived alone for his entire adult life, he was comfortable in his own company and had always preferred it. Spending long days listening to the machinations of other people's disordered minds, he appreciated solitude and silence, in which he could restore his own depleted reserves and allow their chatter to drain away before starting all over again the next day. He'd always told himself it was a blessing not to be obliged to please anybody else with a false smile or insincere words of love and commitment; he was a free agent and that suited him just fine.

And yet, when he shut the door and stepped into the empty living room, he felt a chill that had little to do with temperature. He found himself wishing for more than another warm body to be close to; he wanted a bright mind that matched his own, someone he could talk to and listen to.

There had been women who'd offered that very thing with open arms, and he knew he was to blame for not taking up the opportunities when they'd arisen. He thought of Madeleine, and the time they'd spent together in Paris. Beautiful, troubled Madeleine, with a generous heart and the voice of an angel, who was now engaged to a man he hoped was worthy of her.

Time stood still for nobody.

He thought of Naomi, the psychiatrist from New York. Intelligent and insightful, in many ways she was a perfect match for him. Who better to understand the work they did, and to understand him—as a man? Yet, he hadn't fought for her. Naomi remained at the Buchanan Hospital, in the Catskill Mountains, while he'd returned to London. As he moved around the room turning on the lights, Gregory tried to make sense of his own decision and could draw only one conclusion.

He was a world-class idiot.

He should have begged her to come back to England with him or found a new job closer to where she was. These were the kinds of risks people took, when it came to affairs of the heart. But then, when it came to the heart, he was still just a frightened kid, wasn't he? He'd survived without a mother's love and the only way he'd done it was to build a wall, so thick and so impenetrable it could never be breached.

Naomi had found a way through it, though. She might have been the very first person to have done so, aside from Bill Douglas, and it left him feeling vulnerable.

So, he'd let her go.

He thought of Sarah Jepson, the doctor he'd run into on the South Bank, the previous day. She was another lovely woman who could make someone very happy…but it would not be him.

Who, then?

He knew better than most that it was foolish to seek perfection, especially as one who was so far from being perfect himself. There was no 'ideal' woman and no 'ideal' relationship, come to that, but it might help to find someone who understood the work that he did, that he was *compelled* to do. It was not impossible. He had a detective friend by the name of Ryan, who lived in the North of England and had managed to find the rarest of things: a woman who was his equal, if not his better, who also understood his work and encouraged him to continue seeking justice for the dead.

Lucky man.

Unaccountably, his mind strayed to DCI Ava Hope and, as he wandered through to his bedroom and began to strip off his outer clothes, he found himself wondering where she was at that moment and whether she had anybody to go home to.

Further west of where Gregory stepped beneath the spray of a steaming hot shower, DCI Ava Hope dragged herself through the doorway of her house, where she was accosted immediately by a cat the size of a small pony.

"All right, all right," she said, nudging the door shut behind her. "I missed you, too."

She crouched down to administer a thorough belly rub and then made her way towards the kitchen, with the cat trotting behind her.

As always, the small Victorian terrace she'd bought a couple of years before looked as though a bomb had recently hit, with a pile of clean laundry still sitting in the basket where she'd left it over a week ago, stacks of unopened letters lying on the kitchen table beside all sorts of other clutter that had slowly gathered around the house like creeping ivy.

Luckily, the kitchen, although disordered, was always clean thanks to the efforts of a weekly housekeeping team and her own personal standards when it came to distinguishing between 'mess' and 'filth'. The former she could live with, the latter she could not.

"Hungry, hmm?"

She topped up the cat's water and set out some food, which he began chomping his way through, and then opened the fridge to see what delights awaited her.

A couple of eggs, possibly out of date. Half a carton of milk. A bit of cheddar cheese, olives and a carton of cherry-flavoured yoghurt that smelled distinctly suspect.

She needed to go shopping but, with the Villiers case occupying most of her time, the chances of her making it to the supermarket anytime soon were about as likely as Carter scoring a date with Rihanna anywhere except in his wildest dreams.

"Omelette, it is," she said to herself, reaching for the eggs and the milk.

She turned on the radio and sang along to some old seventies classics for the time it took her to whisk up the eggs and set them away on the hob.

After a couple of mouthfuls, she found herself pushing the plate away.

The sudden loss of appetite had little to do with her culinary skills, which were as good as the next working singleton's with very little energy left at the end of the day, and nothing to do with the case, either, which should have been at the forefront of her mind.

It was Gregory.

As a woman of thirty-four, Ava had some experience of life, and of men. Beyond the relationships she'd had in university and a particularly heart-breaking one that had taken up most of her twenties, she'd met enough of their gender to be able to discern the kind of man who represented stability and reliability versus those who didn't.

And, no, she hadn't always opted for the safe choice—where would have been the fun in that?

Notwithstanding, she'd reached a time in life where she craved something more meaningful. Whilst she doubted that she would ever be the kind of woman to settle down to a humdrum, predictable, nine-to-five existence, that didn't mean she wouldn't have enjoyed a Friday night movie snuggled up on the sofa with a glass of good wine and a stone-baked pizza. She saw couples walking hand in hand and experienced the occasional pang of envy, which reminded her of bittersweet times when she'd had a hand to hold, both physically and metaphorically. She remembered how nice it had been to come home after a difficult day and have somebody to lend a friendly ear or a shoulder to cry on, if things had been particularly hard. She missed the intimacy that came with a long-term relationship—not only in the bedroom…

She stood up suddenly, scraping the chair back against the tiled floor loudly enough to elicit a protesting *miaow* from the cat.

"Sorry," she muttered, and emptied her plate into the bin with more force than was strictly necessary.

The truth was, she was angry at herself for indulging in self-pity. It wasn't in her nature to dwell on the past; she was, essentially, a positive, forward-thinking person.

Why, then, all the introspection?

Gregory again, she supposed.

There was no getting around it and, in the privacy of her own home, she might as well admit the truth, if only to herself and the cat.

She found the man attractive.

All right, *very* attractive.

He was good-looking, but she'd seen better looking men walking the streets of London. What was it about him that captured her interest? There were boundless theories of attraction, which listed factors such as proximity, physical attractiveness, similarity and reciprocity as determining whether one person was likely to fall for another, but she was inclined to think that, in her own case, she was just a glutton for punishment. After all, any fool could see that Alexander Gregory was not in the market for Friday night snuggles on the sofa watching *Sleepless in Seattle*. He was one of the 'complicated' ones, which wasn't something he tried to hide, either. Nobody could accuse him of pretending to be anything other than what he was. They might enjoy a few nights together, during which she'd probably start imagining a future despite him never having promised one, and she'd walk away with the acrid taste of disappointment on her tongue.

Ava shook her head, decisively.

Not worth the heartache.

"Once bitten, twice shy, aren't we, cat?"

The furball didn't look up from where he was, charmingly, licking his own arse.

"Men," she muttered, and stalked upstairs to hurl herself beneath a cold shower.

CHAPTER 19

The following morning dawned crisp and bright, which matched DCI Hope's mood, considering she'd received confirmation of the name and address of the account holder who had been in receipt of regular payments from the late Nigel Villiers. She and DS Carter met Gregory outside King's Cross station shortly after eight o'clock, where they found him ready and waiting with a small cardboard tray of takeaway coffees to drink on the go as they made their way from there to an address on Copenhagen Street, less than a ten-minute walk.

"You read my mind," Carter said, accepting one of the cups with a toast of thanks.

"I wasn't sure how you liked your coffee," Gregory said, turning to Hope. "I guessed flat white."

Damn him for being right, she thought, *and damn him for looking so vitally awake, at that time of the morning.*

"Thanks," she said.

"So, tell me about the man we're going to see," Gregory said, as they began to walk.

"Lance Beckett, formerly Winston Sugden, aged sixty-one. Londoner born and bred," Carter reeled off. "He's an actor and a lifelong friend of the late Nigel Villiers—or so he's always claimed. They came up in the Stagelights together, at Cambridge, and he had a very promising start which seemed to peter out over the years. He does bit parts now—"

"And, apparently, supplements his income by tapping up his old friends," Hope put in.

Gregory nodded. "Any previous?"

"None," she replied, taking a healthy gulp of coffee. "Aside from a couple of drink-driving offences, back in the nineties. He doesn't keep a car, now, so I guess that's why he's managed to avoid any further misdemeanours."

"Seems to fit your profile, Doc," Carter said. "Somebody who feels like they haven't quite met their own expectations...possibly knew something about Villiers and wanted him to pay for it, in more ways than one, but prefers not to get their hands dirty with a messy murder?"

Gregory nodded. "I do believe the person capable of murdering Villiers, or inciting his suicide, is of a non-violent personality type, in general. 'Behaviour mimics personality', so if we look at their style of communication and killing, that's very telling. They aren't the classic 'alpha', and probably aren't likely to enjoy mess or gore; they prefer neat e-mails to handwritten notes, and poison to more bloody acts of murder," he said. "They're methodical and organised, but…"

He trailed off, a small frown furrowing his brow.

"But?" Hope prompted him.

"It's the extortion," he said. "It doesn't fit with the allusion to Socrates or the need to 'right wrongs', because idealism and greed are conflicting psychological goals. Then again, as we've said before, there's always room for surprises when it comes to offender behaviour."

"I guess we'll find out when we talk to Lance Beckett," she said. "I have a feeling he's the breakthrough we've been looking for."

Unfortunately, Lance Beckett's talking days were over.

When they arrived at the unassuming block of flats where he lived, their first clue that something was amiss came in the form of the flashing blue lights of a squad car pulling up outside the main entrance, and the presence of a young woman seated on a low brick wall outside, weeping.

searching look, as if she was trying to see what lay behind his eyes.

"What is it?" he asked.

She shook her head. "I—nothing. You're a safe pair of hands when it comes to this sort of thing, aren't you?"

Gregory held out both hands to demonstrate their lack of tremble. "You can rely on me."

Hope thought of the conversation she'd had with herself the previous evening and was confused all over again.

"I'll be back shortly," was all she said.

"I'm Doctor Alexander Gregory, but you can call me Alex. What's your name?"

Gregory turned to the woman seated beside him and asked an easy, non-threatening question while surreptitiously tucking the blanket around her legs.

"Anya," she whispered.

Tears still leaked from her eyes, which were puffy and sore, and her breathing came in short gasps.

"Nice name," he said, easily. "It sounds like you've had a rough morning, so far, Anya. Do you want to talk about it?"

Her lips trembled. "He—I saw…he was…he was *dead*."

Gregory nodded, and picked up her limp wrist to keep a finger on her pulse, which was beating to an erratic, staccato rhythm.

"It's very difficult to see a dead body," he said, in an even tone. "I remember seeing one for the first time in hospital, but it isn't the same when you're not expecting it."

She nodded, looked up from her focused inspection of the floor, then back down again.

"Can you do something for me, Anya? Can you take a deep breath in through your nose, counting to three, then let it back out through your mouth, counting to three in your head?"

He helped her to breathe for a few minutes, talking softly and counting the breaths in and out in the same even tone he'd used with patients many times before, until he was satisfied that her mind was focused wholly on that one, simple task, and not on what she had seen. Visual trauma was hard to banish and there would be nightmares and flashbacks to contend with, but they'd worry about that later. Before then, he needed to make sure she didn't pass out.

"How do you feel now?"

To her surprise, Anya did feel a little better.

"Shaky, but okay."

"You had a nasty shock," Gregory said. "It's a normal reaction."

"I—I wish I hadn't seen it. I wish I hadn't found him like that."

Gregory nodded. "You did the right thing, calling the police. They came quickly and they'll do all they can for him."

"There's nothing they can do, now," she said, morosely. "He was long gone."

Gently, he directed her towards the facts. Another mental exercise that tended to shut down rising panic.

"I understand you did some housekeeping work for Mr Beckett?"

Anya nodded. "I always start at eight on Mondays," she said. "I have a key, in case he's out, or sometimes he's still sleeping. He said, so long as I didn't hoover before eleven, it was okay to let myself in. So, when I rang the buzzer and nobody answered, I thought he was still in bed or maybe still out somewhere."

"Did he often stay out all night?"

She nodded. "Sometimes, if he's at the casino, he'll be there all night," she said. "I told him, he should stop and try to save something for old age. He couldn't help himself…it was an addiction, I think."

Gregory said nothing, because sometimes silence was best.

"I…I opened the door and went into the flat, and I didn't hear anything, no snores or anything like that," she said. "I thought nobody was home. There was no sign of his coat on the peg in the hallway, where he usually left it. Then, I saw his favourite shoes beside the chair in the living room and I thought, 'I wonder why he didn't wear them?'"

Gregory nodded.

"I…I'm sorry, I put them away in his bedroom," she said. "If I knew, I wouldn't have touched—"

It was a pity, Gregory thought, because he knew the police forensics team would have preferred to have had no interference with the scene, but these things happened.

"Don't worry about that now," he said.

"I cleaned for maybe fifteen minutes," she said, and felt sick at the thought of not having known. "I always do the kitchen, first, then the bathroom…"

She swallowed, and rubbed a hand across her forehead.

"Take it easy," Gregory murmured. "There's no rush."

Anya took a sip of water from the gym bottle she kept in her rucksack, to clear her throat.

"The bathroom door was open, but only ajar," she said. "I had no idea he was in there. I pushed open the door and he was lying in the bath. I—at first, I was embarrassed; I thought I'd walked in and disturbed him, but then, I could see—"

She sucked in a long, shaky breath.

"It was obvious he was dead."

Gregory nodded, and asked a question she hadn't expected. "Anya, when you cleaned the kitchen, did you wash any cups or glasses? Did you see any herbal tea, or anything of that kind?"

She shook her head. "I don't remember any tea," she said. "When I got there, the kitchen was very tidy already, with no dirt on the countertops. The living room, too."

Gregory's eyes sharpened. "Was that usual?"

"I don't like to say, but…no, it wasn't. Mr Beckett wasn't a very tidy man, in general." She looked across with a guilty expression. "I shouldn't have said—"

Gregory gave her a reassuring smile. "You've done the right thing, Anya," he said. "I'm very glad you told me that."

For it was the little pieces and fragments of a life that made up the whole. If Lance Beckett was not known to be a tidy person, it begged the question of how his apartment came to be spotless after he was found dead, apparently having committed suicide. Unless, of course, another person had been so good as to clean all traces, after the fact.

CHAPTER 20

If it weren't for the sickly, morbid pallor of his skin, Lance Beckett might have been sleeping.

He lay stretched out in a shallow bath, his limbs stiff and waxy like a mannequin doll, owing to the effects of rigor mortis, while the underside of his body was red and bloated thanks to livor mortis and the impact of having been submerged in water for several hours.

The fact he happened to be nude seemed inconsequential, by comparison.

"No matter how many times I do this, I always feel like a voyeur," Hope said quietly, as Gregory stepped forward to join her in the bathroom doorway. "It feels so…undignified."

"Death is the last undignified act of the living," Gregory agreed. "Whether by natural causes, self-infliction or by somebody else's hand, it's always brutal."

Hope nodded, understanding him completely.

"You'd think I'd get used to it," she said, with a self-deprecating shrug. "My stomach might have grown stronger, over the years, but it's always a punch to the gut seeing people laid out, raw."

"Better you than anyone else," Gregory said, turning to look at her. "Your discomfort reflects the compassion you retain for the people who once inhabited the bodies in your charge. They had lives, dreams, friends, family...regardless of whether they were 'good' or 'bad' people, whatever those words might mean, you treat them with respect. It's all any of us could hope for, when our time comes."

Hope turned away, wondering whether he knew how much his words affected her.

He couldn't possibly know.

"It doesn't scream suicide, at first glance," Gregory continued, all business again. "No obvious wounds, no bottle of pills..."

"There was a note," she said, and guided him back through to the living area, where two other members of the forensics team rustled about in polypropylene suits while they swept the place for evidence.

She handed him a clear plastic evidence bag containing a printed sheet of paper, which read:

To Whomever May Find Me,

I apologise for the state in which you'll discover my body, when the time comes. Unfortunately, I could see no other recourse than to end things now.

I was inspired by Nigel's bravery in taking the decision to atone for his sins, making the ultimate sacrifice, like Socrates, for the sake of what is right. I knew that I had to make the same sacrifice, for the same reason.

I'm sorry for all my mistakes of the past and hope I will be forgiven, in the end.

Yours faithfully,
Lance Beckett

"What do you make of it?" she asked.

Gregory read the note again.

"I think we can safely assume Beckett wasn't responsible for sending the threatening e-mails to Nigel, for one thing," he replied, and handed it back to her. "If we're to believe Beckett typed this note—which I'm not convinced he did—the content is still relevant, because it reflects what matters to the person who wrote it. Namely, the impetus behind the deaths of Villiers and Beckett; the ideology of Socrates' death; and the allusion to some misdeed in the past. I think it's also a fairly safe assumption Beckett will have died following ingestion of poison hemlock, just like Villiers."

Even if every instinct told her Gregory was correct, part of Hope's job was not to discount potential avenues of enquiry too soon. A former mentor had once told her that, if something looks like a duck and quacks like a duck, it probably is a duck. On that reasoning, if she was presented with a crime scene that looked like suicide, then it probably was, until proven otherwise.

"I won't rule anything out," she said. "Right now, we've got circumstantial evidence that provides motive for Villiers having taken the hemlock himself, and a typed note, ostensibly from Beckett, to say he'd offed himself for the same reason, whatever that may be. Even more than that, I've got Beckett telling us he was inspired by Nigel's act of 'bravery', which ties in with the idea of a noble, self-sacrificing death."

"And yet, we have the threatening e-mails," Gregory said. "That tells us there's a third hand in all of this."

Hope sighed. "Yeah, I know. It stinks."

It was unfortunate that, at that very moment, the coroner's team brought out Beckett's body, which had since been given formal permission for removal to the mortuary. Despite the heavy-duty body bag, their nasal cavities detected the faint but unmistakable aroma of decomposing gases wafting on the air, in their general direction.

"Vicks?" Hope offered him, and held out a little jar of mint-scented gel to dab beneath his nose.

"Don't mind if I do," Gregory replied, and wondered what it said about his personality that she could have offered him gold or diamonds and he wouldn't have been half so pleased.

"No sign of any mobile phone," Carter said, coming to stand beside them. "There was a pretty ancient-looking laptop in one of the cupboards in the spare bedroom, so we've bagged it up."

"What about the cause of death?" Hope asked. "Any little bags of poison hanging around the place?"

They had worn coveralls, masks and gloves not only to protect the integrity of the crime scene, but to protect themselves against the possibility of contamination.

"Nothing suspect," he replied. "Forensics are still searching, but there was nothing obvious. No glasses, cups, or anything like that."

"Maybe the cleaner got to them, first," Hope suggested, but Gregory shook his head.

"I had a word with his cleaner, earlier," he said. "Anya says she cleaned the kitchen, but it was already tidy when she got there, and there weren't any glasses or cups left out. She also said that was unusual, for Beckett."

Hope didn't need to follow any trail of breadcrumbs to understand his line of thought.

"You're thinking somebody might have washed up any remnants? Yes, that's possible," she said.

"It's also possible he swallowed a capsule," Gregory said. "It would only take one of sufficient strength, and there'd be no evidence to clean up afterwards. It's neat, tidy and organised, just like the killer."

Hope looked around the room, which had a musty, 'old man' feeling to it, with all kinds of trinkets and collectibles scattered around bookshelves and on the walls, and thought of Beckett having lived there alone, with just himself and his memories for company. Her next thought was that it could easily be her, in another thirty or forty years, if she didn't start socialising a bit more.

It was a sobering thought.

"There's something else," she said. "The body didn't show any bruising or signs of aggression, which tells me that, if there *was* a third party in here, they didn't have to force their way in or manhandle him."

Gregory agreed. "I think it's highly likely we're looking for someone known to both Villiers and Beckett," he said. "It's the only way they'd have known their routines and how to make contact with either or both of them."

"What I don't understand is, why make it look like suicide?" Carter asked. "Why go to the trouble?"

"To cover themselves," Hope replied.

"To legitimise their cause," Gregory added. "The attempt to make either death look like suicide relies on a lack of evidence to the contrary, rather than anything particularly convincing from a police perspective. The fact Beckett's mobile phone and coat are missing—"

"Coat?" Hope queried.

"The cleaner, Anya, mentioned he had a coat he always wore that he tended to keep hanging on a peg in the hallway," Gregory explained. "When she entered the flat and saw it wasn't there, she assumed he was out. Then, she was confused to find his favourite shoes in the living room, because if he'd worn the coat, he'd usually have worn the shoes. Beckett was a creature of habit, it seems."

Hope eyed the pair of tan leather brogues sitting next to one of the armchairs.

"The coat was probably taken because the killer worried they'd touched it, and there'd be trace evidence left in its fibres," she said. "It's an attempt to be DNA-savvy, but the very act of removing it looks suspicious, and goes against the staging of a suicide."

"They're inexperienced," Gregory surmised. "It's as I said before, I don't think we're looking for a sophisticated killer. This is somebody who's stepped outside their comfort zone to kill both men, at a suitable distance. I wouldn't be surprised if we found that they weren't responsible for putting Beckett in the bath, either; I'd say they would have avoided physical contact at all costs."

"You think he ran the bath himself?"

Gregory nodded. "Most likely. I'm no pathologist, obviously, but would you agree he looked as though he'd been dead somewhere in the region of eight— maybe ten hours? The poison takes time to kick in, so perhaps he thought he'd have a dip before bed."

"I guess there are worse places to die," Carter remarked, thinking of some of the poor souls they'd fished out of rubbish bins and car boots. "Look, you said the person who's done all this is inexperienced, but it seems like they've gone to a lot of trouble…"

"I agree," Gregory said. "There's a reason for it, and they want us to think it's to do with whatever happened in 1979, so I'd say our next logical step should be finding out what it was."

"That could take time," Carter said.

"Time isn't necessarily something we have," Gregory replied. "Before, it was just Villiers. Just one victim and, even then, the outside possibility his death might have been suicide. Now…"

"There's two," Hope finished for him, her eyes dark and troubled. "Are you saying what I think you're saying?"

"Two friends with history," Gregory replied. "Both are dead within the space of a week, both by the same means—because I'm certain you'll find Beckett died following hemlock poisoning, when the tox report comes back. Both deaths seem to be linked to something in their shared past, at a time when they were at university together. It's too much coincidence. Until we know what happened in 1979, we can't be sure that a third person won't die, too."

"You're thinking we've got a serial on our hands?" Carter asked, with a touch of excitement that earned him one of Hope's reproving glances.

"Technically, they're not 'serial killers' until they make it to the magic number three," Gregory replied.

"Then let's make sure they don't make it that far," Hope said, flatly. "One person who might be able to tell us about Villiers and Beckett back in '79 would be your friend, Bill Douglas. I'd appreciate it, if you could let him know we'll be coming to speak to him this afternoon."

Gregory nodded. "He'll be happy to help, I'm sure."

But Hope gave a little shake of her head.

"Think it through, Doctor," she said, quietly. "Villiers, Beckett…and who else, from the old days? Douglas was friends with Villiers, and we don't know if he had any connection with Beckett but, since they moved in the same circle, it's more than likely they knew one another. If there's anything in your friend's past—anything at all—that he should tell us about, then now would be the time because, if what you say is true about there being somebody out there on a mission, he could be next."

Gregory couldn't believe he hadn't made the connection himself…

Denial, he realised. He never wanted to imagine his friend being embroiled in anything underhand, or, worse still, that he might be in danger.

It didn't bear thinking about, but he must.

"In that case, there's one more person you should speak to," he said.

It took a second for the penny to drop, then Hope swore volubly, turning the heads of the forensic team who still hovered nearby.

"The Super," she said, for Carter's benefit. "Campbell makes four of them who were at university together."

"Oh," he said.

"Yeah," she replied, and swore again for good measure.

CHAPTER 21

It was said that it took many good deeds to build a good reputation, and only one bad deed to lose it.

He knew better.

It didn't take a single bad deed; it took only a single word.

The word of one man—one *arrogant* man, with a powerful platform—could be enough to turn the tide. If that man were then multiplied and became two, or even three, there was no chance for an unsuspecting innocent to defend themselves against the onslaught. Soon, others joined the bandwagon, which rolled faster and faster, gathering momentum until it struck like a battering ram, crashing through lives and livelihoods, destroying that most precious thing of all.

Reputation.

It had been Mark Twain who said that "a lie can travel halfway around the world while the truth was putting on its shoes" and he knew that to be the case, from painful, first-hand experience. Once a lie had been spoken, then accepted and propagated again and again *ad nauseum*, what chance did anybody have to contradict it without sounding desperate, or uncredible?

Even in the rare instance that the witch-hunters shelved their pitchforks and turned their focus elsewhere, all that was left of the person they'd tormented was the miserable fragments of a character; broken and irretrievably lost.

Unwanted.

Unemployable.

Feared.

No smoke without fire, people whispered. *They say he didn't do it, but can we really be sure?*

For a while, he'd tried to convince them otherwise. He'd tried to prove them wrong. He'd given his side of the story and borne the curious stares, the false, nodding smiles, and waited for life to return to normal.

It never had.

People remembered, you see. So long as a lie lived in their memories, the truth could never win out. He'd lived with the injustice of that simple premise for a long time—too long, for any person to bear— until reality mingled with paranoia, and he could no longer trust anybody, least of all, himself.

Despair had spiralled, sending him down and down, until he hardly recognised himself any longer. For a while, he thought that was all he had left, and had, to his shame, considered ending it all.

That's when anger had set in.

It was not for him to remove himself from the world; it was for others to be removed. There was a price to pay for what had been taken from him and it was time to collect. He would not entrust that task to their weak, contemptible excuse for a justice system. There was a higher law, a 'natural' law, that every human being was entitled to enforce. Theirs was a social contract, and the terms had been broken.

No more contracts with men and women in uniform, he thought.

No more deference to higher authorities.

He was his own authority, now.

Leaving the scene at Beckett's flat in the capable hands of DS Carter, Hope and Gregory made their way back to King's Cross, where they boarded a train shortly after eleven that would take them to Cambridge in under ninety minutes. It was a journey Gregory had taken many times before but, he had to admit, never in such pleasant company.

"Tell me about your friend, Bill Douglas," Hope said.

Gregory cocked his head. "Do you want the executive summary, or the full works?"

"Let's try the summary, first, and go from there."

"Bill is, without question, the best in his field," Gregory said, quietly. "Which is, very broadly speaking, clinical psychology as applied to violent offenders, although he's mostly an academic these days. He varied his work to include profiling a number of years ago—"

"When you set up your profiling unit," she said. "I remember."

"We decided to re-open it," he said.

She said nothing, but he could read her mind easily.

"You're worried we'll come in for more bad press?" he guessed. "It's always a risk."

"If you know it's a risk that you'll come across more men like Campbell, who'd throw you under the bus as soon as look at you, why do it?" she wondered aloud.

"Why do what *you* do?" he countered. "We do it to prevent harm and to help people, in our different ways."

It took a certain amount of backbone to have suffered the ignominy of professional embarrassment—especially when it was uncalled for—and to have decided, nonetheless, to get back on the proverbial horse and ride again. It demonstrated an integrity that Hope found appealing—an emotion that was in direct contravention of her personal edict about him being firmly, 'off limits'.

"You were telling me about Professor Douglas' specialism," she said, to distract herself. "How did you meet?"

"At Southmoor," he said. "Bill was the senior consultant when I began my clinical training there, after university. We worked closely together, and he taught me everything I know…he's still teaching me, now."

"You have a lot of respect for him, don't you?"

Gregory smiled. "Hard not to," he replied. "He's a very good man."

Hope admired his loyalty.

"Does he still practise?"

"Not really," he said. "I think Bill takes on the odd private case, but he has a fellowship at Hawking College and most of his time is tied up with research and teaching. Whatever spare time he has, he donates to the profiling unit, largely for his own interest."

"I've heard you describe yourself as both a psychologist and psychiatrist," she said. "Which is it?"

Gregory relaxed back against his chair, lulled by the motion of the train and the ease of their conversation.

"Technically speaking, I'm a psychiatrist, and so is Bill," he said. "We have the medical training which entitles us to approach diagnoses with a physical examination of symptoms and we can prescribe medications, if needed. I'm also a psychologist, in the sense that I often prefer to adopt psychotherapy and talking therapies in my treatment of patients and to address abnormal behaviours, rather than falling back wholly on medical training."

"So, the distinction comes down to the treatment?"

He shrugged. "The word, 'psychology' refers to the study of people," he said. "How they think and act, how they react and interact with one another. It looks at all aspects of behaviour and the thoughts, feelings and motivations that underly that behaviour. It's a combination of science and practice, really, and, over the course of my time in a clinical setting, I found a purely medical approach to understanding the mind quite limiting."

"One size doesn't fit all, you mean?"

He nodded. "For that reason, I suppose I think of myself more as a clinical psychologist," he said. "You might say I've been adopted by their cohort, despite having a medical background, but it still comes in handy now and then."

She smiled. "Don't like to be pigeon-holed, do you?"

He met her eyes and shook his head, slowly. "I could say the same of you, Chief Inspector."

Something fluttered in her chest. *Oh dear,* she thought. "Ah…" She dragged her eyes away from his. "So, Douglas became your mentor at Southmoor?"

Gregory nodded. "He became a friend, too—he has an encyclopaedic knowledge, but he's always eager to learn more."

"You're very similar, then," she remarked, and prepared herself to ask a difficult question. "Having a close friendship can be a blessing and a curse, though, can't it? You look up to him, professionally and personally. That could make it hard for Douglas to confide in you, if there was anything he wasn't proud of, couldn't it?"

Gregory had thought the same thing, since their discussion earlier that morning. When he hadn't been looking at the nude corpse of Lance Beckett or dealing with the man's traumatised housekeeper, he'd thought of Bill, and of whether their friendship had blinded him to other facets of his character.

He was, in some areas, a very private man.

Douglas was gay but hadn't come to the realisation until later in life. There had followed a process of re-discovery and a rapid re-assessment of his personal paradigm, which had been built during a different, less enlightened generation. He hadn't been fortunate enough to meet anyone special—yet— but he had a gregarious and optimistic nature that

Gregory felt sure would appeal to many potential partners. However, it was still a new world to him, and Bill was in the process of accepting himself. Until he had, he remained intensely private about his personal life, which Gregory had always respected. When he wanted to talk, if he ever did, he hoped his friend knew that he would be there to listen with a non-judgmental ear.

Aside from that, his life appeared to be an open book—quite literally. Douglas had penned several academic texts, all of which were in wide usage at Cambridge University and beyond. He was often invited, as part of the international speakers' circuit, to lecture at events around the world. He was a doyen who was devoted to his subject and had committed many years of his life to the project of understanding the human psyche, with compassion. His students admired him—loved him, Gregory would go so far as to say—not only because he was a trove of information, but because he knew how to impart his wisdom with panache, distilling it into bitesize chunks that undergraduate students could understand and assimilate. Often, it was a malady of university academics to be so wrapped up in themselves and their own projects that teaching became a poor second...not so with Douglas, who always found time to answer questions and listen to the ideas of more youthful minds than his own, cultivating them where he could.

And yet, the fact remained that Bill was not superhuman, nor infallible. There was always a chance that he had made an error of judgment at some time in his early days which, despite the long passage of time, had come back to haunt him—and Villiers and Beckett, too. Gregory had seen with his own eyes how personalities could shift and develop over time, so it was possible Douglas hadn't always been the same man that he was today.

However, there was one thing that trumped all else, in Gregory's mind, and that was the impact of his own confession to Douglas, regarding his mother, Cathy Jones. When he'd taken the decision to come clean and tell Bill about his professional transgression, it had been the most shameful moment of his life. It had cost him dearly, but had turned out to be his redemption and, rather than losing a friend, his decision to tell Bill the truth had brought them closer together.

The truth shall set you free.

A side-effect of having purged himself was to provide Bill with the perfect opportunity to confide or confess any sins of his own, knowing as he must that Gregory would be the last person to hand down any hypocritical judgment.

*Barring murder, of course…*his treacherous mind whispered.

"I think you're absolutely right," he answered, at length. "Ordinarily, I'd say our friendship might act as a barrier, but Bill knows that I'm no angel, myself. That gives him the perfect opening to tell me anything that's troubling him, because he knows I'd understand."

No angel, she thought. *You could say that, again.*

"Er, I hope we're not talking about anything illegal?" she said.

Gregory shook his head.

"It concerns a professional error of judgment relating to my early childhood," he said, simply. "My mother suffered from a serious illness that compelled her to poison her children, routinely. My brother and sister died, whereas I survived."

He said the words entirely without emotion and Hope looked away, swallowing sudden tears that were all for the little boy he'd once been.

"What happened?" she managed.

"My mother was detained indefinitely under the Mental Health Act, and I went on to various foster homes," he said, with a light shrug.

Where was his father? she wondered, but was tactful enough not to ask. She could always find out, if she really wanted to know.

Which, of course, she did.

"I changed my name, and went on with my life," he said, coolly distilling years of trauma and hard work into a single sentence. "I never expected that, years later, my mother would walk into my consulting room at Southmoor. I preferred not to discuss my past, you see, and my colleagues were unaware of the history between us—as was she, because she didn't recognise me, at all."

Hope began to understand what had happened. "You didn't tell anyone she was your mother?"

He looked away for a moment, out at the passing landscape, and then back into her eyes.

"No, I didn't," he said, softly. "Which only really serves to confirm your point, doesn't it, Ava? Everybody is capable of keeping secrets."

CHAPTER 22

Cambridge was glorious in the early afternoon sunshine.

Its skyline was dominated by church spires and college buildings dating back to the thirteenth century, their history etched into the very fabric of what had once been little more than a settlement but was now a world-renowned centre of learning and culture. The River Cam ran through it all, upon which a handful of the city's thirty-thousand students and tourists punted in wooden boats, gliding along the water in a manner reminiscent of another era while they took in the architectural grandeur of the various colleges from The Backs—a scenic area, where the college buildings backed directly onto the river and their grounds covered both banks in an undulating spread of frosted green grass and willow boughs.

Hope entertained a brief, pleasant daydream about what it might be like to punt along the Cam, perhaps in summertime with a tall, dark-haired man doing the heavy lifting while she nibbled a chicken leg or sipped champagne from a wicker picnic basket. She could almost *feel* the sun against her skin, almost hear the whirring sound of crickets somewhere in the reeded banks of the river...

"Ava?"

She snapped back to attention, aware that Gregory was looking at her expectantly. "Sorry, I was miles away," she said.

"I asked if you'd ever been to Cambridge before."

She shook her head. "Considering it isn't too far from London, it's surprising that I haven't," she said.

Then again, not so very surprising, she amended. Although a bright and able student, she hadn't moved in the kind of circles, nor come from the kind of background where she had even thought of applying to Cambridge University—because nobody had ever suggested it as a possibility. When she'd left school at sixteen, her careers advisor had told her that, with her looks, she should think about working in the beauty industry or as a receptionist. Businessmen would find her very easy on the eye, so she was told.

When she'd mentioned a desire to train as a police officer, the advisor had laughed in her face.

That's a man's job, Ava. Besides, you know how the police can be towards people of colour, even when they're mixed race…

Memories of the Brixton Riots, of 'Stop and Search' scandals and the damning findings of the MacPherson Report still weighed heavily in her community of South London, and therefore, to express fear for a young woman of mixed race who was thinking of entering a work hierarchy that had been found to be racist at an institutional level was not altogether uncalled for.

Still, it had been all the impetus she'd needed to sign up, and Ava had never regretted her decision.

At least, not very often.

Her work had led her to meet some very interesting people, and, if life had taught her one thing, it was to treat all of them the same—whether they happened to be her superintendent, the grieving family of a gangland murder victim or, indeed, an enigmatic psychiatrist-slash-psychologist, who knew so much about everybody else and yet didn't quite know himself.

"I suppose you went to university here?" she said, without any bitterness. Despite his difficult start in life, she could imagine Alex Gregory having been able to make his way in the world, in whichever manner he chose. It wasn't merely that he had the intelligence; he had the right look about him, and the right accent.

He surprised her again. "I've been invited to take up a post here, and I've given plenty of lectures—then, there's the profiling unit, of course," he said. "But, no, I didn't do any of my academic training here. I went to King's College, in London. They have an excellent medical school and access to placements at the Maudsley," he added, referring to one of the most prestigious psychiatric hospitals in the world.

He didn't bother to add that he'd sought the bright lights of London so that he could lose himself; reinvent himself as Alexander Gregory and forget Michael Jones, the boy he'd once been.

"You imagined this would be my kind of place?" he asked, with a twinkle in his eye. "I suppose it is, in some ways. I certainly admire the fact it's home to the largest number of Nobel prize winners, and that it's brought up some of the finest research brains you'd care to mention. The accolades are endless, but, when I was eighteen, it lacked one crucial thing."

"Which was?"

"A decent nightlife," he said, and made her laugh out loud. "C'mon. Hawking College is this way."

Thoughts of murder briefly forgotten, Hope was content to walk side by side through the old streets, dodging bicycles until they came upon a grand stone archway bearing a gilded coat of arms, beyond which was a u-shaped college built of elegant limestone arranged around a glossy green quadrangle.

"Here we are," he said. "What do you think?"

She affected a casual expression. "Looks a bit poky," she said, and made him laugh this time.

Professor Bill Douglas's office occupied an entire floor in the central clock tower of Hawking College, and was a gentle mix of musty, panelled walls and mullioned windows. It managed to stay cool in the summer and warm in the winter, with the aid of a large, roaring fire beside which he'd placed two comfortable wingback chairs and a sagging leather sofa which looked as though it had seen better days.

He welcomed them both with an affable smile.

"Alex, DCI Hope," he said. "Do come in."

"Thank you for finding the time to meet with me, today," Hope said, eager to keep things on a professional footing. "I should ask you, from the outset, whether you're comfortable to have Doctor Gregory in the room with us while we talk?"

She was giving him the opportunity to speak privately if he needed to save face, and Gregory did what he could to support the gesture.

"I could grab some coffees for us all?" he offered, studiously ignoring the coffee machine in the corner of the room.

Douglas looked between the pair of them with a kind of fatherly indulgence.

"It's really very sweet of you both, but I have nothing I wish to hide from my friend," he said. "I'm happy to help your investigation in any way that I can. Now, how about that coffee?"

He moved across to a shiny-looking machine that was all bells and whistles.

"It even does foam, when I can get it to work," he muttered.

"In that case, yes please," Hope said. "I'll have a coffee with milk, if it isn't too much trouble."

It wasn't just that she was thirsty—which she was—it was a matter of putting both men at their ease. The simple act of making coffee was often an icebreaker and she wanted the ice to be well and truly broken, so they could speak freely.

Gregory offered her one of the chairs by the fire, sacrificing himself to the sofa, which almost swallowed him whole.

"Very gallant," she chuckled.

Gregory threw her a devilish look. "Why don't you come over and give me a hand?" he challenged, and was immediately intrigued to see a blush rise up her slender neck.

Interesting.

"Here we are," Douglas said, casting an eye over his friend, then the young woman beside him.

Alex had never encountered any trouble attracting female company, but it seemed to be rather more difficult for him to hold on to it. However, it seemed there was always hope—in more ways than one.

"Well now," he said, taking the remaining chair. "You've both come all this way, so it must be important?"

Gregory remained silent, deferring to Hope's authority in the case.

"I understand Doctor Gregory has already told you about our most recent finding, this morning?" she said.

"Lance Beckett? Yes, he did. Poor fellow."

There was genuine compassion, she thought, but no real grief, which was to be expected since there was no suggestion of them ever having been close friends. Then again, that was what she was here to determine—for Douglas's sake, as much as her own.

"Are you aware that Beckett and Villiers were friends?" she asked.

Douglas nodded. "Yes, Nigel and Lance had known one another for years," he said. "Alex mentioned there's some question mark over whether either death was suicide, despite some contra-indications?"

Hope nodded. "Villiers was sent threatening notes via e-mail, as you know," she said. "And we found a typed note in Beckett's apartment this morning, apparently written by him, explaining why he'd taken his own life." She went on to explain its contents. "We're concerned that a third party developed some sort of crusade against these two men in retribution for an event that occurred many years ago, in 1979."

She watched him closely for any reaction, but there was none except genuine curiosity.

"1979?" He raised a pair of bushy eyebrows. "I didn't start here in Cambridge until 1980, but that would have been Nigel's third year of study and Beckett's second, depending on when he began his course, which I'd have to check."

Gregory felt an enormous weight lift from his chest, one he hadn't consciously realised he'd been carrying. He should have known that Douglas didn't begin his undergraduate studies until 1980, but it made all the difference.

"I see," Hope said, and noted Gregory's relief. "All the same, presumably, you'd have known if there had been any sort of scandal or incident the previous year?"

Douglas pulled an expressive face. "Students talk, certainly," he said. "Gossip is an age-old pursuit, so there's a good chance I'd have heard something, even on the grapevine. On the other hand, things aren't as they are today. There was no dreaded social media, nor any mobile phones or even the internet. The means of communication were old-fashioned and considerably slower which, if I may say, was no bad thing."

He removed his glasses, which were a snazzy shade of dark purple, and began to polish them idly against his woollen jumper.

"It all depends on the nature of the incident," he continued. "No institution is perfect, and the university certainly isn't, either. There's also a chance that something could have been hushed up, so that's why I might not have heard about anything extraordinary happening in the year before my arrival."

Her job would be too easy, Hope thought, *if she simply asked questions and was provided with the precise answers she needed.*

"What about Nigel?" she asked. "Did he ever confide anything to you?"

Douglas replaced his glasses and shook his head. "He wasn't that kind of friend," he explained. "Nigel was the life and soul of the party, but it was all on the surface, all superficial. Great fun to be around, especially at that age, but he wasn't into 'deep and meaningfuls', if you catch my drift. It's highly unlikely Nigel would have confided anything to me, let alone anything of sufficient import to come back and haunt him, almost forty years later."

"What about Beckett?" Gregory asked. "Did you know much about him?"

Douglas cast his mind back as far as it would go. "He was a young man I'd have described as 'chippy,'" he said. "He and I came from similar backgrounds, you know, but he always seemed so *ashamed* of it. He let all *this* addle his self-esteem," he said, gesturing to their surroundings. "It can do that, to some people."

Hope and Gregory both understood.

"Lance wasn't always Lance, you see," Douglas continued. "I'm almost certain he was something like Arthur, or Derek, or Winston; something far more ordinary and less glamorous. But he was a good-looking feller, and knew it, too. Bit of a reputation as a ladies' man, always knocking around in the latest gear."

"Winston Sugden," Hope reminded him. "We ran a basic check on him this morning."

"Lance Beckett sounds more glamourous. Was he talented?" Gregory asked.

"I suppose so," Douglas said. "It really depends on your yardstick. I have to say, I was surprised he and Nigel grew so close. From what I remember, they didn't start out that way."

Hope leaned forward.

"Oh? Why not?"

"I couldn't say," Douglas replied. "All I can remember is people telling me that Nigel used to have no time for him. Called him a peacock and worse, during their first year together. However, by the time I knew them both, they seemed inseparable."

"So, between October 1979 and October 1980, something shifted in their friendship?"

Douglas nodded. "I suppose so," he replied.

"I wonder if it's the same mysterious incident we're looking into," Hope said. "It's amazing how shared experiences can forge friendships."

"Or *schadenfreude*," Gregory said. "Not forgetting that Villiers was making ad hoc payments into Beckett's account, all these years later. Perhaps it was less a case of charity from an old friend, and more a case of paying a levy for silence."

Douglas considered the men he had known, particularly Nigel, and found himself in agreement.

"Nigel simply had no time for those he considered…well, sub-par. He liked to surround himself with successful people, which made him superficial, in his own way, and a bit of a snob. It's hard to imagine why he'd stay in touch with Lance, let alone send him money. Did Rebecca know about it?"

Hope had Rebecca Villiers on her list of people to speak to again.

"We don't know," she replied. "It depends how close he and his wife were, as a couple. Do you have any insight into that?"

"None, except to say that they'd been together a very long time and seemed devoted," Douglas said. "However, they're actors. They'd both know how to put on a good show, if it served a purpose, and it does...or it did."

"They were a golden couple," Hope remarked. "I suppose that made them popular from a PR standpoint."

"Very," Douglas agreed. "That can be lucrative in more ways than one, especially in the world we live in, where 'cancel culture' is rife. Any whiff of bad behaviour and endorsement deals could be snuffed out, film roles snatched away and reputations that were long-established left as little more than embers, overnight. A good reputation is the kind of thing people might pay a hefty toll to keep intact."

There was that word again, Gregory thought.

Reputation.

"What about Simon Campbell?" Hope asked, conscious that time was marching on. "Did you know much about him, back in the old days?"

It was hard to imagine her superintendent as a student—with hair, for one thing, or youthful ideals—but she had to try.

Douglas wondered whether to sugar-coat his response, but innate honesty prevented him.

"Campbell is, and always has been, a toadying crony," he said. "The man had no interest in the theatre, really, but he recognised that Nigel and his gang were the 'in' crowd and he desperately wanted to be a part of it. He was a man who never liked to be left behind, in anything."

"What did he bring to the table?" Gregory asked. "The same logic applies, surely? Villiers wouldn't have let him through the stable door, if he didn't have something to offer."

"Oh, he might have had no interest, but Simon was actually a very gifted comic actor," Douglas said, surprising them both to such a degree that their faces were comical, too. "He was reserved, the sort of chap who'd watch you like a hawk and make notes, for later. But, put him on a stage, and he was a different person. He used to have a broad Glaswegian accent which he played up, for a while, until he decided he'd rather speak like every other plummy Englishman in the city. When he lost his accent, it seemed he lost a bit of himself—and his verve, too. He didn't stick around the theatre company for more than a year."

"When did he join?" Hope asked. "Was Campbell in your academic intake?"

Douglas shook his head.

"No, I was a year younger than all of them," he said. "Campbell knew Nigel, and probably Lance too, by the time I came along, but he'd given up the theatre by the end of the second term of 1980."

"Did he give any reason for the change?"

"I couldn't say," Douglas replied. "I really didn't know Simon very well at all, and I barely recognised him when our paths crossed again, years later."

He didn't mention the name of the case that had thrown them together again; he didn't need to.

"Did he remember you?"

"Yes," Douglas said. "He doesn't strike me as a man who forgets anything, or anyone."

There was a brief lull, while each of them thought of the past, and of how it could have such a bearing on the future.

Then, Gregory broke the silence. "What we really need to know is the names of the permanent fixtures in Villiers' life, at that time," Gregory said. "Perhaps the individual we're looking for now is one of them, or knew one of them, and believes that anyone connected to Nigel deserves to pay a price for whatever happened. At the very least, it would help with the process of elimination."

"Hard, when Villiers was such a social butterfly," Hope remarked.

Douglas snapped his fingers. "I'm sure I can find some old programmes or photos from those days," he said, rising from the chair to make his way across to a large wooden filing cabinet. "If you look at a list of all the people who formed part of the Stagelights revue in 1980 and '81, then you can try to get hold of a similar list for '79 and compare, eh?"

"Where would we go for that?" Hope asked him.

"The CADC Theatre," Douglas said. "It's the home of the Stagelights, and where Nigel, Lance…all of them began."

CHAPTER 23

The CADC Theatre was the oldest university playhouse in the United Kingdom, with plays having been shown there since 1855, when the Cambridge University Arts and Drama Club was founded and the society met and performed in the back room of the Grapes Inn, which used to stand where the theatre building now stood. Technically it was a department of the university, but the theatre was run almost entirely by students with very little involvement from the faculty, and its list of theatre luminaries was long and distinguished, launching the careers of many a well-known name.

The building itself was an unprepossessing, white-painted affair, only a short walk from Hawking College. Armed with the photographs and programmes given to them by Douglas, they left him to his afternoon classes and made the short journey to the theatre in search of more.

"Hello! Can I help you?"

A girl of around nineteen or twenty greeted them from the small box office, as they entered the foyer.

"Yes, please. Can we speak to the theatre manager, or the president of the CUADC, please?"

Hope presented her warrant card, and the girl's eyes rounded into saucers.

"Right," she whispered. "Well, yes, of course… um, Ishpal isn't in, at the moment—he's the manager and he's got a tutorial, this afternoon. But you could speak to Lacey? She's our current president, and she also happens to be one of the leads in our production, so she's on stage rehearsing just now. Do you want to wait for her to finish?"

Hope merely smiled. "I'm afraid our business is quite pressing, and we need to get back to London as soon as possible. I'm sorry for the inconvenience, but I'm afraid your players will need to take a break for fifteen minutes while we speak to their president—*now*, please."

The message was understood, loud and clear, and the 'BACK IN FIVE' sign was hastily put up while they were shown the way to the theatre auditorium, where a group of five actors were illuminated against a plain black cloth backdrop.

"Lacey!" The girl led the way down the aisle, waving her arms to grab the attention of a red-headed young woman dressed in skinny jeans and a nineties-style crop top.

She spun around at the intrusion, already on the offensive. "Poppy, are you kidding me? We're in the middle of a rehearsal!"

Spotting the other two figures hovering beside her, Lacey snapped her mouth shut.

"You've got a couple of visitors," Poppy said, gesticulating towards Gregory and Hope. "They're from the *police*."

Hope watched the girl's face drain of colour beneath the stage lights and wondered whether they'd happened to catch her on the same day she'd invested in some performance-enhancing drugs, or something of the kind.

Ah, youth.

"Um, right, okay," Lacey said. "Let's take a break, everyone, and come back at half past."

———

Lacey Hetherington-Smythe was even skinnier up close than she'd looked on stage and, with skin so pale it was almost translucent, Hope and Gregory felt that, rather than questioning her about theatre history, they ought to be taking her to the nearest pie shop to stuff some carbs inside her malnourished student body. However, it didn't fall under their job descriptions, and so they followed her into the CADC Bar, which was empty at that time of day.

"So—ah—how can I help you?"

"You may have heard of the death of one of your alumni, lately—Nigel Villiers?" Hope began, and saw the girl's bony shoulders sag with relief.

No drugs busting, today.

"Well, yeah, of course," Lacey said, all confidence again. "He was a legend...an inspiration, one of the greats. We held a vigil for him, last week."

"That's very..." Hope cast around for the word. "Nice."

"It's the *least* we could do," Lacey said.

"Well, perhaps there's something you might be able to do for us," Gregory said, and she turned to him. "We're trying to find out a bit of history about who might have made up the revue for the academic year 1979-80?"

Lacey was obviously quite taken with the doctor, for she smiled slowly and, in Hope's opinion, inappropriately for a girl half his age.

Nearly half his age.

All right, a few years younger.

"I can easily find that out for you," Lacey was saying, her chin now resting coquettishly on her hand while she gave Gregory her full attention. "Is there anything else?"

"If you have any photographs, that would be a help," Hope said, bluntly.

Lacey sat up again. "Well, there might even be something on the wall in here," she said, indicating the collection of framed photographs gracing the bar room walls, some dating back to the 1930s and '40s.

They rose from their chairs and took a different wall in turn, scanning each picture for the relevant date placard.

"Here," Gregory said, after a minute, and Hope hurried across to look while Lacey took up a position on his other side in a manner the other woman found distinctly over-familiar.

The black-and-white photograph had aged with time, but still showed a collection of fifteen smiling men and women with long hair, wearing classic seventies garb. The placard beneath read, 'Stagelights Revue, 1979.' Immediately, they recognised Villiers, who stood front and centre of the assembly with his hands in the pockets of his corduroy trousers, looking as if he could take on the world—which, indeed, he had gone on to do. Though his hair was dark and there were considerably fewer lines marring his face, Villiers seemed always to have possessed a certain bearing, which showed even at the tender age of twenty. On his left was a young Lance Beckett, who stood—

or, rather, *posed*—with his body angled slightly to the side, presumably to show off his face and figure to best advantage for posterity. His hair was well cut, his dress impeccable and he wore a knowing, lazily suggestive look in his eye that reminded Hope somewhat of the French actor Alain Delon, at that time. He had one arm slung around the neck of a pretty blonde woman, whose face she didn't recognise at all, and in his other hand he held a half-smoked cigarette that might have been for show, as so much of his life had been.

Hope couldn't help but remember the last time she'd seen Beckett, and wondered if his younger self could ever have imagined the ignominious circumstances of his eventual demise.

Probably not.

It brought a smile to her lips to see the young, carefree faces of several BAFTA and Oscar-winning actors who had once trod the plain boards of the CADC, and she wondered whether, for all their fame and fortune, accolades and notoriety, they ever missed the simple life. Her smile slipped slightly when she spotted her superintendent, Simon Campbell, who stood at the end of the row, his face turned away from the camera as he was captured looking down the row towards Nigel and the others—always looking to see if he was missing out; always wanting to be part of the crowd. He was nondescript, much as he was now, but Hope knew him to be a force to be reckoned with and would have liked to have met the younger version to find out when the character she knew today had begun to develop. She also knew that she couldn't keep putting off the difficult conversation that must be held with him. She resolved to speak to his personal assistant at the first opportunity and hold a meeting the next morning, whether he had prior engagements or not.

Hope dispatched Lacey to retrieve whatever records she could find from that intake and, as soon as she left, turned to Gregory.

"Do you have the pictures Douglas gave you?"

He nodded, and pulled them from the folder tucked beneath his arm, so they could study them.

"Nigel's front and centre in all of them," Gregory said, tapping a finger on each image. "Lance seems always to be next to him, in the first two pictures, at least, although he's missing from the '81 revue."

"He had a job offer, by then," Hope murmured. "He dropped out of his degree to go off in search of his pot of gold."

"Campbell is only present in the first picture," Gregory said, pointing to the one still hanging on the wall. "As for the others…"

They spent a minute studying their faces.

"Villiers stayed on to re-take a year and squeezed a fourth term as CADC President, which is why he features in the '81 picture, despite starting his degree in '77," Hope said. "Douglas is in the pictures from 1980 and '81, as we expected," she added, pointing to the image of Gregory's friend, as he'd been years earlier.

To Gregory's delight, his fashion sense hadn't altered much, and his eyebrows had always been preposterous. He made a note to tease Bill about that, as soon as possible.

"Most of the others from the '79 image stayed right through until '81," Hope continued. "The only ones who didn't were Beckett and Campbell, which we already know, and this woman here."

She indicated the blonde, who stood with Beckett's arm around her shoulders.

"I don't recognise her. Do you?"

Gregory moved to make a closer inspection, then shook his head. At that moment, Lacey returned with a small pile of papers, hurriedly retrieved from the theatre manager's office.

"This is all the stuff I could find from back then," she said, toppling it onto one of the tables in the bar area. "I hope there's something in here, because I don't know where else to look."

"That's great, thanks," Hope said. "Can we borrow these? We'll give you a receipt for them, and return the papers as soon as our investigation is over. If you need to get back to your rehearsal…?"

Lacey looked as if she was going to decline, but one glance at the chief inspector's face told her that the suggestion had been more of a dismissal.

"Right, yeah," she said, casting a disappointed glance in Gregory's direction. On her way back from the office, she'd enjoyed a very nice daydream in which he'd asked her out that evening and they'd talked of nothing but Chekov.

Some things were not meant to be…

Once she'd departed, their two heads bent once more, this time to look over the old list of names belonging to the 1979 theatrical company. There had only been four women in that revue year, three of which they already knew of and would be able to eliminate from their enquiries easily enough.

The fourth name belonged to the mystery blonde.

"Sally Fletcher," Gregory read. "Reading History of Art…wants to be an actress one day. Or, should I say, 'actor'?"

"Dunno," she said. "But I'll keep it in mind, the next time I run into one of them on the red carpet."

Gregory turned to her with an appreciative smile, and found their faces were much closer than expected.

He didn't move away and, for a few seconds at least, neither did she.

"Better be heading back," she said. "I'll see you in the foyer, in a minute."

With that, she scooped up the papers and hurried out.

CHAPTER 24

There was an art to execution.

He would not call it, 'revenge'. That would be to imply something base and ragged; an act committed by a person who had lost their sanity and succumbed to anger and rage.

He was perfectly sane.

He understood the difference between 'right' and 'wrong'—in fact, it was *because* he understood the difference so well that he was driven to redress the balance. Scales were a symbol of justice, weren't they? There was even a golden statue of Lady Justice on top of the Old Bailey in London, depicting her with a sword in one hand and scales in the other. A symbol of fairness, or so he'd once thought.

What a joke.

True justice took a certain amount of planning, which he'd soon realised after the first, over-zealous attempt he'd made a while ago. Looking back, he could admit that he'd acted in haste, without much clue of where to begin. A red mist had descended, blinding him to practical considerations, and he was bloody lucky not to have been caught.

He'd learned from that mistake and realised that he needed to do what everyone else did, when they were learning a new skill.

Practise.

The first and most obvious consideration was surveillance. Could he watch someone closely, learning their habits, the patterns of their behaviour and daily life, without ever being seen? He was no spook, but the internet was really a *marvellous* place where one could learn how others had gone about such things before him. Some of their advice was on the Dark Web, of course, but it was worth the risk to gain the knowledge.

Then, there was the matter of finding the weak spots in their home, so he could enter without raising the alarm. Better still, enter and leave again, without them ever having known it.

He'd been able to do the former, but was still working on the latter.

He rolled his neck, trying to ease out the kinks that had formed during the forty-five minutes he'd been lying beneath the child's bed while he waited for the woman to run her usual late-night bath following her shift at the café. It was the third time he'd been able to gain access to the little one-bedroom flat she occupied on the ground floor of the council block, and he had to admit that practise was starting to make perfect. He knew which window was old and rotten, and easy to jimmy. *That was the problem with council-owned buildings*, he thought sagely. *You never knew when they'd get the maintenance men around to take care of things.*

Finally, he heard the water start to run in the bathroom across the narrow hallway, and froze when the bottom of her feet came into view in the child's doorway, silhouetted by dim light beyond. He saw her painted toenails approach, holding his breath as she crouched down so that her face was on a level with the sleeping boy's.

"I love you, Ollie," Anika whispered. "I'm going to do everything I can to give you the best life."

In the shadows beneath the cotton pelmet, his grip on the knife loosened, in shock.

"Things are tough, at the moment, but they'll get better, I promise," she said, almost inaudibly. "Trust me."

He heard her lean across to bestow a gentle kiss, watched her feet retreat from the room out of sight, then the gentle click of the bathroom door.

As he'd maintained many, many times, he was not an unfair man. He lived by a code and a set of morals that were higher than man's law.

He'd needed some sort of sacrifice in order to achieve a higher goal; a means to an end, if you wanted to think of it, like that.

But he wasn't a monster.

He wasn't.

Besides, he was ready now. He could continue without any sacrifice.

Slowly, and with infinite care, he edged from beneath the bed, keeping low while projected images of stars swam across the walls. Only when he'd made it to the window did he rise up and sheath the knife, sliding it back into the waistband of his trousers. Reaching for the latch on the window with gloved hands, he took one last look at the sleeping boy.

Sweet, really.

He'd been a boy once, he remembered. He'd had his whole life ahead of him, until it was snatched away.

He left quickly, before the mist descended again.

"This is all we need."

As the train chugged its way back to London, Hope looked up from her inspection of her news feed and handed it to Gregory, so he could read the contents.

It featured a 'breaking news' story and the headline, 'STAGELIGHTS PACT CLAIMS SECOND LIFE', followed by a sensationalist round-up of Villiers' death and an image of Lance Beckett, who'd been found dead only a week later. Somebody had managed to dredge up some photos of the men with smiling faces, looking like the best of friends, beneath which read:

Theatre and film fans around the world were rocked by the news of Sir Nigel Villiers' untimely death, last week, during the opening performance of 'King Lear' at The Old Palace Theatre in London, the place he has come to call 'home' during his tenure as co-owner of the popular stage venue. Although his death was widely thought to have been caused by a heart attack, the police are now understood to have upgraded their investigation to 'suspicious'. Earlier today, Villiers' lifelong friend and fellow actor, Lance Beckett, was found dead at his home in trendy Islington, in an apparent suicide. Sources close to the investigation have confirmed that Mr Beckett left a suicide note that strongly indicates a pact between the two men brought about through their shared connection with the Cambridge Stagelights. Fears are now circulating around the possibility of there being further members of what some are calling a 'secret society'...

Gregory handed the mobile phone back to Hope with a sigh of frustration. "I know we need a free press," he said. "I understand the value of investigative reporting, but—"

"It can be a pain in the arse?" Hope put in.

"I was going to say, 'it can inhibit the smooth running of a police investigation', but I think I like your version, better."

She sighed. "I knew something like this would hit, sooner or later," she said. "In fact, I'm surprised we've lasted this long without there being more of a media frenzy."

"It's like Bill was saying earlier. News moves so swiftly, nowadays, every big story gets subsumed by the next," he said.

Hope rubbed a tired hand over her forehead. "I hope you're right," she said. "I'll have the Super breathing down my neck about this, tomorrow, and it'll be an awkward conversation as it is."

"Maybe you should do a little breathing of your own?"

She nodded. "I had one of the analysts run a search for any recorded incidents relating to the CADC, the Stagelights or involving any members of the company in '79-'80," she said. "Nothing's coming up, so far."

"That doesn't mean nothing happened."

"I know, which is why I also asked them to do some digging around Sally Fletcher," she said, tapping her phone, which contained the e-mail responses from her team. "You know what flagged up?"

Gregory waited.

"A death certificate," she said quietly. "Recorded 1st June 1979, which would have been right at the end of her first academic year at Cambridge, and only two months after that photograph of her was taken."

"What was the cause of death?"

"Non-accidental drug overdose," she said. "Plain, old-fashioned paracetamol."

Gregory thought of a young life, half-lived, and was sorry for it. "Any history of depression?" he asked. "Have you been able to dig up any medical records?"

"There must have been an inquest at the time," she said. "The funny thing is, we haven't been able to find any official record. Back then, things were paper-based and it was a slow process to transfer things across to digital records. It's possible something fell through the cracks."

"Anything is possible," Gregory said, but thought again of his friend in the North of England, who never believed in coincidences. "What about university records?"

"Nothing," she said. "I think it's fairly safe to say the pastoral care wasn't quite as good then as it may be now."

Which left them with no clue as to how or why Sally Fletcher had decided to take her own life.

"Does she have any family left?" he asked.

Hope smiled, because she'd had the same line of thought.

"There's a sister," she said. "A hot-shot pharmaceuticals barrister by the name of Amy

Fletcher-Vale. I thought we might look her up—there's probably just enough time to make it across town this evening."

"It's a date," Gregory said, and watched something flicker in her eyes.

"Unless it involves a curry or a steak, it doesn't count," she shot back.

"Duly noted," he replied.

CHAPTER 25

Detective Chief Superintendent Simon Campbell was a man of meticulous standards and taste, so he liked to imagine. He came from a long line of grafters—men who worked with their hands and had taken every opportunity presented to them—which, in his father and grandfather's case, had been few and far between. However, things had been different for Simon, and he'd learned to grasp and claw his way up the metaphorical ladder until he hit a ceiling—at which point he'd invariably built an extension to that ladder, smashed through the ceiling and carried on, regardless.

His intelligence afforded a good degree of introspection and lateral thinking, which allowed him to come to terms with the fact that, in all probability, he was a sociopath—perhaps, even, a psychopath.

Was there really any difference?

He was sure a man like Gregory would know the difference and it irked him, slightly, to think that he'd see through him, past the shell to his very core.

Then again, he wasn't ashamed. Far from it.

He'd known from a very early age that he wasn't like other people. Not only because he was *vastly* more intelligent than most, but because he didn't experience the same kind of weak-headed emotions as many of them did. He could emulate emotions, certainly...but truly feel them? Never. He hadn't cried when the family dog died, as his brother had. He hadn't even cried when his mother died, although he'd tried to, for the sake of appearances. Gruesome images of crime scenes didn't faze him; nor did the fact his wife had left him recently and taken the children with her.

The house was blessedly quiet, now, and there were no toys cluttering his fine furniture.

Simon liked the best of everything, even when it was not strictly within his means. Especially, when it came to women. He preferred them to be high-class and well-dressed, because they looked better on his arm, and in the bedroom. For a while, he'd found escorts the most agreeable but, lately, he'd found his Russian girlfriend to be just as amenable and, if not cheaper, exactly, she was far more cost effective, overall. He knew that she sent money home to her family and that she had a child of some description whom she was desperately trying to hide, but he wasn't bothered about that. If anything, it was a good incentive for her to toe the line and keep him happy.

He wasn't about to move her in, though. He predicted another two, maybe three months, and he'd put her out to pasture.

There was a shelf life to everything, wasn't there?

Which led him to consider his present situation, and how frustrating it was becoming that he hadn't been offered another promotion in the past twelve months. He felt certain that would have happened, by now, if a few more cases had been closed. Still, he was confident that, if they closed the Villiers case in a timely fashion, that would count for a lot the next time he was having dinner with the Commissioner.

Thinking of the Villiers case didn't bring back any special, poignant memories of his time at Cambridge with Nigel—although, back then, he'd valued the man's company for the doors that had opened to him. It was why they'd kept in touch, through the years.

Amongst other reasons.

Nigel had always been a useful person to know, but, as with Natalya, there was a shelf life and his old friend had outlived his, long ago.

As for Lance—or, rather, Winston…

Poor old Win.

Simon stepped out of the marble jacuzzi shower he'd installed, at great cost, a couple of months before, and reached for one of the fluffy white towels he kept folded in identical rows on the shelf beside it. Wrapping one around his waist, he padded towards the double vanity unit which, he was glad to say, he had all to himself, nowadays.

He stared at his face in the mirror for long minutes, turning this way and that, scrutinizing his skin for any new lines or blemishes. So enthralled was he, that he failed to notice the sudden chill in the air, nor the rustle of the curtains in the bedroom beyond.

For such a large city, London's legal world was surprisingly small.

There might have been thousands of paralegals, interns, solicitors, barristers and their clerks, judges, court clerks and everything in between, but when it came to a certain elite crowd, they all tended to gather within the same square mile. Gregory and Hope found themselves heading towards an area known as the 'Inns of Court', tucked away from the masses via a series of gated alleyways accessible from Fleet Street and the Strand, which held the Royal Courts of Justice, and leading to a rarefied world of wig-toting, gown-wearing individuals with rights of audience who were called upon to speak on behalf of those who could not—whether they be ordinary people accused of affray, or corporate entities seeking to avoid liability.

There were, in fact, four inns of court—Gray's, Lincoln's, Inner Temple and Middle Temple—serving as the professional associations for barristers in England and Wales. Each had supervisory and disciplinary functions over their members, offered accommodation and dining, library facilities as well as a church or chapel, which meant that the inns formed a kind of precinct where member barristers could practise their trade from offices known as 'chambers' and be amongst other similarly-minded people, in a collegiate environment that was probably very comforting to those who had recently left Oxford, Cambridge or Durham.

Of all the churches belonging to the Inns, Temple Church was the most impressive. It was also the most recognisable to those outside of the profession, having featured in films such as *The Da Vinci Code* thanks to its crusading history and aesthetic beauty, and had been built during the twelfth century by the Knights Templar.

"I keep expecting to run into Tom Hanks," Hope joked, as she and Gregory passed by the church and made their way towards the chambers where Amy Fletcher-Vale QC kept her legal office.

Gregory grinned. "It feels like a different world around here," he agreed. "It's only a couple of streets back from the main road, but it's so quiet."

They passed rows of attractive, stone-built buildings with mullioned windows, dodging harassed-looking men and women making their way back from court, until they came to one with a large, black painted door bearing a brass plaque that read, 'ONE TEMPLAR BUILDINGS'. To the left of it was another plaque holding several smaller rectangular wooden slats, each displaying the hand-painted name of a barrister who was a tenant of that building.

"This is the place," Hope declared, pointing to one such slat with Fletcher-Vale's name on it.

They pressed the buzzer and made their way inside a plush hallway decorated in a classic style, where they were met by the disembodied sound of a bellowing cockney voice from one of the rooms beyond.

"Through 'ere!"

They followed the voice through a panelled doorway into what turned out to be the clerks' room. It was a large, high-ceilinged workspace with five enormous desks, a wall full of pigeon-holes, each marked up with the name of a different barrister, and stacks upon stacks of files and papers. In the middle of it all was a man of fifty or so, with a belly like Santa Claus and a beard to match.

"Aft'noon!" he said, leaning back in his ergonomic chair. "'ow can I 'elp yer?"

Hope took out her warrant card and made the introductions.

"Well, now," the Head Clerk, whose name turned out to be Ernie, said. "Ms Fletcher-Vale's very busy… but let me see what I can do."

He reached for the telephone on his desk and held a brief, hushed conversation, sent Hope a ludicrous wink, then replaced the receiver.

"She says she'll see you both," he said, and Hope held back an urge to laugh. Usually, a general deference to authority meant that people made time for the police, *especially* her department, but she'd forgotten they weren't dealing with 'usual' people in that neck of the woods. Barristers such as Fletcher-Vale were probably so used to dealing with the police—and cross-examining them in court— that any deference had long since worn off and was unlikely ever to return.

"Head up to the second floor," Ernie continued. "There's a conference room there, first on your left."

They thanked him and climbed the narrow, carpeted stairs.

"Much as I'm loath to give in to stereotypes, I have to admit our friend Ernie isn't what I'd have expected from a place like this," Gregory said, once they were out of earshot.

Hope shook her head.

"He's exactly right," she countered. "It might be the barristers who do the legal work and notch up the wins in court, but it's the clerks who're the savviest of the lot. They negotiate fees, allocate work, manage everything, really, and they must have a good knowledge of the law to be able to decide how much time and work will go into a particular case. They usually start out as a junior clerk and learn from the older clerks in the room. It's not about having letters behind their name; it's about having commercial intelligence."

"You know a lot about it," he observed.

"I've met plenty of them," she said, and didn't bother to mention that her former fiancé had been a clerk himself and worked just around the corner.

They were met on the second-floor landing by the quick tread of footsteps from the floor above, and presently Amy Fletcher-Vale QC appeared. She was a slim reed of a woman in her late fifties with a cap of shining blonde hair, bright blue eyes, and a restless energy that belied her age.

"DCI Hope? Doctor Gregory?"

She shook their hands, and indicated a doorway leading to an impressive conference room dominated by an enormous antique table.

"How can I help you?" she asked, once they'd seated themselves. "I'm afraid I don't usually take consultations this late in the day, and I must tell you that the majority of my work is civil, not criminal—"

"We're not here to discuss a new instruction," Hope told her. "We're here to talk about your sister, Sally."

Instantly, a shadow seemed to fall across the other woman's face, and beneath the low-hanging lights she looked every one of her years.

"I'm not often surprised," she said, tremulously. "But I am now. You must be a part of the team investigating the deaths of Nigel Villiers and Lance Beckett."

Hope raised an eyebrow. "What makes you say that?"

"It's a logical assumption," Amy said, incisively. "There's no other reason to think that the police would wish to talk to me about my sister, who died more than thirty years ago, unless a connection had been made between her and the people she spent her time with, before she died."

"What do you believe that connection to be?" Gregory asked.

Amy Fletcher-Vale looked between them both with dawning understanding.

"Oh, I see," she said. "You don't know, do you? You haven't spoken with my mother, then?"

Hope shook her head. "What don't we know?"

"Why Sally killed herself," Amy replied, in a flat, accusatory voice. "She was sexually assaulted, multiple times. Her attackers maintained their innocence, claiming everything was consensual and above board. Sally said otherwise, but her reputation was slandered around the university and people called her a 'slut'. Lewd pictures were posted on common room noticeboards...you can imagine. My sister was a sensitive, artistic soul, Chief Inspector, and she couldn't stand it, nor the shame of being disbelieved. She took her own life on 1st June 1979, and my family has never been the same, since."

Hope and Gregory took a second to process the information, and its meaning for their present investigation.

"I'm very sorry for your loss," Hope said, softly. "Did your sister say who her attackers were?"

Really, she could guess.

"Their names were Nigel Villiers, Lance Beckett and Simon Campbell," the other woman said, enunciating every syllable clearly.

Hope heard the final name and closed her eyes, briefly, thinking of the implications, then fell back on due process. There were procedures to follow, and they were there for a reason.

"Did your sister ever make a formal complaint?" she asked. "We've found no record of any police or university report having been made."

"You wouldn't," Amy replied. "Sally made a statement to the Dean, but the university convinced her to retract it. She was under intense pressure and veiled threats had been made about how appropriate it was for her to remain at the university, at all. Women were outnumbered, back then, and they closed ranks against her."

"Why haven't you said anything about this before now?" Gregory asked. He couldn't imagine a woman of her stature keeping quiet about such a thing, especially now that she occupied a senior legal position, with a ready list of contacts she could call upon for help.

"It was my sister's wish," she said. "Sally didn't want any further humiliation, nor any more opportunities to be torn apart by men who tried to convince her it had all been in her imagination. She didn't have pictures of her injuries or any forensic evidence, you see. Just her word against theirs."

She looked away, swallowing the old anger she'd tried so hard to banish. Perhaps that's why she'd gone into the legal profession: with every case she won, she could tell herself it was one for Sally.

"My mother is still alive," she added. "She's very clear about protecting Sally's memory and didn't want her name sullied, which is undoubtedly what would have happened if any of us had tried to raise it against Villiers or his band of merry men. They're of a type—well-connected with access to means beyond my family's disposal."

It wasn't how justice should be, Amy thought, which was why she took on more than her share of pro bono work, to help those in need of a good legal brain.

It was what Sally would have wanted.

"Can I ask where you were, on the evening of Saturday last?" Hope asked her.

Fletcher-Vale gave a funny little smile. "I was at home," she said. "I'm afraid my husband was away, on business, so I was alone. I realise this isn't particularly helpful, but all I can do is tell you that I didn't administer any hemlock to those men. What I will say is this: I believe for every action there is a consequence and, in this case, karma came for them in the end. It might have taken thirty years, but it did. I won't pretend to be sorry about that, and I won't stop there. Already, I've seen ridiculous vigils being held for Villiers, as though the man was a saint…well, none of us are that, but he, especially, was far from it. The same could be said of Beckett, and of Campbell, who lied through their teeth to cover themselves rather than own up to their actions. I won't stand for Villiers and Beckett being inducted into any golden hall of fame; just as soon as my mother passes, and no longer cares about protecting my sister's name, I will fight with every fibre of my being and with the full force of the law to have this matter resolved, posthumously."

Hope and Gregory listened, and it was hard not be moved by her love for her sister and impressed by her conviction. There was a kind of showmanship to public speaking, just as there was to acting, and it was easy to be persuaded.

On the other hand, Amy Fletcher-Vale was the only person with any firm motive to want Nigel Villiers and Lance Beckett dead, and she had no alibi.

That was persuasive too.

CHAPTER 26

Later, as the sun fell off the edge of the horizon and the city of London was sheathed in darkness, Hope and Gregory stepped out into the cold evening and made their way back through the cloisters towards the hustle and bustle of ordinary life.

"What do you make of it?" she asked him, after a few minutes had passed.

Gregory looked up at the sky, which was a deep, velvety blue, and then at her.

"I can't think of any reason for Amy Fletcher-Vale to have lied about her sister's circumstances," he said. "There was a wealth of pain there for all to see, as well as plenty of anger and bitterness. I presume you'll be checking on her whereabouts, during the relevant period?"

Hope's lips quirked, and she nodded.

"There's that cynicism again," she said. "And, yes, I've already asked Carter to check her out."

"The circumstances of what happened would explain a lot," Gregory said. "The scandal, if it were to come out, would be enough to ruin the reputations of Villiers and Campbell, certainly…but…"

He shook his head, and, by mutual accord, they paused for a moment outside Temple Church, which was lit by the dim glow of several old-style streetlamps.

"The problem is Beckett," he said. "Lance Beckett was almost completely unknown to this generation and forgotten by the last. It wouldn't have been any great shakes for the world to have discovered he'd attacked a girl thirty years ago, except they'd have likely felt sympathy for Fletcher's family."

Hope agreed. "That's the outside perspective," she said. "*Internally*, from his own paradigm, Beckett thought he was someone special. If we believe that he took his own life, then he'd have done it believing he had a reputation to save and it was a noble act of repentance, or something of that kind."

"Do you believe he took his own life?"

Looking up at him in the semi-darkness, she felt a tremor run over her skin—but it wasn't unpleasant. "No, not really," she said.

"In which case, we look at the killer's motivations," he replied. "If we're to believe there's somebody out there looking to exact revenge for what happened to Sally Fletcher. and possibly others that we know nothing about, then there's at least one other person on their hit list."

"Campbell," she said, grimly. "I'm sure it comes as no surprise when I tell you that he didn't make any of us aware of his connection with Sally, or of Villiers and Beckett's involvement in an assault, back in '79."

They began to walk again, and Gregory blew onto his hands, for warmth. "He's one of the ones with a reputation to protect. Besides which, he's probably forgotten all about it, for the most part."

She looked at him with a kind of horror. "How could he have forgotten something like that?"

"He's a sociopath," Gregory replied. "A high-functioning one, who doesn't experience emotions in the same way that we do. He wouldn't feel guilt or remorse; he is entirely self-serving."

She couldn't argue with that. "Still, if he's in any danger, I have a duty," she said, and reached for her mobile phone to put a call through to his office, but the number rang out, signalling that the superintendent and his personal assistant had already left for the day.

"Do you have his mobile?" Gregory asked.

She nodded, and tried calling it, only to find it had been switched off.

"Is it usual for his phone to be turned off?"

"Not that I know of," she said. "He's like a doctor on call—he likes to be kept up to date with everything. He gave instructions only the other day that he should be kept in the loop with everything to do with the Villiers case."

Gregory played Devil's Advocate. "It's possible his phone ran out of battery on the way home, and there's nothing to worry about," he said, but he understood better than most the potential significance of behaviour that was out of character.

Hope made a fast decision and put a call through to her sergeant, who was still at his desk.

"Ben? I need a team dispatched to the Super's home address…I'll tell you all the details later, but just trust me. I think there could be a real danger to life. Another thing, while you're at it? I want a surveillance team set up to follow Amy Fletcher-Vale," she said. "I'll answer any questions later—just make it happen."

She slipped the phone back into her pocket, and they walked towards Fleet Street, where they could hail a cab.

"Where are we going?" Gregory asked.

Hope could have said 'we' weren't going anywhere, but she didn't. "Campbell doesn't live in London," she replied, throwing out an arm to hail an oncoming taxi. "He lives out in Kent, in some demi-mansion in the middle of nowhere."

Secluded, Gregory thought. *Easy to surveil.*

"How far?"

"At least an hour by road, possibly longer. We'll stop off and pick up my car—unless you have one nearby?"

He did, and gave directions to the cabby.

"I've told Carter to get a local team across to Campbell's address, but that'll still take time," she said, as the cab flew across Blackfriars Bridge and made a sharp left towards Southwark and, beyond it, to Shad Thames. "I've got a bad feeling about this, Alex."

He did, too, but still allowed himself to enjoy the private pleasure of hearing her use his first name, and not 'Doctor Gregory'.

"There comes a point where we can save ourselves," he said, thinking of his own life and the decisions he'd made. "We have to face the darkest parts of our mind, look at them clearly, and decide whether we want to change. If what Amy Fletcher-Vale has told us about her sister is true, then Campbell must have suspected a connection almost as soon as he read the contents of those threatening e-mails and the suicide note we found at Beckett's place. He must have known there was a possibility, but still chose to say nothing. That's a clear decision, and he made it in favour of maintaining his professional reputation rather than safeguarding his own life. We all have that kind of agency, Ava, and you can only do what's within your own power."

She nodded slowly, and then did something she hadn't meant to do.

There, in the darkness of the taxi, she reached across and held his hand, and, when there came an answering squeeze, she no longer felt alone.

CHAPTER 27

As it happened, Gregory was right about one thing.

Campbell's mobile phone *had* run out of battery charge, a fact he was irritated to discover after leaving the bathroom to check for any messages whilst he'd been showering. He located a charger and plugged it in, looking up at the sound of heavy rain pattering against the panes of his bedroom window, and remembered that the forecast had been for heavy winds and rain overnight.

He always liked to be prepared, so he could dress appropriately.

He discarded the towel and wrapped himself in a fine cashmere dressing gown, then turned on the television on the wall opposite his bed, lounging on top of the covers while he checked the news.

Following the death of sixty-one-year-old Lance Beckett, long-time friend of the late Sir Nigel Villiers and fellow actor of stage and screen, sources close to the police investigation say the two deaths are now being treated as linked, with speculation around the possibility of there being a secret suicide pact between the two men relating to unsubstantiated historic allegations of assault...

Campbell sat up again, swearing softly.

Where had the leak come from?

Nobody in the Met knew about what happened with that girl, back in Cambridge. He'd made sure of that, and had made sure to let her mother know just how viciously he would fight her allegations, should she or her other daughter decide to try and make life difficult.

He could produce statements, from other young men at the time, to say that Sally been ready and willing for anything.

Bought and paid for, of course.

He could produce images, taken by his own fair hand, of Sally in the most compromising positions... and he couldn't be sure they wouldn't find their way into the gutter press.

It had been years, and her family had always maintained their silence.

How, then, had the connection been made?

He was still mulling it over when, suddenly, the lights went out.

Campbell did not fear the darkness, nor what it might hold.

He assumed the electrical lines had been affected by the gathering storm outside, or that a fuse had blown, and was doubly irritated. He began to reach for his phone, before remembering it was still out of battery and would be no use to him.

"Bloody hell," he muttered, and inched towards the bedroom door in search of a torch or a candle.

Did he even own one, come to that?

He left such trivial matters to his wife, or rather, his housekeeper nowadays. Since there hadn't been a blackout in recent memory, he wasn't convinced she'd have purchased matches or candles.

Then, he remembered the cloying, scented candle his girlfriend had insisted upon leaving in the guest bathroom, which she lit while she bathed herself and read all manner of fashion magazines, no doubt circling the expensive shoes she wanted him to buy for her.

If there was a candle, shouldn't there be a matchbox or a lighter?

Campbell moved down the hall, keeping one hand to the wall as he tried to feel his way through the enveloping darkness, but the downside to having purchased a house in the country was a lack of neighbours or streetlamps to relieve the blackness outside, which was all-encompassing.

He caught his hip on a console table on the landing and swore, stubbing his toe again in the process.

Enraged, he decided that the very first thing he'd do the following morning was contact the electric company to make a complaint. What use was it, having a certain degree of power, if he couldn't flex his muscles, now and then?

Somebody would pay for this.

A few minutes later, he held an unlit scented candle in one hand as he made his way down the wide, Georgian staircase towards his kitchen in search of something to light it. Campbell was not a man given to flights of fancy, nor any suggestiveness when it came to things that went bump in the night. However, he could admit to feeling a certain discomfort as he waded through the oppressive darkness. His eyes might have been blind, but his hearing was attuned to every creak and moan in the house, every rush of wind and rattle of rain against the old slate roof.

Pushing away these weak thoughts, he crossed the marble hallway to the kitchen and hurried across to a bank of drawers where utensils and other knick-knacks were kept. Gingerly, trying to avoid the sharper objects, he felt around for a box of matches and was delighted when his fingers met with the very thing.

"About time," he said to himself, and struck a match.

In the seconds it took to burn down, he caught a pale reflection of himself in the mirrored splashback of the Aga, before the light was gone again and he was plunged back into darkness.

Quickly, he struck another, and held its flickering ember to the candle wick.

"Come on," he muttered.

It lit, and soon his nostrils were assaulted by a steady flow of frangipani and jasmine-scented smoke. Holding it aloft, he turned and, catching sight of a figure in the window, almost dropped it immediately.

Until he realised the figure was himself.

"Been reading too many novels," he said, and gave a nervous laugh.

He made directly for the door leading from the kitchen to the garage, which was attached to one side of the house and held the electrical fuse box. He thrust it open and felt an immediate gust of cold air against his bare skin.

One of the garage doors was open.

He was certain he'd closed and locked it, after parking his car for the evening.

Shivering, Campbell hurried across to tug it shut, struggling one-handed against the force of the wind outside, while trying to hold the candle in his other. Eventually, it slammed shut and he turned the handle quickly, breathing a sigh of relief.

Next, he went in search of the fuse box.

But when he opened it and held up the flickering light, his heart gave one hard thump against the wall of his chest while his mind tried to make sense of what he was seeing.

The fuse box had been cut to shreds.

Wires hung limply inside the metal box, where they'd been ripped and torn.

Campbell gave a slight shake of his head, and then spun around, eyes wide in the darkness. His skin crawled, icy tentacles of fear rippling up his spine while he considered his options.

The car.

His Tesla was parked right there in the garage, fully charged and ready to go. All he had to do was open the garage door again, and he could get away…

Listening intently, he stood there for a moment, sweating despite the cold.

One…

Two…

Three!

He ran across to the garage door and turned the handle to release the catch again, thrusting it open. Breathing heavily now, he spun around, waving the meagre light from the candle this way and that, trying to peer into the corners of the garage, but he could barely see beyond a few metres.

Behind him, the wind rushed against his back as if to urge him forward, and he did, running towards the driver's side of the car.

That's when he saw the tyres.

They were in tatters, slashed in a series of jagged cuts, so that the car rested at a limp, awkward angle on its chassis.

He backed away, panic taking a stranglehold.

What now?

Think.

Think!

There was a landline telephone in the kitchen, and a ready supply of knives.

He had to try.

Simon moved slowly, inching his way towards the kitchen door.

In his hand, he clutched the candle still, though its light was running low. Beyond the howling wind, he heard the rush of his own blood in his ears and could feel the thudding of his own heart beating against his chest like the wings of a bird.

There was no mistaking that the fuse box had been tampered with, and no mistaking the angry slash of tyres.

Somebody else had been in the house.

Perhaps they were still there.

But where?

He almost tripped over a bucket, and sent it clattering across the concrete floor. He shrank back against the wall, listening for the tell-tale sound of soft footsteps or a figure looming towards him through the darkness, but, when nothing came, he gathered his strength and peeled himself away from the wall.

He was breathing heavily through his teeth by the time he made it back inside. Every few seconds, he paused to listen, trying to sense whether another warm body was in the room, waiting.

Swallowing bile, he lurched towards the countertop that held the landline, snatching it up with a shaking hand.

No dial tone…

Then, far away, he heard the distant ring of his mobile phone, which must have recharged sufficiently to receive calls. But there was no time to make a run for it, no time to wonder who was calling and might have been able to help him.

Fate had other plans for Simon Campbell.

In the corner of his eye, he saw the flicker of the candle's wick, less than a second before the first blow came crashing down upon his head.

CHAPTER 28

"Can't you go any faster?"

Gregory looked at the speedometer, which read eighty-five miles per hour. "We're going as quickly as we can," he said.

She was a woman who preferred to be in the driver's seat, he realised, and it wasn't something he minded.

"Any word from Carter?" he asked.

She shook her head. "Apparently, they're sending out a squad car—"

She broke off as her phone began to ring.

"Speak of the devil," she said, and held it to her ear. "DCI Hope."

Gregory heard Carter's voice in the background, too jumbled for him to make out the words.

"You're sure?" she said. "All right. We're on our way now, so we might as well swing by...yeah, all right. Thanks, Ben."

She ended the call and stared straight ahead, watching the windscreen wipers swish back and forth as they made their way along the motorway out of London towards the neighbouring county of Kent.

"Carter says the squad car did a drive-by to check on Campbell, but he doesn't appear to be at home. Lights are off, no car on the driveway, doors are locked and nobody's answering."

Gregory flicked the indicator to overtake a passing lorry.

"He could be out," he said.

"Mm hmm."

"On the other hand—"

"That's what I'm worrying about," she muttered.

It was a big call to make, on top of an evening of big calls, but Hope decided to make it all the same.

"I'm going to give the order for them to go back and force entry," she said. "There's a chance I'll incur the wrath of my Superintendent and kiss goodbye to any promotional opportunities in the foreseeable future. Still, it's better than the alternative."

She made the call, and hoped it was the right one.

He'd seen the squad car arrive and was glad he'd chosen to park his own car well away from the house, hidden by some of the ample woodland in that part of the world.

Of course, he'd chosen the spot carefully.

It meant that he had to walk back through the rain, but he could handle that. It would wash away some of the sweat that caked his body inside the overalls he wore, for one thing, and get rid of the blood that had managed to work its way behind his goggles.

Messy business.

It had been tempting to take a quick dip inside Campbell's swanky looking shower, but he'd read that forensics teams could take apart whole plumbing systems to check for DNA samples, so it wasn't worth the risk. He'd look forward to a nice bubble bath when he got home.

Maybe he'd light a scented candle, too.

The squad car had given him a bad moment, and his cortisol levels were still abnormally high. Despite all his planning, all his preparation, the police had surprised him…

Why? How?

Who had called them?

Nobody could have known tonight was the night. Only *he* had known, and he'd been as giddy as a child at Christmas on the journey down from London.

He hadn't been disappointed.

Even now, as he remembered the feeling, the *power* that came from taking control again and watching fear dance in the eyes of his tormentor, he became aroused—which surprised him. He'd read about that happening to some killers, but hadn't expected to experience it; after all, he was only exacting justice, nothing more.

It certainly wasn't for his own *pleasure*—he wanted that to be perfectly understood.

Of course, he'd taken pictures afterwards, but that was for posterity. As a memento, not as something he planned to look at regularly.

As it turned out, the squad car left barely five minutes after it had arrived, and clearly the two flat-foots who'd been sent out to check on the house were eager to get home, because they made a cursory check of the doors, peered through a couple of windows and then left again.

Nothing to worry about.

He'd taken his time, leaving everything exactly as he'd planned. Once he was satisfied, he let himself back out of the garage door and took a torch from his rucksack, tugging a hood over his head as he began the return journey.

Ten minutes later, when he saw the flashing blue lights of more oncoming squad cars on the country lane, he turned off the torch and moved back from the road. It was a precaution, really, because in the downpour he knew the police would struggle to see much of anything, especially as his dark clothing was as good as invisible against the hedgerow.

Sure enough, they sped past him, their brief, blinding wails swallowed by the night.

Too late, he thought, with a grin.

Much too late.

He began to whistle an old show tune, before disappearing into the undergrowth.

Gregory steered the car along a network of winding country lanes until they reached the tiny hamlet of Eastbridge, in Kent. From what little they could see through the driving rain, it consisted of a smattering of cottages and an ancient-looking church, but they didn't stop to sightsee. At Hope's request, the team of first responders sent out by Kent Constabulary had returned to Campbell's home and forced entry, finding the place in darkness with the power off. They'd proceeded to conduct a full sweep of the house, discovering the superintendent's car parked in the garage with its tyres slashed, but no sign of the man himself.

"He has to be there, somewhere," Hope said, as Gregory slowed the car to make a final turn into Campbell's driveway.

"Agreed," he said. "However, if it's another case of hemlock poisoning, he could have wandered off somewhere before the effects kicked in. It isn't an instant death."

He brought the car to a standstill outside a beautiful Georgian rectory, with Virginia creeper crawling up the frontage and over the edge of a grand entrance portico.

"I thought public sector salaries were supposed to be modest?" he said.

"They are," Hope muttered. "Campbell gives a lot of after-dinner speeches."

Slamming out of the car, they made their way through the rain towards the front door, where a local constable was huddled beneath the entrance portico in a heavy service-issue parka.

"Constable?"

Belatedly, he came to attention.

"Chief inspector…Hope, is it?"

She nodded towards the door behind him. "Are you the only one here?"

"My partner's just nipped in to—ah—" He glanced back over his shoulder, obviously embarrassed.

"I hope you're not about to tell me he or she is in there helping themselves to the facilities?"

His face said it all. "I'm sorry, ma'am, but we'd already checked out the premises and found it unoccupied, so—"

"I strongly advise you not to finish that sentence," Hope growled. "I'll be writing you both up for a disciplinary as it is—"

Any further remonstration was interrupted by the arrival of the errant, weak-bladdered constable, who exited the front door at a run, almost barrelling into them. No introductions were made, nor any lectures about professional conduct, because one look into the whites of the man's eyes told them something was seriously wrong.

Sure enough, the uniformed officer pushed past them to find a clear spot on the driveway before emptying his stomach of the burger and fries he'd picked up from the drive-thru in Ashford, earlier that evening.

"He—I've found him," he said, once he'd recovered himself.

"Campbell?" Hope demanded, blinking rainwater from her eyes. "He's in there?"

He nodded weakly, scrubbing a hand over his mouth as if to dispel the taste of vomit.

"We…we thought the place was empty, but we forgot to look in the downstairs cloakroom. It's a blood bath, ma'am."

Beneath the glare of the late Superintendent Campbell's security lights, Gregory frowned.

Blood bath?

That made no sense at all.

CHAPTER 29

Detective Chief Superintendent Simon Campbell had always wished to leave behind a dignified legacy, and a name others would remember and venerate in the corridors of the Metropolitan Police. The 'Campbell Method', they'd say, or the 'Campbell Way', when they spoke of best practices or legendary collars. Unfortunately for him, any dreams he might have had on that score were quashed by the manner of his untimely demise, for his body had been found in the nude, propped on top of an expensive toilet pan with a book stuffed inside his gaping mouth.

And he was no Elvis Presley with a discography of hits to fall back on.

"Jesus," Hope muttered, as she and Gregory took in the miserable sight of him from the open doorway.

Her eyes ran over the angry slash at Campbell's throat, from which blood still trickled down his neck and torso in long, red rivulets, mingling with the myriad of angry stab wounds peppering his chest. There were no footprints, aside from the skid marks made by the constable who'd stumbled upon the grisly find less than five minutes before and trampled the pool of blood in his haste, but there was a murder weapon—a carving knife had been driven through the dead man's jaw to hold the book in place, like a suckling pig set to roast.

"Campbell always wanted to be remembered," Gregory said. "Perhaps he'll have his wish, after all."

Hope made a sound of agreement, and realised that a small, mean-spirited part of her wondered whether Campbell had earned a humiliating death, rather than one that would inspire rousing speeches over a parapet.

"He might not have been my favourite person, but I wouldn't have wished this on him—or anyone," Gregory continued, as if he'd read her mind. "All the same, I have to wonder whether there isn't a certain amount of karma at work here."

"I wouldn't have pegged you as someone to believe in all that," she said.

"I don't," he replied. "As far as I'm concerned, karma was a real, live person here, not some unseen cosmic force."

"I agree with you, and this is a lot worse than hemlock poisoning," she said, gesturing to the mess in front of them. "Do you think the killer is escalating? Maybe they saw Campbell as more 'guilty' than the other two?"

Gregory didn't answer directly. "What's the book inside his mouth?" he asked, trying to angle himself to read the spine that was just visible through layers of congealed blood.

Gingerly, and without disturbing the scene, Hope leaned forward slightly and tilted her head.

"*Othello*," she said. "Another work of Shakespeare, so our perp must have a preference."

He could not bring himself to agree. "From what I remember, it's a tragedy about passion, jealousy and race issues, set against the backdrop of the Ottoman-Venetian War during the sixteenth century," he said slowly. "But it covers other themes."

"Such as?"

A muscle ticked in his jaw. "Loss of reputation," he said, shortly.

"It must be linked," Hope said. "From what we already know of the perp, they wanted their victims to atone for past misconduct, so it would make sense for their killer to leave a symbol of this kind, relating to someone's fall from grace—"

"The MO doesn't conform to the personality type," he interjected. "Everything we know so far speaks of a character who prefers the 'hands off' approach to murder, not aggression on this kind of scale. However personal their reasons for executing

Nigel and Lance, the *mode* of their execution was all business…detached, almost clinical. Remember, *behaviour mimics personality*."

Hope looked back at Campbell's limp body and understood immediately. This was no detached execution, no clean, fuss-free murder.

It was a frenzy.

"What are you saying?" she asked him, with a touch of irritation. "Are you telling me your profile was wrong?"

If Gregory was hurt by the imputation, he allowed none of it to show on his face, nor in the tone of his voice.

It was only business, after all.

"I don't believe my profile was inaccurate, based on the information available to me at the time of writing," he said. "It's possible the killer has escalated but, given the differences in style and degree of violence employed in each, I'd say it was far more likely you're looking for a second person, or perhaps an accomplice."

Hope heard the coolness in his voice, understood it, and matched it with her own. There would be hard questions to answer back at The Yard about whether this calamity could have been prevented and she needed to be sure she could answer them without prejudice or bias—something she was far from sure of, having lost sight of her objectivity along the way, somewhere between the flat white coffees and cosy train rides to Cambridge.

"It's still possible we're looking for the same perp," she persisted. "Although they went to town on Campbell, it wasn't without a degree of planning, just like the other two. They needed to know where he lived, when he'd be home and how to gain access to the property to kill him without leaving obvious traces. That's an organised killer who likes symbolism, the same as the other two."

Gregory paced away to clear his head, thinking through the patterns in all three deaths as he stared unseeingly at a large, ugly piece of modern artwork hanging on Campbell's wall.

"The symbolism is different," he said, definitively. "You remember, I told you that the kind of person to kill Villiers and Beckett has a code and a process they follow every time. Every communication of theirs has referenced Socrates and the events of 1979, whereas there's no sign of anything to do with either of those things left at the scene here. Even the *method* of communication is different—on the one hand, typed e-mails and letters, on the other hand, a book wedged inside a dead man's mouth."

"Like I said, they've escalated," Hope argued, a bit desperately. "Besides, there's every chance we'll find some sort of reference to Socrates written inside the book, once we've extracted it."

Gregory thought it unlikely. "Perhaps most damning of all is the move away from any staged suicide," he said, and watched the truth of that statement hit home. "In the case of both Villiers and Beckett their deaths were staged to resemble suicide or cause us to query the possibility. In the case of Simon Campbell, no effort has been made to stage his death as anything other than what it was—a vicious attack he would have been incapable of inflicting upon himself."

Hope stared at him in the semi-darkness of her former superintendent's hallway while she tried to make sense of the conflicting evidence, and what it meant for her investigation.

*If it looked like a duck...*she remembered.

"You may be right," she said softly. "But I can't rely on conjecture or theories, I need to look at the facts in hand, and they're telling me we have a third dead man who we *know* to have been connected to Sally Fletcher's suicide, back in 1979. We *know* Campbell's killer wanted us to consider *Othello,* for one reason or another—which I will, in detail. We *know* Campbell's killer wanted to end his life painfully and to degrade him afterwards, so he'd be remembered this way and not for anything else he might have done—"

"Don't you see the discrepancy in motivation?" Gregory burst out. "If the goal was to have these men fall on their own swords, to *atone*, or have it look as though they'd atoned for past misconduct, then it's plainly obvious there's none of that in the way Campbell died, tonight. Think about it, Ava: by killing Campbell the way they did, nobody will recall anything he might have done or not done in 1979; all they'll remember is that he was found on a toilet seat, naked, like a poor man's Elvis. There's no deeper message to that, no reference to any specific incident, only a general loss of reputation that will eventually be yesterday's news."

Hope heard the logic and might have agreed with it, but she had a job to do and her own processes to follow—some of which would take her through to the early hours of the morning. As if on cue, flashing blue lights pulled into the driveway beyond, signalling that the cavalry had arrived.

"I appreciate your insights," she said, politely. "And I'll certainly bear them in mind, but now I need to work the scene. Thanks again for the lift, Doctor—I can take things from here."

Gregory gave her a funny half-smile that didn't reach his eyes, then left without another word.

CHAPTER 30

Two days later

A light drizzle began to fall as Gregory and Douglas stood outside the imposing façade of Southmoor Psychiatric Hospital. They looked upon its stark, uncompromising lines with a heady mix of nostalgia and apprehension, each man having spent a significant chunk of his working life inside its fenced perimeter, walking its rubber-lined, pink-painted hallways tending to the disturbed minds of those who resided within.

For his part, it had been several years since Douglas had been employed there as a Senior Consultant—long enough to allow bad memories to fade and good ones to prevail.

"It's hardly changed a bit," he declared. "Nice to see they've installed another bench in the garden."

Gregory thought the old brick building with its lawn-and-concrete 'garden' possessed all the kerb appeal to be expected of a purpose-built Victorian lunatic asylum for the criminally insane, and a wooden bench did little to change that.

"One of the families donated it, in memory of their relative," he said, thinking of the young man who'd murdered four people before finally turning that violence upon himself, using a shiv fashioned from a plastic comb. "They wanted other patients to be able to sit and enjoy the fresh air."

Douglas nodded, then stole a glance at his friend. "How does it feel to be back?" he asked. "It must be strange, after such a long break."

Gregory sucked in a deep breath, wincing as the cold air hit his teeth. "It's familiar and alien, at the same time," he said. "It hasn't been that long since I left, but it feels like a lifetime."

"Has too much water passed under the bridge for you to come back?"

Gregory had thought of little else during the long, sleepless hours of the previous night.

"More to the point, I don't know whether the hospital will have me back," he said. "They may feel my actions were tantamount to gross misconduct, so the question of whether things have changed or whether *I've* changed too much to come back is moot at this point."

Douglas made a small sound of frustration. "Gross misconduct is conducting an illicit affair with a patient or breaching confidentiality," he muttered. "You spoke with your mother every week to try to help her, and yourself. There are worse things."

Gregory smiled. "Tell that to the panel," he said, but was grateful for his friend's unwavering support. "Look, Bill—whatever happens today, I'm at peace with it. I knew what the consequences could be when I confessed everything to Parminder."

He referred to Doctor Parminder Aggarwal, the Clinical Director at Southmoor.

"In fact, I knew what could happen long *before* then—that very first day, when I realised who my new patient was, and when I took the decision not to make the hospital aware she was my mother."

Douglas sighed, and put a hand on his friend's shoulder in silent support.

"Even if the hearing goes well, the more important question to ask yourself is whether you *want* to go back to treating patients, Alex."

"You think I'm burnt out?"

"Not at all," Douglas averred. "In fact, very much the opposite. You're still on the ascent, unlike an old codger such as myself, who's getting decidedly long in the tooth."

Gregory merely raised an eyebrow. "I'll remember this, when I'm buying you your next packet of Werther's Originals."

"Heaven forbid!" Douglas shuddered.

Gregory chuckled, and then grew serious again. "I enjoy helping people," he said quietly. "My work here at Southmoor has meant…"

His throat contracted, and he was embarrassed to find himself overcome by emotion. His life at Southmoor had plugged a hole in his life, had given him purpose and meaning for so long, he hardly knew where he would be without it.

"I know," Douglas said, and patted his friend's back again. "It takes a certain kind of person to spend time with those who've lost their way, without becoming lost themselves."

Gregory wondered whether there was anyone who didn't find themselves lost, sometimes.

"You've helped an awful lot of people in these walls, Alex, but don't forget you've helped plenty of people outside of them, too," Douglas continued. "Life doesn't begin and end at Southmoor."

Gregory looked up at the clocktower, noted the time, and knew it was growing late. Still, there were things to say.

"I might have helped them, but the people here helped me, too," he admitted. "They reminded me that I wasn't alone in dealing with trauma. There's a whole world full of messed up people, Bill—I'm just one of them, and an insignificant one, at that."

Douglas shook his head. "You matter to many people, Alex," he said, and wondered if he should mention the e-mail he'd received from one of those people that very morning.

Later, he decided. His friend needed no more distractions before heading into one of the most important meetings of his professional career.

"If not clinical work, what would I do to fill my days?" Gregory wondered aloud.

"Profiling, for one thing," Douglas replied. "We've a list of enquiries as long as your arm from police forces across the UK and further afield. You'd never be short of work, and you could devote yourself to it, full-time, rather than squeezing it around your day job."

Gregory had considered the possibility and had to admit it held some appeal, but the impact of recent events had forced him to re-evaluate his own skills in that area.

"Is it worthwhile?" he asked. "More worthwhile than treating patients?"

Douglas was surprised. His young friend was a leading light in the profiling world thanks to his unique ability to step into the minds of the people he met, and even those he hadn't. Imagining the character and characteristics of violent perpetrators was no easy task.

"Where's this coming from?" he asked. "If you're thinking of Carl Deere, or Theodor Andersson again…"

"I wasn't," Gregory replied. "Actually, I was thinking of Simon Campbell. Everything about his death was contrary to the profile we'd built for the killer, but there are enough similarities for the police to believe there's a connection with Villiers and Beckett."

"In other words, they think the profile is wrong?"

Douglas's affronted face was comical enough to lighten the mood, and Gregory smiled. "I can't blame them, entirely. The circumstances threw me off, for a minute."

"But?"

"I think the same as I did before," he said, firmly. "Whoever killed Campbell didn't lift a finger to the other two men, I'm sure of it."

In a flash of understanding, Douglas realised it wasn't self-doubt that had upset his friend, but the doubt of another. "Ah," he said, and began to stroll towards the entrance.

Gregory matched his stride. "What does 'ah' mean?"

Douglas whistled a line or two from *Singin' in the Rain* before answering. "It means, you wish a certain brown-eyed chief inspector shared your confidence."

Gregory opened his mouth to issue a denial, but the lie wouldn't come. "Does it ever get old?"

"What's that?"

"Being right, all the time."

Douglas gave him a smug smile. "Rarely," he replied. "You'll find I'm right about a great many other things too, my boy, and today's hearing is one of them. It'll come out right, but you have to fight for it."

"Is it worth fighting for?"

"All the best things are," Douglas replied, and held open the door.

CHAPTER 31

"Have a seat, Doctor Gregory."

Alex settled himself on the proffered chair, an uncomfortable plastic tub affair that had seen better days, and faced the panel of three professionals who would ultimately decide the pathway his life would take. He knew one of the three, Parminder Aggarwal, while the remaining two were senior consultants who'd been drafted in from the wider hospital trust to satisfy the need for a supposedly unbiased and independent hearing.

In her role as Chair, Aggarwal made the introductions, checked to see that the tape recording had begun, and noted the date and time for the record.

"If you would kindly state your full name," she began, in a neutral tone.

Michael Jones, his mind whispered.

"Alexander Gregory," he replied clearly.

"You're aware of the reasons we've assembled today," she continued, linking her fingers on top of his file. "Two months ago, you disclosed to me that, contrary to hospital procedures and professional guidelines, you had undertaken to treat your mother, Catherine Jones, and had furthermore withheld that information—from the hospital, and from her. Under the Trust's professional conduct procedures, I had no option but to refer the matter for independent review. Following that review, it was the appointed case manager's opinion that this disciplinary hearing be convened, in which you'll be facing an allegation of gross misconduct."

Her lip quivered slightly, and he was sorry all over again. Parminder had always been a friend, and it pained him to see her in distress—however well she tried to hide it.

"I must tell you that an allegation of this gravity, if borne out, will lead to your dismissal," she continued, forcing the words from her mouth. "Do you understand, Doctor?"

"I do," he said, without inflection.

"Do you also understand that you may be investigated separately by the British Psychological Society, and, if they find your behaviour to have breached their own code of conduct, you may have your professional membership revoked?"

"I do," he said again.

She cleared her throat. "Good. In that case, let's get down to it."

She spent a minute or two outlining the formalities and running order of the hearing, then summarised the facts.

"The procedures we follow are set out in a document entitled, 'Maintaining High Professional Standards in the Modern NHS'," she said. "Are you familiar with this document?"

"I am," he replied.

She cited a couple of relevant passages.

"Did you have your professional obligations and these procedures in mind when you decided to accept your mother as a patient?"

Gregory swallowed. "Yes, I did." He could not pretend otherwise.

Aggarwal already knew his reasons for ignoring the rules, as did her colleagues on the panel, but it never hurt to hear them from the horse's mouth.

"Would you kindly explain, in your own words, why you chose to override these procedures?"

Gregory looked from her open expression to the closed, faintly bored expressions of her fellow panellists, and knew that, at least for them, the outcome was already decided. It was tempting to get up and walk away then and there, to avoid the humiliation and debasement of trying to explain the hurt and suffering, the sleepless nights and visual hallucinations, the intrusive memories and nightmares that had plagued him since boyhood. How could he sit in that stuffy room that smelled faintly of chicken casserole, and explain the magnitude of emotion and yearning that had risen up, the first time Cathy Jones had walked into his consulting room? How could he convey his pathetic hope that she'd recognise him and throw herself upon his mercy, apologising profusely for the illness that had caused her to harm him and his siblings?

Shame...a fear of rejection, he realised, carefully picking apart his own brain to look upon its hidden, innermost crevices.

And yet...

All the best things are worth fighting for, Douglas had told him.

He looked down at his hands, then at the tiny but permanent scar on his wrist where once a cannula had been inserted, feeding his child's body much needed fluids to flush out his mother's poison.

Why?

That's all he'd wanted to know. It's all he'd ever wanted to know.

He tipped up his chin. "I did it because I knew it was the last opportunity that I'd ever be likely to have," he said, quietly.

"Opportunity? For what?" one of the panel asked him.

A couple of seconds ticked by while rain ran down the panes of UPVC windows at their backs, and Gregory was transported far away, to a time many years before, when he'd lain in another room and stared at another window from behind a locked door.

Why, Alex? his mother's voice whispered. *Were you hoping I'd recognise you? Did you think I'd say 'sorry'?*

He shook his head.

"It was an opportunity to forgive her," he said softly. "I wanted...I hoped that, by talking to her in a professional capacity, detaching myself from the familial connection, she might open up to me. Understanding her was the key to forgiving her and letting go of the past."

"Did you—forgive her, that is?" Aggarwal couldn't help asking.

The question hung on the air while Gregory searched his soul for the answer.

"No," he replied, painfully. "I didn't. I couldn't."

He reached for the glass of water and snatched it up, drinking thirstily to wash away the bad taste in his mouth.

"Professor Douglas, let me start by welcoming you back to Southmoor. I wish the circumstances were different."

"Not at all," Douglas said. "It's no hardship for me to provide a character reference for Doctor Gregory."

Aggarwal smiled.

Half an hour had passed, during which time Gregory felt as though his innards had been laid bare. He'd been asked to recount almost every interaction he could recall, despite every one of his meetings with Cathy Jones having been committed to record, both in writing and on tape.

He supposed it came down to motivation, and their need to understand what *his* had been.

Now, exhausted and wrung out, he made way for his friend to take the hot seat and found that he couldn't muster the energy to care what the outcome might be, after Douglas said his piece.

Fortunately for him, there were others who cared.

While his friend took up a chair at the back of the room, Douglas faced the panellists and, being fully aware of his influence in the sphere, was gratified to see a measure of professional deference. Whilst he was not generally a man to be much affected by reputation, there were times when it came in handy.

"Professor, you're here to speak to us about Doctor Gregory's character," Aggarwal reminded him. "The facts are generally agreed, and we understand you were not privy to them at the time of the—ah—"

Offence, she'd almost said.

"Alleged infraction," she continued.

"That's correct," he said.

"Perhaps you could start by telling us how long you've known one another?"

"More than ten years," Douglas replied. "As you know, he took up a position here at Southmoor to complete the final stage of his clinical training, where he worked under my supervision—and was the best clinical trainee I'd had in years, I might add. We began as colleagues, but quickly became friends. That friendship has developed over the past decade, and we've worked together many times since."

"Do you trust him?" one of the panel asked.

"Implicitly," Douglas replied, without hesitation.

"Even though he didn't tell you about the fact he was treating his own mother?" they pressed. "Didn't you feel betrayed?"

At the back of the room, Gregory felt his chest tighten, a physical by-product of acute shame.

"*No,* I didn't," Douglas said, and looked down his sizeable nose at the man who'd dared to ask. "As a clinician, I recognised that my friend's decision had absolutely nothing to do with me, and everything to do with the boy."

"The boy?"

"Young Michael Jones, of course," Douglas said, and realised he was speaking to a dimwit. "The boy he once was. It's taken Alex—I beg your pardon, Doctor Gregory—years of hard introspection and personal development to heal wounds that might have broken a lesser person. That alone is laudable, but if we consider that his reaction was not only to try to heal himself but to use his personal skills to try to heal *others*, too…well, there you have the mark of the man."

"And yet, it's clear that his own healing process was more important to him than that of Catherine Jones, considering he prioritised that above all else when the opportunity arose," the man persisted.

Aggarwal stole a glance at Gregory, who was seated at the back of the room, saw the flash of pain flit across his face and was sorry for it.

"I think that's very much a matter of opinion," Douglas said. "Knowing him as I do, I would say Doctor Gregory was trying to help Cathy Jones, whom he regarded as a patient, and hoped to receive some answers and personal healing as a side-effect—nothing more. I would refer you to the meticulous records that were kept, documenting every communication they shared, which is in line with hospital and BPS expectations."

"I've checked the records myself," Aggarwal murmured. "They're full and complete."

"Was there anything untoward in their content?" Douglas asked, reversing the scrutiny. "Was there anything in his clinical approach that stepped outside of professional boundaries, or would have given you cause for concern? Anything that you, as a clinician, would have done differently?"

"Nothing whatsoever," Aggarwal was pleased to say.

Douglas was unsurprised. "As I say, my friend is a man of high moral fibre. He's also *human*, as we all are, and he made an error of judgment. However, that error caused no harm to the patient in question, nor brought the hospital into disrepute or endangered any other patients or staff."

"The patient *did* commit suicide, didn't she?" one of the panellists pointed out.

"The circumstances of her death were fully investigated," Aggarwal muttered. "They bear no relationship to the matters in hand. Jones took her own life whilst Doctor Gregory wasn't even in the country, and there were no red flags in the weeks prior."

Gregory focused on a spot on the far wall, trying not to remember the pain of losing her, even after all that had gone before.

"Look," Douglas said, steering the conversation back to safer ground. "There's no denying Alex and his mother shared a complicated past. It's easy for us to be distracted by that kind of drama, and to think that every action and motivation would have to be informed by it. I'd say you'd do far better to look at the present reality—and the reality is that you have a highly competent clinician whose behaviour in all else has been beyond reproach. Even when treating Catherine Jones, he kept up his due diligence. Look beyond the veil to the heart of the matter—"

At the back of the room, Gregory's eyes sharpened.

Look beyond the veil.

Don't be distracted by the drama of the past...look at the present reality...

"...look at the true nature of the beast..." Douglas was saying.

And, in a rush, it came to him.

All thoughts of Cathy Jones forgotten, Gregory stood up suddenly and made a grab for his coat.

"Doctor—? I'm afraid we're not finished here," Aggarwal said.

He paused. "Do you need to ask me anything else?"

"Well...no, I suppose not—"

"In that case, I have somewhere I need to be," he said, and, with one last grateful nod for his friend, he strode towards the door and flung it open.

As his footsteps receded down the corridor, Douglas removed his glasses and began to polish them against the edge of his trousers.

"Did I mention he's also single-minded in his pursuit of the truth?"

He gave them a winning smile, and hoped it would be enough.

CHAPTER 32

Darkness had fallen by the time Gregory made it back into Central London but, rather than going home, he headed west and found a parking spot on one of the leafy suburban streets not far from upmarket Chiswick—close enough to be desirable, far enough to be affordable. He made his way along a short pathway to a front door painted bright red, raising an eyebrow at the sight of a brass knocker fashioned in the shape of a naked woman's bust. Feeling decidedly naughty, he grasped it and gave a couple of loud raps against the wooden frame.

Almost immediately, the door opened.

"*Alex*?" DCI Hope stood in the doorway dressed in leggings and a t-shirt with a faded Aerosmith motif emblazoned across the front.

She didn't look happy to see him, neither did she look unhappy.

She looked…

Self-conscious.

Immediately, he was contrite. "I'm sorry to trouble you at home," he said. "DS Carter told me where to find you…"

"Oh, he did, did he?" she muttered, and irritated herself by wishing she'd had time to run a brush through her hair.

"I can come ba—"

Gregory trailed off as he caught sight of what, at first glance, appeared to be a giant hairball but thereafter turned out to be an enormous cat. After a long, yellow-eyed stare, it stepped daintily over the threshold and waddled towards him to conduct a more thorough inspection, sniffing his ankles before rubbing its considerable bulk against his trouser leg and purring like a steam engine.

"What the hell is it?" he had to ask. "A panther?"

She chuckled, despite herself. "He's an ordinary cat, with an extraordinary appetite," she said. "The vet says he's healthy, just…ah…"

"Cuddly?" Gregory offered, and almost braced a hand against the wall for support.

"It's been Christmas," she said defensively. "Anyway, are you going to tell me why you've turned up on my doorstep—unannounced?"

He nodded, remembering the reason he'd come.

"It's about the Villiers case," he said. "I need to talk to you."

"I gathered that," she said. "Can't this wait until the morning? I can meet you at the office—"

"It can't wait—that's why I came here."

If she invited him into her home, an invisible boundary line would be crossed and there would be no going back. On the other hand, the tension crackling between them could be entirely in her own mind and she was making a fuss over nothing.

Professional curiosity warred with natural reserve, and the former won, as it always did.

"Come in," she said, and gestured for him to precede her.

"Quite a place you've got here," Gregory said, parroting the words Hope had used when she'd first visited his apartment in Shad Thames.

She leaned back against the kitchen counter and folded her arms. "Come to the point, Alex."

He nodded. "What if Villiers' death had nothing to do with Sally Fletcher," he said baldly. "Nothing to do with anything that happened in 1979?"

She frowned. "What happened to Sally Fletcher is the only thing connecting Villiers, Beckett... and Campbell," she said, despite their disagreement on the last. "It's referred to in the communications relating to each death, bar one—"

He held up his hands. "Bear with me," he said. "It struck me, earlier today, that we might have been led up the garden path. Nobody's denying what happened to Sally Fletcher back in '79 was terrible. But what if that *isn't* the reason Villiers died? What if it was used as convenient distraction for us all, a rabbit hole we could fall into and follow further and further away from the truth?"

"Which is?"

"Far more prosaic," he said. "If we strip away the drama of the past and focus on the present, what are we left with? Ordinary motivations."

"You mean, bog-standard jealousy, money, lust, revenge...all that?"

"Exactly. You'd be looking for a perpetrator who wasn't necessarily connected to Villiers' past in any way—or Beckett's, or Campbell's, for that matter. Someone from the here and now, who only knew about the events of 1979 incidentally and used it to their advantage to cover their tracks, as a kind of smokescreen."

Hope was unconvinced. "That doesn't explain the e-mails," she said. "If what you're saying is true, and everything was a smokescreen, why would someone write those e-mails and alert Villiers to the threat? Surely, there'd be no need."

Gregory had an answer for that, but needed to check something, first.

"Do you have a copy of the file here?"

"Yes, but—"

"Can I see it, please?"

She sighed, but had no real objection since he remained their consultant. With one of her long, meaningful stares, she reached for her laptop and brought up the file.

"Help yourself," she said, swivelling the screen towards him.

Gregory thanked her and took a chair at the kitchen table, where she watched his long fingers tap a few keys, scrolling to find a particular document. She moved to stand at his shoulder, partly so that she could keep an eye on what he was doing and partly...

Partly to be close to him.

Their eyes met, and she wrapped her arms around herself in a gesture that had nothing whatsoever to do with feeling threatened and everything to do with feeling needy. The worst of it was that he'd probably read her body language and drawn all the right conclusions.

She felt vulnerable, and he hadn't even said a word.

"What are you looking for?" she asked, a bit sharply.

"Ah...do you have a note of Villiers' movements in the week prior to his death? A timeline?"

Hope leaned across to search for the correct file, and he felt the brush of her hair against his face—nothing more than a fleeting whisper, but enough to divert his attention from murder to far more pleasant pursuits.

"There's a list of times and dates, as far as we've been able to gather. Why do you ask?"

Gregory dragged himself back to reality and focused on the screen, cross-checking Villiers' known movements with the timings listed on the e-mail chain.

"I doubt very much that Villiers ever read these e-mails, let alone deleted them," he said, after a long silence.

Hope digested Gregory's statement, trying to follow his line of thought, and then it hit her like a thunderbolt.

"He couldn't have deleted them," she realised. "The timings don't match. That's what you're saying, isn't it?"

Gregory nodded. "The first e-mail was deleted at 5.47p.m. on 3rd January," he said. "But Villiers was on stage rehearsing at that time."

"Might have had his phone with him," she suggested. "Maybe he had his e-mail account hooked up to the phone, which means he could have deleted it on his mobile device."

Gregory shook his head. "Villiers hated technology," he reminded her. "It was a foible of his. He was also a consummate professional. There's no way he would have been the type to check his phone mid-rehearsal, if he kept it on his person at all. Remember, you found his mobile phone back at his apartment, not at the theatre."

She nodded, scanning the list on screen to be doubly sure.

"Who handled his correspondence?" Gregory queried. "Who took care of his diary, and would have had access to his e-mails?"

"That would have been Marcus Hale, or possibly his wife," Hope replied, straightening up again. "The password for his e-mail account was 'OSCAR2012!', which refers to the last Oscar he was awarded, for *Sins of the Father*—"

"Any good?"

She stared at him. "What?"

"The film…is it any good?"

She was incredulous. "We're in the middle of a discussion about murder and you want to know if some film was worth the price of a ticket?"

Gregory shrugged. "It helps me to know if Villiers lived up to his fame."

"All right," she relented. "It was a great film, completely immersive. There's no denying he knew his craft."

"In that case, maybe I'll get a takeaway pizza and watch it some Friday night," he said to himself, then realised she was staring at him again. "Something the matter?" he asked.

She thought of her earlier assumption regarding him not being the kind of personality to enjoy a Friday night movie, and was forced to adjust the parameters of her understanding once again.

"No," she said quietly. "Nothing's the matter."

"Okay," he said. "You were telling me the password to his e-mail account—?"

"Right. Well, according to his wife, and since he was such a creature of habit, Villiers had that same password since 2012 and never changed it. It wouldn't have taken an MI6 code-breaker to crack that one."

"Which means that anybody could, theoretically, have logged into his account and deleted the e-mails after sending them?" Gregory said.

"They could, but why would anybody *want* to do that?" she said, stopping to look at him again. "Why send an e-mail then delete it yourself before the recipient can read it?"

"I believe it's all part of the smokescreen," Gregory said. "Send a threatening e-mail that paints a false picture of why a man dies, in advance of his murder. Delete the e-mails so he never sees—but the police do. They must have *known* you'd look at Villiers' devices and communications history, and must also have known you'd find the deleted e-mails in the trash folder. That would make it look as though Villiers had been aware of the e-mails, had been unnerved enough by the prospect of repercussions or loss of reputation, and built the picture of a man choosing to kill himself on stage rather than face it all."

She reached out a hand to ruffle the cat's ears when he lolloped onto the chair beside her.

"Let's say I believe your theory about Villiers' death having nothing to do with Sally Fletcher, or the past," she said. "Where does that leave Beckett? The thing that connected them was 1979, and their university history."

Gregory shook his head. "Basic motivations again," he said. "What do we know of Beckett? We know he was an avaricious, grasping sort of character who valued money, prestige and success—or his definition of it. The events of 1979 told us something useful, which is that he and Villiers weren't natural friends; even Bill Douglas told us that he was surprised Villiers ever gave Beckett the time of day. Why keep in touch with a man you barely like, for all these years? Why pay him an occasional stipend?"

"Blackmail," Hope muttered.

"Exactly," Gregory replied. "Villiers kept his enemy close. They shared something shameful, but, out of the two of them, he was the one with the most to lose. He kept paying Beckett to ensure his silence, and we can see the payments get bigger or more frequent, in line with Villiers' rising success."

"Inflation," Hope said, and gave a short laugh. "Economic principles apply, even in the extortion game."

Gregory nodded again. "Beckett was, essentially, the same character he'd always been," he continued. "It's why we thought of him as a suspect, for a while, because his character fits the profile in many respects. But, rather than being the perpetrator, perhaps he found himself in possession of certain valuable information. Perhaps he knew or suspected who had killed Villiers—at least, enough to try his hand for a little quid pro quo."

"Which would mean that his death had nothing to do with what happened back in 1979, and everything to do with his own greed," Hope said. "He went to Villiers' killer and asked for hush money, and thought he'd been successful. Instead, they decided to end him in the same way."

"It would have been risky, because the killer was taken by surprise," Gregory said. "The first murder required some planning, and they could afford to take their time. The second was a rush-job, by necessity, which required some nifty alteration to their overall scheme. The profile still fits an organised type," he explained. "You've got someone who prefers to be prepared for all eventualities, but isn't averse to a bit of risky business, either. They capitalised on Villers' past connection with Beckett and extended the rationale to include him—the press played into their hands, in that respect. All the reporting about a cult, or a suicide pact, playing on their membership of the Stagelights? That was perfect, as far as they were concerned, because it's exactly what the killer wanted us to think. How they must have laughed."

Hope rubbed a hand over the back of her neck, which was starting to ache. "If somebody other than Villiers deleted those e-mails—the same somebody who murdered Beckett to keep him quiet—it must have been someone who *wasn't* involved from the past, otherwise, why potentially implicate themselves?"

"Agreed."

"That still leaves a wide pool of suspects," she said.

"But only so many who could have sent those e-mails at those times," Gregory reminded her. "The timings are highly significant."

"There were some discrepancies in the whereabouts of some of the cast," Hope said. "Which means that some timings may be unreliable."

"You mean, the fifteen-minute question mark over Peter Gray and Margot Winters, when they each claim to have been in their dressing rooms, but weren't?" he said. "Yes, I assume they have an arrangement where she supplies him with a bag of coke, whenever the need arises. They were probably huddled somewhere discreet."

Hope stared at him. "How the *hell* did you know that?" she demanded. "We had a lead from the Drugs Squad yesterday, and I paid Mr Gray a personal visit this morning. He sang like a canary."

Gregory shrugged. "I've seen a lot of people who've abused substances," he said. "It's easy to recognise the physical signs. As for Margot, that's pure guesswork, but the timings fit for both of them, and she strikes me as a 'fixer'."

"A…fixer?"

"A personality who values order, smooth running plans…getting from A to B without mishap," he said. "Somebody who opts for short-term fixes rather than long-term strategies. Margot would value Peter being able to deliver his performance on-stage, on-time, over and above his long-term health. She'd have helped to procure a four-leafed clover, if he'd told her that it would ensure his being on top form for opening night."

Hope nodded, feeling unnerved by his insight.

"What about Villiers' wife, or his PA? They'd have access to Villiers' e-mail account."

"Yes, particularly via his home computer," Gregory agreed. "Especially since Marcus likely spends a lot of time there, with Rebecca."

Hope stared at him again. "What are you implying?"

"That Marcus Hale and Rebecca Villiers are conducting an affair," he said, as if it were obvious.

She laughed, and wondered if the man were psychic after all. "There's absolutely no way you could have known *that*," she decided. "Carter had to lean on Rebecca's doorman—heavily, I might add— to find out that particular nugget of information."

"Beckett's last movements," he explained. "It's in the file that he visited Rebecca before he died, and that Marcus was already there when he arrived. It was early morning, which seemed odd to me. I made an educated guess."

"Apparently, your cynicism is even greater than mine."

"Stop, you'll make me blush."

She grinned, which prompted an answering smile in return.

"The point is, Rebecca doesn't have much to gain from killing her husband," she said. "She's independently wealthy and has plenty of her own fame to fall back on. If anything, their brands were intertwined, which is why she worked so hard to keep any scandal out of the public eye."

"I agree," he said. "The same logic applies to Marcus Hale. It wouldn't be in his interests to kill Villiers; he's a social climber and he'd hitched his wagon to Nigel and Rebecca. He might have kept her happy in the bedroom, but I don't imagine he had any plans to marry her since he's been courting his next mark, in America."

Hope lifted a hand and let it fall away again. "I might as well ask...how did you know that?"

"*Hello!* magazine," he said.

"I wouldn't have thought you were a fan of glossy magazines."

Gregory shrugged. "They have their moments, especially when constructing a picture of a well-known celebrity. For example, I happened to notice that Marcus was papped at three separate parties standing in conversation with Henry Neville, who's in line to be the next big action hero—or, so the 'unnamed sources' in *Hello!* tell me."

She snorted.

"Anyway, Marcus and Henry looked cosy, and there wasn't a Villiers in sight. Again, it's just guesswork, but these things often add up."

"He's been looking at real estate, quietly, in Los Angeles," Hope told him. "I'd say you're right about him planning a big move, and I agree it wouldn't have served him to kill his employer to get there. It doesn't look good as a reference."

She paused, yawning hugely.

"Sorry," she said. "It's been a long week. Look, I'll speak to Carter in the morning, and we can start digging into the timings, eliminate a few more people—"

"That may be too late."

Her eyes refocused, and she realised something she hadn't before.

"You know who did this, don't you?"

Gregory thought of all the reasons he should be cautious and keep his trap shut, but there were lives at stake.

"I have a strong suspicion, yes."

He mentioned a name and, after the initial surprise passed, she found she could imagine it.

Yes, she could see it.

"We have no proof," she said, calculating the steps she could take to get it. "I can ask Digital Forensics to dig into the financial side, but that will take time."

"How much time?"

"Couple of days, possibly more."

He shook his head. "Every day that passes is another day evidence could be disposed of," he said. "We have to take the chance there's still something to find."

"You don't know that."

"No, I don't," he agreed. "But I have a measure of their character. The profile of the person we're looking for describes an over-confident personality, but even that has its limits. Once the initial thrill of killing—and, ostensibly, getting away with it—passes, the planning side to their personality will take over once more and they'll need to clean up shop. When that happens, there'll be nothing for us to find."

"There may be nothing to find, anyway," she muttered.

"That's possible," he agreed. "But, if the financials don't come through, you won't have any hard evidence at all, whereas there's still an outside chance the hemlock hasn't yet been disposed of. We have to try, Ava."

She met his eyes across the table, thought of all the reasons why she shouldn't chase a thread of a theory. "Hold up your hands," she muttered.

He gave her an odd look. "My hands?"

"Humour me."

He raised his hands, which were rock steady.

"All right," she whispered. "We'll execute a raid—"

"You won't find anything that way," he said, lowering his hands again. "We don't know for sure where the hemlock is being kept. It could be anywhere."

"What do you suggest, then?"

"Provoke a response," he murmured. He proceeded to set out the plan he'd been considering during the drive back from Southmoor.

"I don't like it," she said. "It's risky, and I'm not that personality type."

"Yes, you are," he said, with a slow smile that made her flush for reasons she understood completely.

"All right, smarty pants, I don't mind the risk, but…" She snapped her mouth shut, but he leaned forward and edged his hand across the table towards her.

"You're worried about me?" he said, softly.

She swallowed. "I don't want you on my conscience, that's all. It'll look bad in the report."

He covered her hand with his own and gave it a gentle squeeze. "I don't have many people to worry about me," he admitted. "Thank you for being one of them."

"It's—"

"Purely professional, I know."

She looked down at their joined hands and returned the squeeze before tugging her fingers away. "Ah, you know, this is all well and good, but what about Campbell? Do you still believe his death is unconnected?" she asked.

It was rocky ground between them, and he trod carefully. "I still believe the mode of his killing is inconsistent with a cold assassination," he said. "Campbell's death was personal, unlike the other two."

"Opportunity, again?" she asked. "Somebody he sent down in the past, come back to haunt him, maybe?"

Gregory stared at her, and the germ of an idea bloomed, one that was too terrifying to contemplate. "Perhaps it was a ghost, of sorts."

If it was, then he may have more in common with the late Simon Campbell than he cared to imagine.

CHAPTER 33

The next morning

It was funny how dabbling in a little murder could spice up an otherwise humdrum life.

Jasper Pugh thought this as he adjusted his tie in the small mirror fixed to the back of his office door, and congratulated himself on a job well done—both the tie, and the murders.

He almost jumped when there came a knock at the door. "Ah—" He cast his eye around the room, found everything in order, then opened it with a smile already in place for whichever usher or actor he found standing there.

It was neither.

"Doctor Gregory," he said, and looked past him to the empty corridor beyond. "No police escort, today?"

"Not today," the other agreed, and stepped inside. "What I have to tell you is best said without an audience."

Pugh closed the door carefully, while his mind raced. "Sounds serious," he said. "If you're here to offer your services, I'm afraid I already have a very good therapist by the name of Maureen. Wonderful woman, who listens to my rants and rambles every week without complaint."

"Well, therapists can't pick up on every little thing, can they?" Gregory said, with a knowing smile. "We rely on the information our clients tell us, but, if they're less than open about the lives they lead, there isn't always much we can do to help them. Is there, Jasper?"

Pugh's lips twisted into a thin smile. "Why don't you have a seat, Doctor? Can I offer you a drink? I was about to make one, myself," he lied.

"Well, if it isn't too much trouble, I'll have a coffee—black."

"No trouble at all," Pugh murmured, and headed towards the back of the room where he kept the coffee machine, slowing his stride so as not to appear too eager. "If not to help me deal with the trauma of losing my *dear* friend, what is it you could possibly wish to speak to me about?"

He kept his back to the room and reached for a small tub of dissolvable pills he always kept on his person. Swiftly, he tapped one into the bottom of a china teacup, then added a second for good measure.

"Well, Doctor? What brings you back to the theatre?" he pressed. "Are you looking for a free ticket?"

Gregory crossed one leg over the other and gave Pugh a self-deprecating smile. "I suppose you could say that."

"Really? Well, in that case, I'll speak to the Box Office and make sure a couple of tickets are left behind the front desk for you," Pugh said, as he watched the little compressed hemlock tablets mingle with steaming brown liquid. "I should have thought to do it before now. We're all so grateful for your efforts with Nigel."

"I'm afraid I'm looking for something more generous than theatre tickets," Gregory said. "My clinical work pays well, but not as well as the theatre business—especially if you don't have to share the earnings with a business partner—wouldn't you agree?"

Pugh's fingers curled into fists, but he told himself to remain calm. There was nothing that Gregory could know for certain; absolutely nothing.

"That may be true, Doctor Gregory, but I'm sure I don't need to tell you that I'd be far happier having my friend and partner back here with us in the land of the living—profit margins be damned."

Gregory gave a little chuckle. "If you say so."

Pugh reached for the cups and set them on the desk, careful not to spill any of the liquid onto his skin. He'd chosen strong coffee, and its scent overrode the faint aroma of rotting vegetables hemlock carried with it.

"As for the rewards of our respective professions... well, I can assure you there may not be quite so much leverage in the theatre business as you seem to imagine."

"Certainly, if one were to believe the figures you submitted for your last tax return, then I'd agree with you," Gregory replied. "But I've a sneaking suspicion those figures don't quite tell the full story—do they?"

"I'm afraid I don't follow," Jasper said, with one of his airy smiles.

"Then let me explain," Gregory replied. "The police aren't buying the suicide pact. They think the e-mails were a smokescreen and Nigel never saw them, let alone deleted them. They're coming back around to thinking it's murder."

He reached for his cup but overshot himself, knocking it against a picture frame propped up on the desk and sending the frame crashing to the floor. "So sorry," he said. "Let me get that—"

"It's not important," Pugh said, irritably, ducking beneath the desk to retrieve the silver frame of himself as a younger man, dressed in full costume.

Seconds later, he reappeared, just in time to see Gregory take his first sip of coffee.

Pugh smiled broadly. "No harm done," he said, tapping the frame. "You were saying something about the police thinking the e-mails weren't genuine.

What does that have to do with me—or you, for that matter? As for them investigating murder, well, I'd be glad to see whichever maniac killed Nigel properly brought to book—"

"Unusual for someone to self-reference as a 'maniac,'" Gregory mused. "But it does happen."

Pugh stared at him over the rim of his cup, sipped, then set it back down again. "Be careful, Doctor."

There was a short, heavy silence while both men stared at one another over the width of the desk, then Gregory set his cup back down.

"Let me speak plainly, Jasper. I know it was you who poisoned Nigel, and I think I know why. You've been embezzling money from the business, a little bit here and there, and perhaps nobody noticed for a while. I can imagine Nigel was happy for you to handle the administrative side, wasn't he?"

It was a rhetorical question, but Jasper applauded him privately for his accuracy thus far.

"Please, go on," he said, giving a little regal wave of his hand. "I'm enjoying this immensely."

Gregory nodded. "Perhaps he surprised you, one day, by asking to look at the books," he said. "He noticed the figures didn't add up and started poking around, asking questions, making life difficult for you—didn't he?"

Again, Jasper neither confirmed nor denied, but remembered the vicious row they'd had in that very office. He recalled his old friend standing in the middle of the room hurling accusations, his face red as a tomato as he'd issued his ultimatum: return the money, in full, by Lear's opening night, or be reported to the police. The reputation and esteem he'd built up over the years would be gone. Nobody in the industry would trust him again. The invitations to openings and red-carpet events would dry up, as would the steady stream of young starlets who'd been willing to overlook his age in favour of a dollop of specious charm and passable good looks.

It was always true love, until it ended.

All of this had passed through his mind while Nigel ranted, until suddenly the solution presented itself. He'd already spent the money, so he couldn't return it even if he'd wanted to, but perhaps there was another way to rid himself of the problem.

How do I know you haven't already told someone about this? he'd asked.

I've grown soft, in my old age, Nigel said. *I wanted to give you a chance to put this right, Jasper. Besides, I'd rather not have my name mixed up with anything as grubby as embezzlement. You pay the money back and nobody's the wiser. After a suitable period, you'll decide you're ready for pastures new and I'll buy you out.*

What if I don't want to leave?

You don't have a choice. You gave up that luxury when you decided to steal from me, Jasper. As for our friendship, that's gone the way of the dodo.

He'd made a show of apologising, even worked up a few crocodile tears, then agreed to Nigel's deadline to give himself time to figure out the best way to kill the man. He'd spent days and nights racking his brain to find a weakness, anything he could use as a counterweight, and dimly recalled Rebecca telling him something about Nigel being touchy about his Stagelights days. Mind you, she'd had a few too many, and wasn't so hot on the details. At the time, he hadn't given it another thought...only then did he wish he'd paid more attention. Still, it was enough to get the ball rolling and set the scene for suicide.

Then, Fate had played a blinder, in the form of Lance Beckett.

Turns out, Nigel had bent the truth a bit, himself. For starters, he'd blabbed to Beckett about his suspicions about the books having been cooked a couple of weeks before it had been confirmed. Later, once Beckett heard that Villiers had dropped dead and that the circumstances were suspicious, he'd put two and two together and come up with the correct number. Beckett's handwritten note had come as a bolt from the blue, but he'd rallied.

After you'd killed once, it became old hat.

His only regret in all of it was not having known that Nigel had been paying Beckett through the nose, all those years. Hell, it might have saved the man's life—rather than offing him, they could have lived in an awkward truce, like nations with access to nuclear weaponry: each party armed and unwilling to deploy unless attacked first, and the threat would remain potent enough to keep either from becoming the aggressor.

On the other hand, perhaps he'd have taken the same path, regardless. Nothing could beat the sight of the great Sir Nigel Villiers hitting the stage with a thud, eyes wide, no longer a vibrant *tour de force* but a frail old man on the cusp of death.

It had been glorious.

"Let's say you're right," he said, cutting back to the present. "What do you propose to do about it, Doctor?"

"The police aren't quite there yet," Gregory said. "I could make it my business to steer them in another direction—for the right incentive."

Jasper glanced at the cup and estimated the volume Gregory had ingested would be more than enough to do the trick. In a couple of hours, once the hemlock worked its way around his bloodstream, he would find himself in a grave predicament.

"There's one thing I don't understand," Gregory continued. "I wonder if you'd clear it up for me—for my own peace of mind?"

Jasper raised an eyebrow.

"I understand why you killed Lance Beckett," Gregory said. "But why Simon Campbell? More window dressing?"

He watched genuine confusion spread across the man's face.

"Campbell? I don't know anyone by that name."

Gregory nodded. It was just as he'd thought, and his heart began to beat wildly, a film of sweat coating the skin beneath his clothes.

He needed to get out of there, and fast.

"We have a deal, then?"

Jasper laughed softly. "No, Doctor. I'm afraid I'll have to decline your offer—thanks, all the same. As I say, I had absolutely nothing to do with my friend's death, nor that of Lance Beckett—or this Campbell fellow."

"That's a bold move," Gregory said, rubbing his hand against his chest to ease the burn. "However, I'll respect your decision. I hope you understand I have no choice but to inform the police."

Jasper leaned forward and an ugly smile spread across his face.

"Are you feeling all right, Doctor? You don't look quite yourself."

Hemlock, Gregory thought. *He'd used the hemlock.*

CHAPTER 34

Gregory reached for his coffee cup and drained the remaining liquid, and Jasper watched him with a degree of incomprehension, wondering why the man was still drinking when, surely, he must know the fluid was contaminated.

"In answer to your question, I'm feeling very well, thank you," Gregory said. "The more pertinent question to ask is: how are *you* feeling?"

Jasper gave a barely perceptible shake of his head. "Me?" He laughed. "Never better, in fact—"

His eyes fell on the spent coffee cup on his side of the desk, then strayed to the cup in front of Gregory. Identical mugs, identical contents.

Fear rippled through his body in one powerful rush.

"I know you have it somewhere in here," Gregory said quietly. "Tell me where the hemlock is, before it's too late."

Jasper searched the man's face for early signs of illness but found none. On the other hand, he was beginning to feel distinctly nauseous.

It was just nerves, he told himself. There was no way he had made a mistake with the cups. He'd allowed the man to spook him, that was all.

"I don't know what you're talking about," he said, with renewed confidence. "I've never touched hemlock."

"No, I imagine you've been very careful when handling it," Gregory said. "The instructions probably told you not to allow it to come into direct contact with your skin, didn't they? I suppose it's been distilled into capsules, so you could administer quickly and easily?"

Jasper felt the little pill bottle burning a hole in his trouser pocket and a line of sweat trickled from the nape of his neck down his back.

"You're looking a little hot under the collar, there," Gregory continued. "You know, the longer you delay, the longer the hemlock will have to absorb into your bloodstream. You know how swiftly it works."

"I—don't know what you mean. I've never seen hemlock in my life, let alone poisoned anyone with it."

Gregory smiled broadly. "Then you have nothing to worry about, when I tell you that I swapped our coffee cups," he said, and watched the man's pupils dilate. "It won't matter to you, at all, to know that you drank the coffee that was intended for me."

"You—you're lying—"

"You're probably wondering when I swapped the cups," Gregory carried on, conversationally. "I did it while you were picking the frame up, off the floor."

"That only took me a couple of seconds," Jasper whispered.

"Which was all I needed," Gregory said, and leaned forward to pin the man with a hard stare. "Tell me where the hemlock is, and we'll get you to the nearest hospital before the damage becomes irreparable."

He was bluffing again, Jasper thought. *Trying to draw him out.*

"Think about it," Gregory crooned. "Think about your friend, Nigel, and of how he looked, the last time you saw him. In a couple of hours, maybe less, you'll be joining him. Unless—"

Jasper began to hyperventilate, the air wheezing through his lungs in harsh breaths that sounded around the room.

"What?" he managed. "Unless *what*?"

"As I say, tell me where you keep the hemlock and I'll get you to the hospital."

Jasper watched him with eyes full of hatred. Could he be sure—*completely* sure—that he hadn't drunk the contaminated coffee? He began to imagine the coffee had tasted sour, after all, and that his limbs were no longer working as they should.

No, he couldn't be completely sure.

All because of the interfering man sitting before him, who wore the smug smile of one who knew they had won. He had him between the proverbial rock and a hard place, and there was no escape. He knew very well that he couldn't charm his way out of this predicament, and every second that ticked by brought him closer to death.

How the mighty have fallen, a voice seemed to whisper, and he fancied it was Nigel. *Everything you've done was all for nothing.*

Rage welled up and he sprang from his chair, eyes wild. "I won't end like this!" he hissed. "I won't have everything taken from me!"

Gregory had only a second to prepare before the man launched himself across the desk towards him, fingers extended like claws, teeth bared. The force of his body sent them sprawling backward onto the floor where those claws clamped around his neck like a vice.

The breath snatched from his body, he grasped Jasper's wrists and tried to prise them away, but gravity was against him, and they wouldn't budge. Looming above him, the man's face was lit with madness, his laughter maniacal.

"You've...ruined...*everything*..." he rasped, as he bore down even harder against Gregory's throat.

Starved of oxygen, hearing the pounding of his own heartbeat, Gregory brought the heel of his hand up sharply against the underside of Jasper's jaw, so hard he heard the *crack* of bone.

With a howl, the man fell backwards, releasing the pressure from Gregory's throat so that he could take several deep, painful breaths, dragging air back into his lungs.

Gathering himself quickly, he sat up to find Jasper clutching his face.

"*Where*?" Gregory croaked. "Where is it?"

Unwittingly, Jasper's hand reached out to grasp the bottle in his trouser pocket but found it gone. "No," he growled. "*No!*"

There was a tense, frantic moment in which both men searched the floor to see where it had fallen and, at the precise moment Jasper's fingers clasped the little brown bottle, the door burst open.

"You took your time." Gregory rubbed a hand across the bruised skin of his neck as DCI Hope entered the room, with DS Carter and a couple of heavyweight constables in tow.

"Sorry," she said, cheerfully. "What have I missed?"

Thinking fast, Jasper raised an accusatory finger towards Gregory.

"He—he poisoned me!" he said tremulously, while the pain in his jaw intensified. "Then he assaulted me—"

"*Poisoned* you?" Gregory said. "What on Earth are you talking about?"

Jasper had begun to drool, and he raised a shaking hand to swipe it from his chin.

"The hemlock," he said, turning to Hope. "He—he put some in my coffee, then attacked me. He—he tried to blackmail me. Said he'd plant hemlock in here and tell the police it was me who'd killed Nigel and Lance, if I didn't pay him. Then, when I didn't agree, he poisoned my coffee and said he'd prevent me seeking help, if I didn't go along with it. I—I tried to escape, and he—he attacked me. The man's dangerous, Chief Inspector…arrest him!"

Hope turned to Gregory. "You attacked him? That wasn't part of the plan."

He held up his hands. "Now, just wait a minute," he said. "He jumped me and had his hands around my throat. It was purely self-defence."

"Plan?" Jasper said. "What plan? I need to get to a hospital!"

"Don't worry, we'll have somebody see to your jaw, as soon as we've read you your rights," Hope told him.

"Not the jaw," Jasper cried out. "The *hemlock*, for God's sake! We can't wait any longer!"

"What hemlock?"

"*This!*" he shouted, brandishing the pill bottle. "It's in here!"

With careful, gloved hands, Hope plucked it from his fingers and dropped it into a sealed evidence bag.

"Am I to understand that you believe you've accidentally ingested some of this poison hemlock?"

"There was no accident," Jasper lied. "*That man* put some in my drink, as I've told you."

"Really?" Hope tutted. "Are you sure?"

Before he could respond, Gregory wandered back to the desk and crouched down to indicate a small wet patch on the carpeted floor at the foot of the chair where he'd recently been seated.

"Ask the forensics team to analyse the fibres here," he said, rising to full height again. "You'll find a concentrated solution of hemlock mixed with coffee."

Jasper looked between the pair of them with sudden understanding.

"You—didn't swap the coffee," he realised, and let out a harsh laugh. "You threw it on the floor."

Gregory held up his hands.

"Hand's quicker than the eye, so they say."

"I didn't drink any hemlock, after all," Jasper mumbled, his speech slurred by the pain in his jaw.

"And nor did I," Gregory said. "Despite your best efforts."

Hope nodded towards Carter, who stepped forward to lift the man to his feet, in preparation for an arrest.

But, before he could recite the words, Jasper turned to look around his office one last time.

"Thirty years," he said. "It took me thirty years to get here."

"Console yourself," Hope said. "It'll take you less than thirty minutes to get down to The Yard."

CHAPTER 35

"Are you coming with us?"

Hope addressed the question to Gregory as they stepped out into the late morning sunshine and it was on the tip of his tongue to accept her invitation, before he remembered something far more urgent.

Campbell.

He stepped forward and grasped her shoulders, taking her by surprise. "Ava—in there, Jasper told me he had no idea who Campbell was—I believe him."

Her eyes searched his face, which was strained. "Okay," she said, conscious that her staff were watching their exchange. "If Pugh isn't our man, we'll find Campbell's killer another day—"

"He isn't," Gregory said simply. "But I think I know who it was."

Now, she was all ears. "Well?"

"I have no proof—"

"What a shocker."

For once, he didn't smile. "I think it could have been Carl Deere."

"Boss? Are you coming?" Carter called across to Hope from the squad car that was parked on the kerb, attracting attention from passers-by.

But she held up a hand for him to give her another minute.

"Carl Deere?" she said, in disbelief. "The man wrongfully convicted of the Andersson murders? Alex, the man was a victim, not an aggressor."

He thought of his original profile, and of how it had fit the personality, if not the crime.

"Think about it," he said, trying not to let frustration get the better of him. "The passages from *Othello*, left at the scene. The frenzied killing, the staging, the execution…it was punishment, Ava, inflicted by someone who had reason to hate Simon Campbell."

"He wasn't a popular man," she argued. "There may be plenty of people with an axe to grind."

Gregory didn't have time to debate the matter, not when every instinct told him to act.

Act, now!

"If I'm right, then there are others who may be under threat," he said, releasing her shoulders from his grip, conscious that he'd been holding on to her a little too tightly, a little too desperately. "Other members of the police team who arrested and detained him. The prosecution team who put him behind bars. The trial judge who gave such a damning summation—His Honour Judge Whittaker, I think it was—and even the jury. The press who vilified him and…"

"And?"

"Me," he said. "And *Bill*."

She saw naked fear in his eyes now—a son for a father.

"Hey," she said, and took his shoulder in her own gentle grip. "We'll look into it. We'll find Deere's current address, do a routine check…I promise you, Alex, I'll do what I can, as soon as I've booked in Jasper Pugh…"

It wasn't fast enough, he thought. "Please, ask a team to check Bill's home address, in Cambridge."

"I—okay, but if you'll only wait, we can go and speak to him together."

He shook his head, already thinking of train timetables. "I have to go."

Gregory heard her calling after him, but he didn't stop to look back. He ran, legs pumping hard and fast until he reached the tube station, where he disappeared into the murky London tunnels and didn't stop until he reached King's Cross.

Murder was easy.

He hadn't imagined it would be so simple, nor so satisfying. He'd castigated himself for far too long, worrying and fretting about hell and damnation, but now that he'd notched one up on his tally, he could hardly remember a time when the prospect had seemed daunting, or wrong.

Wrong.

There was a loaded word, laden with normative values that society had built up and thrust upon good people like himself, who were simply trying to get by—and would have done so, were it not for the catastrophic interference of a minority few.

Sinful.

There was another word, even more laden with judgment. Sinful according to whom? To God? Which one? To society? He rejected a nation of people who used invisible deities as their moral compass; why not use their own common-sense yardstick? Human beings were animals, at their base, and animals had to defend themselves from attack or risk extinction.

That's all he was doing now…defending himself.

More than that, he was defending *others*. By removing those who had wronged him, he was preventing them from inflicting similar harm to others. Like a soldier, who was given permission to kill in the name of patriotism, he too had a territory and people to defend.

Carl thought of all this and more as he stood across the street from the old stone building, with its attractive windows and high gables. He watched birds circle overhead and wondered if they saw him as just another speck on an enormous patchwork of green and grey.

Presently, the clock above the arched entrance struck the hour. Soon after, people began to spill out of the main doors into the street, chattering amongst themselves. He searched every face, comparing them with the image branded upon his mind's eye…

Then, he spotted the face he was waiting for, as unmistakable to him as his own.

"Bastard," he whispered.

He wore a classic two-piece suit in some sort of old-fashioned tweed, carried a scuffed leather briefcase in one hand and an eco-friendly coffee cup in the other. He was around sixty, with silver-grey hair brushed back from a still-handsome face.

A proud man, who walked tall, Carl thought. Not at all the type of person who carried around any measure of guilt or remorse.

He'd be sorry, before long.

Carl walked along the opposite pavement to his quarry, keeping pace with the other man's footsteps and never losing sight of him as they weaved through the streets. Eventually, Carl watched him enter a smart town house decorated with a pretty wreath left over from Christmas and knew there would be no interruptions because the man lived alone. There would be no housekeeper there today, because she had a day off on Fridays, nor anyone else to interrupt their reunion. All that remained was for him to let himself into the house using the little cloakroom window he'd found unlocked on every one of his previous reconnaissance visits.

He ducked his head, tugging the cap further over down his forehead, and crossed the street.

Just another speck in the patchwork.

There was an agonizing ten-minute wait until Gregory could board the next train to Cambridge. When he wasn't pacing the floor of the train platform, he tried calling Bill Douglas numerous times, before remembering he was probably in lectures or tutorials. He wouldn't answer his phone in those circumstances, and never had before.

There was no reason to panic.

Still, he wished he could have pushed the train faster along its tracks, rather than being forced to endure what seemed to be an interminably slow journey. Nothing good ever came of having too much time on his hands, and that was never truer than then, as he stared out of the discoloured train windows at passing fields, seeing none of them.

All he saw was Simon Campbell's mutilated body, bloodied and broken. Except, it wasn't Campbell his mind conjured up in glorious technicolour.

It was Bill Douglas.

CHAPTER 36

Oblivious to his friend's anguish, Professor Bill Douglas collected up his papers after an enjoyable session with some of his PhD hopefuls, stopping to chat with several of them before his stomach rumbled sufficiently to encourage him to head home. Several times per week, he chose to dine in college with the students, or at one of the local cafés or restaurants with his many friends and colleagues, but on Fridays he finished early and went home to slip his feet into the cosy moccasins Alex had gifted him the previous Christmas and pour himself a glass of fine Montepulciano to enjoy over a good book.

Such was the luxury of simple things, at his time of life.

It was important to appreciate everyday joys—such as reading and fermented grapes—otherwise work had a nasty habit of overtaking life which was, after all, for living. He thought of his friend, who might have been the son he'd never had, and wished Alex would learn that lesson. The boy never stopped until his body reached the verge of collapse, regularly burning the candle at both ends until he was fit to drop. His stamina and drive were impressive to behold, but they were also deceptive, for they could not last forever.

Time, he'd told him so often, *was something that could not be bought.*

Thoughts of his friend, and of Nigel, so recently taken from the world, preoccupied him so that he missed the hands raised in greeting from students he passed on the street. They were faces in a crowd, which was a blur as he made his way slowly through the cobbled back roads towards the house he owned on a residential road, not far from the Cambridge Arts and Drama Club Theatre.

It was comforting to be so near to a place that had played a large part in his formative years. Indeed, he often went there to enjoy a play, and got to know each new committee as they were elected. He supposed some would call his decision to remain in Cambridge a failure to move on with his life, or an obsession with the past...he'd call it self-knowledge, and an appreciation for the arts and for education in all its forms.

Reaching his house, Douglas retrieved the key to his front door, pausing to adjust the wreath adorning its painted frontage.

"Must take it down, sometime," he said to himself.

Carl made his way to the back of the row of terraced town houses, finding the spot in the brick wall where it was easy to climb up and over, with a bit of help from the wheelie bins helpfully stacked against it. It was a simple matter for a fit, energetic man to vault over the wall with hardly a whisper of sound—not that anyone would have heard him at that time of day, when the city traffic loomed large and drowned out the sound of his approach.

He kept to the side walls, moving slowly and purposefully, watching the French doors for any sign of life, ready to freeze should someone decide to look out at the garden.

Nobody did.

Soon, he reached the back wall of the house and dipped low beneath the kitchen window to avoid being seen, moving cat-like towards a small window at the end.

It was unlatched, as he'd known it would be.

He pushed the sash with gloved hands and then levered himself up, slipping into the house in one smooth motion.

By the time the train pulled into Cambridge, Gregory was the first to bound out of its electric doors.

He ran along the platform, oblivious to the curious stares of those he passed, stopping only to present his ticket at the turnstiles before picking up his feet again in the direction of Douglas's home address which was within walking distance. Once again, the city was a beautiful wash of blues and mellow yellow stone, but he hardly noticed. The cold air burned his tender throat as he laboured, urging himself to run faster, or pay the price for his delay.

Back on the train, his mobile phone began to ring, where he'd left it lying on the seat in his haste to leave.

Douglas tried calling Gregory back, but gave up when the number rang through to voicemail, reasoning that his friend would surely try calling again if it was important. In the meantime, he made his way through to the kitchen and went in search of lunch and that glass of red wine he'd earned over the course of the week.

Faculty meetings.

Alex's hearing.

The Villiers case…

He'd certainly earned an afternoon off.

He turned the radio on and uncorked a bottle, letting it air on the countertop as he moved around the room, humming along to Louis Armstrong.

He thought of all the years he'd lived alone, never a fully active participant in any of his past relationships, always looking outward trying to help others without ever helping himself. All that had changed, now, and he felt re-born, ready to take on the world as a man who seemed far younger than his advancing years. His only regret was that it had taken him so long to understand himself, to lift the veil and to be at peace with what he found beneath.

It didn't matter, now.

He had all the time in the world.

Carl watched the man moving around his kitchen from the shadows of the hallway, his footsteps unheard over the sound of the radio. He'd already taken the trouble to lock and bar the exits and had been careful not to brush against any of the walls or doorways as he moved silently through the house. Now, all that remained was to select a weapon of choice and make his intentions known.

But he stood there for a moment longer, head cocked to one side, imagining what the man's insides would look like and became aroused, just thinking about it.

Who could have known that an act of public service could be so stimulating?

His eye fell on the knife block beside the cooker, no more than two or three paces away from where he now stood.

Just then, the man at the window turned around, having finished his washing up. It was amusing to watch his face shift between initial shock, to a sort of relief, before circling back around to fear.

"*Carl?*"

Of course, he remembered him. He'd have been angry if he hadn't.

But then, who wouldn't remember the man whose life they'd ruined?

"Why are you here? How did you get in here?"

The man's eyes darted around the room, looking for some means of defence or escape. Watching him, Carl could feel the rage burn in his belly, just like before.

"You can't run," he said softly. "The doors are barred."

The man's jaw went slack, his eyes widened with fear. "Carl, please—"

"They teach you that, don't they? To use a person's first name. It's supposed to create a feeling of intimacy and understanding, so you can talk your way out of difficult situations," he said. "But you won't talk your way out of this."

He crossed the room and grasped the carving knife from the block, using its sharpened tip to nudge the man down onto one of the kitchen chairs arranged around a central table.

"This court comes to order," he rasped. "You are hereby charged with the following offences…"

Carl proceeded to set out his crimes, for which the penalty was death.

"Any last words?"

When Gregory arrived at Douglas's front door, he was panting following a half-mile sprint from the station.

He raised a fist to bang on the door, and rang the doorbell several times for good measure.

No answer.

He tried again, longer and louder than before, which drew some strange looks from pedestrians on the street, but he didn't care.

When there was still no response, he let out a small cry of frustration and ran around to the nearest alley, which led to the street that ran along the back of the row of smart terraces. He found the wooden gate leading into Douglas's garden locked, so he used a nearby wheelie bin to help him scale the wall.

Once over, he made straight for the back door, which was similarly locked.

Peering through the kitchen window which overlooked the garden, he saw the lights were on and he heard music playing, but there was no sign of his friend.

"Bill!" He shouted through the glass, rattling it with his fist, reasoning that the sound of another person making a commotion might be enough to disturb an intruder.

"*Bill!*"

Over the fence, his neighbour—an elderly woman by the name of Elizabeth—emerged from her own back door to see what the fuss was about.

"Hey there! I'll call the police if you don't stop making that racket!"

"Call them!" he shouted back, and continued banging against the door frame, eager to see his friend's face appear at the window.

But he didn't.

Gregory removed his jacket and wrapped it around one hand, shivering slightly as the wind permeated his skin beneath the thin wool jumper he wore beneath and, to Elizabeth's horror, smashed it through the glass panel of the door.

Reaching inside the broken panel, ignoring the pain in his hand and the jagged fragments of glass, he unlatched the door and hurried inside.

In the distance, he heard the faint whine of a police siren.

CHAPTER 37

"*Alex*?"

Gregory made it from the kitchen to the hallway before he heard Douglas's voice calling to him from somewhere above, and he didn't hesitate before bounding upstairs, taking them two at a time. He checked every room, until all that was left was the bathroom.

He stepped inside, steeling himself against whatever he might find, visions of Simon Campbell replaying in his mind.

"Bill?"

His friend might have been bleeding but it was not from a series of violent injuries.

"Managed to catch my bloody finger on the bloody potato peeler," Douglas grumbled, as he sat on the edge of his bath wrapping a length of gauze around the nasty cut on his middle finger.

He looked up. "Was that you banging and crashing all around the place? I heard the doorbell going but I'd just sliced half my fingertip off and needed to wrap it up…"

Douglas paused, taking in Gregory's ashen face and trembling body, the jacket hanging limply from one hand.

He rose to his feet. "What's happened, Alex? What's wrong?"

Gregory felt tears of gratitude well up in his throat, and found he couldn't speak.

"Is it the panel? Have they given you some bad news?"

The panel?

Gregory could have laughed, but the sound wouldn't come. He shook his head and then closed the distance between them and wrapped his arms tightly around the older man, holding him close to be sure he was real.

"Hey! What's all this?" Douglas asked, but brought his arms up to clasp them around the man he would always think of as 'his boy'.

They stayed that way for a moment or two, Douglas murmuring soothing sounds to Gregory, who drank in the familiar scent of his friend, thanking whichever god might be listening for the fact he was still there, living and breathing.

Before he could explain himself, the doorbell rang again, and the disembodied voice of a police officer could be heard through the letterbox.

"Professor Douglas? Is everything all right in there? Can you open the door, please?"

Gregory released him from the safety of his embrace and Douglas looked into his eyes, which were suspiciously moist.

"Well, Alex? Is everything all right?"

Gregory scrubbed the heels of his hands over his face and nodded, letting the adrenaline drain from his body.

"Yes, Bill. Everything's all right."

For now.

Carl Deere left the smart townhouse owned by His Honour Judge Quentin Whittaker QC the same way he had come—discreetly, leaving little trace of himself behind. He wondered when the man's remains would be discovered; the next day, probably, when his housekeeper came back to do her regular dust and polish. Really, he felt sorry for the cleaners of the world. Within a certain echelon of society, it seemed they were always the ones to find the dead bodies.

Ah, well. Couldn't be helped.

Unlike the other day, when darkness had concealed his bloodied attire, he acknowledged it was probably not wise to wander the streets of London in broad daylight wearing blood-stained plastic overalls and a hairnet. He'd therefore taken a moment to stuff the plastic back inside his little travel rucksack and had given himself a quick check in the large gilt mirror in the man's living room before heading out into the world again, like a butterfly emerging from its cocoon.

As he made his way towards his favourite café in another part of the city, his heart felt lighter, as did his mind, momentarily relieved of the oppressive weight of the obsessive, compulsive thoughts that usually dominated his every waking hour. There was no 'talking therapy' or magic pill he could take to cure that kind of malaise, and he'd tried both. There was only *one* solution, which was to remove the problem at its source and thus the cause of his sickness.

No, no.

Not sickness. More of a temporary affliction brought on by things outside of his control.

Two down, he thought. *Many more to go.*

But which one to dispose of next?

He was spoilt for choice.

Gregory guarded his friend through the long hours of the night, listening for the soft tread of a footstep on a creaking floorboard, or the sound of a door handle being forced open. When dawn rose over the city of Cambridge, he'd tried once again to convince

Bill to come and stay with him at his apartment in London, which had the benefit of gated security and an intercom system.

At least until we find out what happened to Campbell, he'd argued.

But Bill would not abandon his students, not when a new term had only recently begun.

If Bill would not come to London, Gregory thought, *then he'd move to Cambridge.*

He needed to pick up a few essentials, so Gregory found himself back at his flat in London, moving swiftly around his bedroom stuffing things into a suitcase, including his laptop, which he decided to check before heading off again to catch the next available train.

He found a couple of e-mails waiting for him:

Dear Dr Gregory,

Thank you for your attendance at the panel hearing, yesterday.

I write to inform you that, after due consideration of all the available information, including your testimony and that of Professor Douglas, the committee has decided that your behaviour, whilst misguided, did not amount to gross misconduct. However, we do feel that you would benefit from mandatory attendance of certain refresher courses, as a stipulation of your returning to work at Southmoor...

He sank back against his sofa, waiting for a feeling of elation that didn't come, and wondered why he found the news so anti-climactic. As he mulled it over, he clicked open the next e-mail, from an address he didn't recognise, at first:

From: np2022@hotmail.com
Dear Alex,
I hope life is treating you well, since we last saw one another.
I'm sorry it's taken me so long to write. I don't really know whether it's a good idea for me to be writing to you now, but…anyway, I thought I'd let you know I've been asked to give a guest lecture in Cambridge, as part of the European leg of my publishing tour. Did I tell you I wrote a book? Well, I finally finished it, and the publishers liked it, so my name will be on the cover of a very long and boring tome covering aspects of abnormal psychology. Maybe you could read it, sometime, if you need something to help you sleep?
I'll be in the UK next month, for around a week. I wrote to Bill, who says I can stay with him for a couple of nights while I'm in Cambridge. I haven't replied to his invitation yet—I wanted to talk to you, first.
Would you like to see me? I would like to see you, very much.
Naomi

Gregory re-read the e-mail and each time his eye fell upon the name 'Naomi', his heart quickened. He remembered a woman with dark, intelligent eyes he'd almost drowned in, during the single dance they'd shared. He remembered the feel of her lips against his, when he'd kissed her, and the sound of her voice as she'd healed him, during the long hours they'd talked in her office at the Buchanan Hospital. There was only one answer to the question she'd asked him.

I'd always like to see you, Naomi. Stay with Bill—I'll be there too.
I've missed you.
Alex

He could have said so much more, but he left it at that and clicked 'send' before he lost his nerve.

———

Carl watched the window on the second floor of the old warehouse conversion in Shad Thames, knowing it was the apartment belonging to Doctor Alexander Gregory. He'd seen the man hurrying inside the main entrance, keying in a code that buzzed open the doors—which was a waste of time, as far as he could tell, considering the number of people who seemed to hold them open for delivery drivers and other visitors claiming to know one or another of the occupants.

He noted the time in his little book and took a picture of the exterior of the building on his smartphone, so he could study it later.

He checked his watch.

Plenty of time to pay a few more house visits, before the day was out.

He blew a kiss towards the second-floor window and was tempted to break his own rules, but he knew that all the best things in life were worth waiting for.

His day would come, soon enough.

AUTHOR'S NOTE

The idea for *Mania* came about after reflecting on some of the changes the '#MeToo' movement brought about across many industries and areas of life, and the domino effect it had upon those who considered themselves beyond reproach. Of course, the idea of one gender oppressing another and moreover using a position of power to manipulate and control is not a new phenomenon in the world. Indeed, I'm sure it's been happening since the dawn of mankind but, every so often, there is a catalyst which forces society to re-engage with the discussion in a meaningful way and encourage us to continue to make baby steps towards treating the 'other'—whoever that 'other' may be—with the respect they deserve.

My decision to use the world of celebrity as a medium for this theme came from an acknowledgement that, whilst fame carries the power to whitewash, it also has the capacity to shine a light on issues that matter. Films, television, audio and stage productions, books and social media stardom can each provide a platform to showcase the experiences had by 'everyday' people, for whom there is no microphone nor any spotlight. For that reason, the personalities who make up the cast of characters in *Mania* could just as easily have been welders or teachers or bankers, rather than actors, but in the real world we'd be less likely to hear about them and less likely to take an interest in changing things for the better. In that regard, celebrity serves a real purpose, albeit as a double-edged sword.

I discuss the importance of reputation—in particular, when it is *justified*, and when it is *unjustified* that a person should lose it—and herein lies the tragedy for Carl Deere, who began life as an innocent man wronged by the justice system and who is now the pariah the world always suspected him to be, which begs the question of whether his loss of reputation became a self-fulfilling prophecy. If the world were to think the very worst of any of us, could we continue to defend ourselves indefinitely? Could we continue to hold our heads high at the supermarket, the post office or when picking up our children from school? Injustice is never desirable but, for some, it could drive them mad.

Or perhaps Gregory is right, and Carl Deere always had the capacity to be a killer.

They say there's a killer inside all of us…

In my case, I restrict myself to the pages of a book, and I hope you do, too!

Until next time.

LJ ROSS
January 2022

ACKNOWLEDGEMENTS

I would like to begin by thanking you, the reader, for your patience in waiting for this next instalment of Doctor Gregory thrillers. Since his last outing in *Bedlam,* much has happened— a worldwide pandemic, for one thing—but not least a bereavement in our family that hit us very hard and was relieved only by the arrival of our daughter, Ella, who brought joy to all of us from the moment she was born. They do say that, as one door closes, another opens…perhaps there's something in that. In any event, these events delayed my finishing *Mania* and several other stories. However, amidst the delay, I came up with a story I liked far better than the first concept I'd imagined, so perhaps it all worked out for the best!

In a similar vein, I'd like to express my thanks to Laura Smith and the rest of the team at W.F. Howes, to my agent Millie Hoskins, and to the wonderful narrator of these Gregory stories, Richard Armitage, for their patience and understanding. It has been much appreciated by all of us in the Ross household, and I can only hope that reading *Mania* has brought a couple of smiles at the parody of a profession which is, I'm sure, vastly different to the one I've portrayed on these pages ("Oh, no it isn't!" etc.).

The biggest thanks always go to my family and friends—in particular, James, who has been a tower of strength over this past year and whose kindness and care has been pivotal in keeping my love of writing and reading alive. With his encouragement, I was able to bring together fifty-five bestselling and acclaimed authors across the spectrum of publishing to produce an anthology of short stories entitled *Everyday Kindness,* the proceeds of which all go to Shelter, a charity that works to prevent homelessness and bad housing here in the UK, and provided a positive focus throughout the first and second lockdown periods in England. As Doctor Gregory would attest, through our own periods of turmoil, helping others can be a great healer—so please do pick up a copy of *Everyday Kindness* if you love a good story and would like to support a good cause!

ABOUT THE AUTHOR

LJ Ross is an international bestselling author, best known for creating atmospheric mystery and thriller novels, including the DCI Ryan series of Northumbrian murder mysteries which have sold over seven million copies worldwide.

Her debut, *Holy Island*, was released in January 2015 and reached number one in the UK and Australian charts. Since then, she has released a further 22 novels, all of which have been top three global bestsellers and almost all of which have been UK #1 bestsellers. Louise has garnered an army of loyal readers through her storytelling and, thanks to them, many of her books reached the coveted #1 spot whilst only available to pre-order ahead of release.

Louise was born in Northumberland, England. She studied undergraduate and postgraduate Law at King's College, University of London and then abroad in Paris and Florence. She spent much of her working life in London, where she was a lawyer for a number of years until taking the decision to change career and pursue her dream to write. Now, she writes full time and lives with her family in Northumberland. She enjoys reading all manner of books, travelling and spending time with family and friends.

If you enjoyed *Mania*, please consider leaving a review online.

If you would like to be kept up to date with new releases from LJ Ross, please complete an e-mail contact form on her Facebook page or website, www.ljrossauthor.com

If you enjoyed *Mania*, why not try the
bestselling DCI Ryan Mysteries by LJ Ross?

HOLY ISLAND

A DCI RYAN MYSTERY (Book #1)

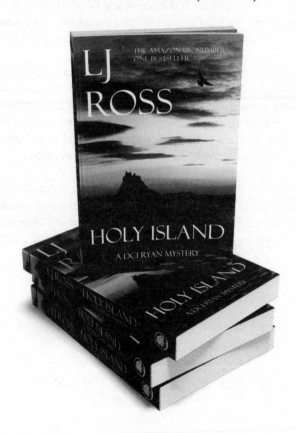

Detective Chief Inspector Ryan retreats to Holy Island seeking sanctuary when he is forced to take sabbatical leave from his duties as a homicide detective. A few days before Christmas, his peace is shattered, and he is thrust back into the murky world of murder when a young woman is found dead amongst the ancient ruins of the nearby Priory.

When former local girl Dr Anna Taylor arrives back on the island as a police consultant, old memories swim to the surface making her confront her difficult past. She and Ryan struggle to work together to hunt a killer who hides in plain sight, while pagan ritual and small-town politics muddy the waters of their investigation.

Murder and mystery are peppered with a sprinkling of romance and humour in this fast-paced crime whodunnit set on the spectacular Northumbrian island of Lindisfarne, cut off from the English mainland by a tidal causeway.

THE COVE

A SUMMER SUSPENSE MYSTERY (BOOK #1)

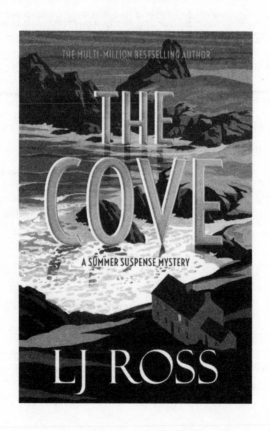

The perfect escape...

Gabrielle Adams has it all – brains, beauty, a handsome fiancé, and a dream job in publishing. Until, one day, everything changes.

The 'Underground Killer' takes his victims when they least expect it: standing on the edge of a busy Tube platform, as they wait for a train to arrive through the murky underground tunnels of London.

Gabrielle soon learns that being a survivor is harder than being a victim, and she struggles to return to her old life. Desperate to break free from the endless nightmares, she snatches up an opportunity to run a tiny bookshop in a picturesque cove in rural Cornwall.

She thinks she's found the perfect escape, but has she swapped one nightmare for another?

Suspense and mystery are peppered with romance and humour in this fast-paced thriller, set amidst the spectacular Cornish landscape.

"LJ Ross keeps company with the best mystery writers"
—*The Times*

"A literary phenomenon"
—*Evening Chronicle*

THE COVE is available in all good bookshops from 22nd July 2021

LOVE READING?

JOIN THE CLUB...

Join the LJ Ross Book Club to connect with a thriving community of fellow book lovers! To receive a free monthly newsletter with exclusive author interviews and giveaways, sign up at www.ljrossauthor.com or follow the LJ Ross Book Club on social media:

 #LJBookClubTweet

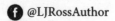 @LJRossAuthor

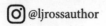 @ljrossauthor